BARLOW AT CHRISTMAS

by

John McAllister

BY THE SAME AUTHOR

THE BARLOW SERIES

The Station Sergeant

Barlow by the Book

Barlow Laid Bare

Barlow Goes Forth

JIMMY & DOC SERIES

Fight or Flight

Pursuit

Line of Flight

SHORT STORY COLLECTION

The Fly Pool

This Book is dedicated to

Stella Hughes

Who has been with Barlow all the way.
Thank you Stella for years of unfailing and generously given knowledge of all things medical.

Sometimes I accepted what you said
Sometimes, like all good patients, I ignored best advice
Sometimes I copied your advice straight onto the page

Published by Glenlish Publications

ISBN: 978-1-8384176-0-4

Blank Page

Friday
December 16th

1

Station Sergeant Barlow thumped the door of the Woman Police Constables' office and called out, 'Man on board.' He counted three before shoving the door open. It cannoned into someone.

'Oh!' said a female voice that Barlow didn't recognise. The voice was alto in range, with a good cadence and definitely annoyed.

Barlow shoved on until the door swung wide. The room was dark and cramped, leaving barely any space between desks and the door. Three WPCs stood at easy attention in front of the desks, their faces set blank, not daring to show any emotion.

A female sergeant flexed her damaged ankle. 'It's manners to wait …'

Barlow talked over her. 'You three, you've got your orders.' He nodded to the neat, dark-haired one. 'You, the garage.' To the larger dark-haired one, 'The kennels,' and to the blonde, WPC Stella Hughes, 'The armoury.'

'I'm briefing my officers,' the sergeant said.

'Briefings are done at the morning parade. Any other discussions or get-togethers, only with my prior permission.' He jerked a thumb at the door. 'Out.'

The WPCs scrambled to find their hats.

He turned his attention back to the sergeant. 'And you are?'

But the sergeant wasn't listening to Barlow. Her eyes were focused on someone behind him. The WPCs, having sourced their hats, stood smiling in welcome. A woman stood in the doorway. She had the lightness of a dancer in every step.

She said, 'The WPCs… I came to see… Sorry.'

She disappeared with a swing of her colourful dress: reds and greens on a white background.

'Do civilians normally wander around the station unescorted?' asked the sergeant.

'That's Mrs Harvey, the DIs wife,' said the neat, dark-haired WPC, Clare Keane.

'She's lovely,' WPC Hughes said as Constable Frank Wilson, his face a mixture of laughter and concern, appeared in the doorway. Hughes' face immediately went all soft and soulful.

Wilson ignored her. 'We got a call from a Mrs Collins. Apparently she was burgled last night by a ghost.'

He obviously expected Barlow to laugh. Instead Barlow frowned. 'Mrs Collins from the Larne Line?'

'Yes, Sarge.' Wilson hadn't picked up on the warning signs. 'I think the old doll's gone gaga.'

Barlow said, 'Mrs Collins is a very nice lady, and don't you forget it.' He turned to the WPCs. 'Are you lot still here?'

'We're gone,' WPC Keane said.

They piled out the door, carrying Wilson along with them. Wilson was good looking and set for a high rank. He also blushed easily.

Barlow shouted after him. 'I'll take the call myself.'

'That's the waste of a senior officer's time,' said the female sergeant.

Barlow eased himself to his full height, allowing him to scowl down on this new arrival. 'What did you say your name was?'

'Thompson. Sergeant Thompson.'

He pointed at her jacket buttons. 'Make those crests run straight up and down, and not hang sideways like a drunken sailor. Attention to detail, Sergeant. The way you would have done if you had attended Morning Parade.'

'Mr Harvey…'

'Doesn't get in any day before eight-thirty.'

'Told me to report to him direct.'

Barlow stood back and folded his arms. 'You should know better than that Sergeant *Sybil Eloise* Thompson, formerly of the Tennent Street station, Belfast, then Newry, Enniskillen and Armagh, in that order. Senior ranks may give orders, but the man you obey is the Station Sergeant. You make your number with me first, then you go suck up to any officer you want to.'

She busied herself straightening the buttons. 'You weren't supposed to know…'

'That it's now Ballymena's turn to have you? No.' He paused in the doorway. 'Make your number with Mr Harvey and then report back. You are coming with me.'

2

'You could always open it,' Barlow said.

He didn't seem to notice Thompson seethe as she edged past him to open the door leading into the station yard. She was the junior officer, and he had no intention of having to reach for antacid tablets every time she appeared.

Nor did he notice Thompson's start of surprise when she saw WPC Keane wiping a dipstick with an oily cloth.

'What do you think you're doing?' she demanded as she stepped into the enclosed yard, with its garages and open sheds for bikes.

Keane nodded to the squad car with the bonnet hooked up. 'Oil, air and water. We check them every day and reset the points weekly.'

'That is not the job for a woman police constable.'

Keane said, 'I'd rather do this than clean out the kennels, like WPC Milton.'

Thompson looked like she would explode, especially when a policeman, with a generous amount of muscle and fat, waved a duster in greeting from inside the car. 'Welcome to Ballymena, Sybil.'

'*Sergeant* Thompson.'

'That's Acting Sergeant Gillespie,' Barlow said.

'Soon to be an inspector, then I'll sort your hash, Barlow,' Gillespie said, getting out of the car to shake Thompson's hand.

Some of Thompson's seethe eased at finding another officer who didn't like Barlow. Again Barlow pretended not to notice. It was barely nine o'clock and already the day seemed to be full of him not noticing things. Like the back door opening behind him and someone giving a tetch of annoyance.

'I need you to run us out the Larne Line,' Barlow said.

Gillespie replied, 'I'm not available, Sergeant, I'm taking Mr Harvey to an important meeting at Headquarters. However, WPC Keane is available.'

Barlow noted the warning in the formality of Gillespie's answer, but still snorted. 'The last thing she drove was a pedal car.'

'Thanks,' Keane said.

She and Thompson had come to attention.

'Really, Barlow!' said a sharp little voice behind him.

Barlow turned and saluted District Inspector Harvey. 'Good morning, sir. I didn't see you there.'

'Your attitude, Barlow. Really! This is December nineteen sixty. On the 9th of January 1961 – barely two weeks from now – woman police officers will be authorised to serve summons and execute warrants, deal with traffic offences and family disputes.'

'I don't know what the world's coming to,' Barlow said.

'Keane will drive you to wherever you're going. That is an order.'

'Very good, sir,' Barlow said and continued not to notice things, like Keane trying to catch his eye and her nose screwing up as she winked.

Satisfied that he had put Barlow in his place, Harvey turned his attention on Gillespie. 'Today's meeting has been rescheduled for later this afternoon.' He looked at his watch as if time was pressing. 'In the meantime, I require some items in the town.'

Gillespie muttered, 'Bloody cigarettes.'

For once Barlow noticed things. Like having to hold open the door of Harvey's personal squad car while Harvey got in. Like Harvey taking his time while he fussed himself comfortable. Finally, Barlow could close the door and Gillespie drove off.

By then, Keane had replaced the dipstick in the oil sump and closed down the bonnet of the first car. Barlow settled himself in the front passenger seat while Thompson got into the back.

Keane swung herself into the driver's seat, all anxious to get going. 'Where to, Sarge?'

'Mrs Collins' house on the Larne Line.'

'Is that the big house beside Lorrimers' furniture factory?'

'That's it.'

Keane's face shone with eagerness. 'Lights and bell?'

She might be from Fermanagh, where half the county was permanently under water and her voice still had something of the soft cadence from there, but she'd taken the trouble to learn her way around Ballymena.

'This time, keep it below a hundred.'

3

Settled comfortably in the car, Barlow folded his hands over his stomach and felt a bulge from too many fries. Something he'd have to deal with after Christmas. He liked the steadiness on the chicane as Keane took the car over the bridge into the Harryville area of the town. Happy that they were on the right road, he closed his eyes for a bit of a think about Mrs Collins.

Mrs Collins had to be a fair age and maybe gone a bit gaga since he'd last called. All the same, he didn't want Thompson reporting her to Social Services unless the old dear could no longer cope on her own.

The edge of the town and Collins' house came up almost too soon. The house was built of dark lava stone and was surrounded by a matching high wall. The garden was a determined green of hacked-back shrubberies and cropped grass. Barlow's shoulders and back ached from the memory of pushing a lawnmower up and down lawns where the grass was forever too high.

Keane braked to a halt at the front door. Thompson rushed ahead of Barlow to pull on the old bell handle.

She was on the second pull before Barlow caught up with her. 'It hasn't worked in a lifetime.'

'Why didn't you say?'

'I just have.'

Thompson gave a grunt of annoyance and rapped on the door with her knuckles.

'And there's no staff so you have to go around the back.'

She turned on him, teeth clenched. 'You…' But Keane was out of the car and watching with interest, so she bit back the angry words. She marched stiff-legged across the front of the house and disappeared around the gable wall.

Barlow told Keane to stay with the car and followed. He found Thompson waiting for him near the turn leading to the back of the house: buttons straight up and down, the cap set firmly on her head.

'Sergeant Barlow, I object most strongly to your repeated attempts to humiliate me in front of my constables. I intend to submit an official complaint regarding your behaviour.'

He couldn't resist leaning into her face. 'Thompson, you're the one whose been making a fool of yourself. And if you want to report me to Harvey, feel free. He's already got a cabinet full of complaints against me, most of them his own.'

'All the same …'

Barlow said, 'Thompson, this job doesn't need *attitude.* It needs attention to detail.' He pointed beyond her. 'Like there, in the shrubbery at the bottom of the garden.'

'What about it?'

'I can see a body.'

4

The body lay alongside a flagged path that stretched across the lawn into the shrubbery. A trouser leg had ridden up to display bare skin and a thick grey sock.

'Stop,' Barlow said to Thompson.

She stood teetering on her toes, anxious to rush on. 'He might still be alive.'

Flaming townies, he thought. 'There's dew on the grass around the body, so it hasn't moved in a long time.'

'We still have to check.'

He joined her, and made himself stand solid, refusing to give into his own anxieties about failing to render prompt assistance to an injured person. 'Bearing in mind that Detective Sergeant Leary is unbearable if a crime scene is contaminated, what do you suggest?'

She frowned at him, more in thought than annoyance. 'We take the path and be careful where we step.'

'Sergeant Thompson, you have the lead.'

Nearing the shrubbery, they could see scuff marks on the grass and churned leaf mould around the body. The path ended at the boundary wall and a postern gate. The gate led into the old stable yard. The bolt was undone but when Barlow cautiously leaned forward and pushed the door refused to move.

'It could be swollen,' Thompson said.

'There's another bolt on the other side,' he said and turned back to the body. There was no need to go close, the crushed-in skull confirmed death.

At least it's a man, thought Barlow. The man was middle-aged, clean shaven and wearing a dark suit. Barlow gave a short prayer of relief. He hated dealing with women fatalities.

He concentrated on the churned up earth where he could see the imprint of footsteps. Large ones, they had to be a man's. Toe prints showed deeper than the heels, where the assailant had leaned forward to strike at the victim's skull. A torn cigarette packet lay nearby. There was something about a partly burnt match lying on top of the body that disturbed Barlow.

He looked at Thompson. Colour had gone out of her face. He felt the same way and hoped it didn't show. 'Back to the car and call it in.'

They went back the way they'd come. Once at the car she leaned in, reached for the microphone and held it out for Barlow to take.

'You make the call,' he said.

She asked to be put through to DI Harvey's secretary, Miss Fetterman.

Miss Fetterman was a new invention at the station. Miss Fetterman had no sense of humour. She wore her skirts long and kept her hair in a tight bun. Harvey had hired her to deal with his correspondence because he didn't trust the WPCs to keep things from Barlow.

Miss Fetterman conceded that Mr Harvey was in. However Mr Harvey had given strict instructions that he was not to be disturbed. If Sergeant Thompson cared to leave a message she would pass it on at the earliest possible moment.

Miss Fetterman would not be swayed by the declared urgency of the situation.

Barlow took the microphone out of Thompson's hand. 'Miss Footerman…'

'Fetterman!'

'Flutterman,' he corrected himself. 'Please tell Mr Harvey that we came across a body of a man in Mrs Collins' garden. The back of the head has been beaten to pulp and the brains are running down the back of the victim's shirt. His throat may have been slit, but it's hard to tell because there's so many flies around the body. The eyes have popped out and are dangling and I think this rat…'

Keane looked wide-eyed and, unbelievably, Thompson was smiling at his inventive description.

'I'll put you through.'

Barlow handed the microphone back to Thompson. 'You update Mr Harvey. I'll go check on Mrs Collins.

5

A good tap-tap on the back door got a prompt answer from Mrs Collins. She might have been pushing eighty and the eyes weren't too good, but her mind appeared sharp enough.

She canted her head to the left and then to the right while she had a good look at the man on her doorstep. 'Why John Barlow, son, you're all growed up.'

Barlow patted his stomach. 'I'm still carrying your wheaten bread.'

'Nonsense, you were like a whippet in those days. A whippet.'

'You had a bit of bother last night,' he said.

'I don't know why I rang at all.'

He knew her well enough to sense uneasiness. 'Well you did call and I'm here, and I've missed my morning cup of tea. Now if there was still something in the pot and a slice or two of that wheaten going spare…'

'I'm forgetting my manners.' She made way for him. 'Come in, son, come in.'

The man that removed his cap and stepped into the house might now be in his late forties but, in his mind, Barlow was a young teenager stepping into that house for the first time. The red floor tiles in the back hall that led into the kitchen, still glowed, and the stove had a shine to give a Sergeant Major's heart a lift. Only the old gas cooker showed wear – a couple of knobs had fallen off. A cobweb hung high up in the far corner. In the old days that would never have been tolerated.

Thompson joined them and Barlow made the introductions. Keane, he could see out the window, had been delegated to stand guard over the body and positioned far enough back not to risk contaminating the crime scene. He nodded at that. Thompson knew her job.

Mrs Collins showed them to a chair and made a fresh pot of tea, and hunted out a packet of biscuits. 'No wheaten bread, son. There's just me now.'

There was sadness in her voice though she tried to hide it.

'Do you see much of the children?' he asked.

'Summer and Christmas they have me to visit, turn about.'

He knew of stepmothers treated better than that. And a lot worse.

'And they never come here?'

'What would bring them back? They've made their lives in the city.'

She made it sound like the other side of the earth, instead of twenty-eight miles up a good road.

Thompson pulled out her notebook and pen. 'You said you had a burglar last night?'

'Did I? Och, it was just an old woman panicking over nothing.'

'So what caused you to panic last night?' he asked.

'The wind, something rattled.'

It had been a frosty night with plenty of stars, little cloud and hardly a breath of wind. He knew that because at bedtime he had walked in the garden with the dog.

Mrs Collins had her back to them while she poured the tea. He caught Thompson's eye and jerked his head in the direction of the door leading into the back hall. She slipped soundlessly out of the room. Mrs Collins turned, cups in hand, and looked startled at seeing only him sitting there.

'So something rattled and you got up?' he asked to distract her.

'I saw nothing and heard nothing. I checked the back door and went back to bed.'

There was something in her tone.

'It's not much of a backdoor,' he said.

'It's like me, son, it's getting on.'

'A good rattle would open it.'

'Where's that woman gone?' she asked.

Her brain still too sharp to bluff, so he said, 'Routine. Your eyes aren't as good as they used to be and you might have missed something.'

'The captain won't like it.'

He could have sworn her husband had never been in the army and, anyway, he was long dead.

Thompson reappeared in the doorway. 'Sergeant, could I have a word?'

Mrs Collins tried to block his way. 'Now, son, you know you're not allowed in there.'

'Sorry,' he said and held her arms to steady her as he edged past. He followed Thompson along the back hall and through the door leading to the front of the house.

Walking into the great hall with its baronial pretensions was like walking into a butcher's chill room. Thompson looked frosty around the edges.

She nodded to a table displaying little silver knickknacks. 'Take a look.'

There was a patina of dust on the table. Not enough for failing eyes to spot, but enough to show that ornaments had been picked up and put down again, but not in the same place.

Thompson pointed at spots of dark matter on the oak floor, and at a large brass platter on the wall among the ancient weapons and family portraits. Something dark smeared the bottom of the platter.

Thompson said, 'Barlow, I think the old woman murdered that man out there. Beat him to death.'

6

Mrs Collins murder someone? A woman he'd seen catch bees in a duster and release them into the yard rather than kill them? All the same, she was hiding something, he could feel it in his water.

'Right, Thompson, you wait outside and brief the detectives when they arrive. Meantime I'll have a word with Mrs Collins.'

Thompson shivered. 'With pleasure. Outside is warmer than in here.' Then she jerked back into her original seethe. 'We should search the house.'

Barlow said, 'We don't know what we're up against, so I want you and Keane locked in the car for safety.'

'Let me tell you, Barlow…'

'I know, I know. Women are as good as men any day.' He pointed to the stairs. 'When we search this house, it will be done by men who served in the army, and they'll keep their guns handy.'

Mrs Collins stood in the doorway leading to the back hall. 'You've got to come back. He does that when he's annoyed.'

'Does what?' asked Barlow.

'Who's "he",' asked Thompson.

Mrs Collins gave something between a shake and a shiver and retreated. Barlow again followed her into the kitchen. Thompson, still stiff with annoyance, went on outside to collect Keane and wait in the car for backup to arrive.

Barlow watched her go. In his own good time, he'd sort out Thompson and her constant questioning of his authority. In the meantime, she and Keane were safe.

He sat at the table, this time selecting a chair where he could sit with his back to the wall. He sipped at his tea while Mrs Collins busied herself around the kitchen. She never had been a great one for sitting down.

Barlow cleared his throat to get her attention. 'There was no wind last night, so what wakened you?'

She dumped Thompson's undrunk tea in the sink. 'This old house is always creaking. It just seemed worse than usual.'

'So you came downstairs to check?'

'I did that.'

'Are you still in the same bedroom?'

'I'm used to it,' she said.

As a youth working around the house, it was something he could never understand. Mr and Mrs Collins lived in the back of the house and used the servants' stairs to access their bedroom. The rooms to the front, the morning room and the drawing room, lay all but abandoned.

'So you heard something and came down the main stairs?'

'Oh goodness no.'

In some ways she was still the District Nurse calling to tend to Mr Collins' ailing first wife.

'But you came into the great hall?'

'There was nothing, nothing. It was just an old woman's imagination.'

She was passing close to him, fussing over some little tidy-up. He caught her hands and eased her into a chair beside him. 'Mrs Collins, there's blood in the great hall and a platter on the wall with blood on it, and we found the body of a man in the garden.'

'He didn't hit him that hard,' she said. 'Just a bump on the nose to make him go away.'

'Who's "he"?'

She started to cry into her apron. 'The captain will be upset when he hears. I know he gets grumpy at times, but he'd never hurt a soul.'

Barlow was part shocked, part amused at Mrs Collins having a gentleman friend. And at her age? Embarrassing and all as it might be for her when people found out, there was no way she could protect this man.

He moved his chair so that he could put an arm around her shoulders. 'Listen, love, it's a bad do when someone gets killed. Lots of questions and the police aren't all like me. Some of them can get very nasty when they don't get the right answers.'

7

Mrs Collins was shaking. Barlow didn't know if she was trembling with fear, or if it was just old age catching up with her. The body he had his arm around was merely bone. He remembered when it had plenty of homely padding.

'Come on,' he whispered, as if it would be a secret between them.

'He woke me,' she said.

'Who did?'

'The captain. He always pulls the bedclothes off when he wants me to get up.'

Barlow blinked at this intimate detail. 'What did you say his name was?' he asked, knowing that she hadn't.

'Oh, I always call him "Captain".'

That answer worried him. The old lady was risking a charge of Withholding Information by trying to protect the man.

Mrs Collins pushed on with her story. 'So I went down and I heard these men in the great hall, two of them, and they were arguing.'

He let her talk on. That way he could spot other gaps in what she said. 'And?'

'They saw me and the big one came at me. I was really frightened, so the captain lifted the big platter off the wall and hit him with it.'

He knew she was lying. The brass platter hung at least ten foot up, and there wasn't a chair handy for this captain fellow to step on. Whatever happened had to be premeditated.

'Mrs Collins, please, tell me the truth.'

Her voice quavered at the memory. 'I am. Then the captain rushed me back to my bedroom and made me lock myself in. He wouldn't let me out again 'til daylight.'

'So the man you call "Captain" is still in the house?'

'Oh yes, yes. He never leaves.'

That made him wonder if she was trying to set up an alibi for the captain, whoever he was. If he never left the house then he couldn't have murdered the man in the shrubbery.

Now Barlow was really worried. If he didn't get things sorted before Harvey appeared the old lady was facing a charge of Accessory to

Murder. He had to get his hands on this man and force the truth out of him.

'So take me to him.'

'I don't think… I mean…'

'Is he still in the bedroom?'

She brushed her clothes straight, somehow reminding him of a maidservant answering her mistresses call. 'At this time he's usually in the morning room.'

The morning room? That had to be a room facing east that caught the early sun. His heart thumped as he helped her to her feet. When she wasn't looking he unsnapped the flap of his holster. Maybe it was the wrong thing to do, but Mrs Collins' presence might make this captain fellow come quietly. 'So we'll go there then.'

He followed her down the back passage into the great hall. The sun coming in the glass panels around the front door must have heated it because it was no longer cold. All the time he was conscious of the creaks and groans of the old house echoing through the building. Was someone creeping up on him? He kept a hand near his gun.

In the morning room, the wooden shutters were closed over, making the room dark and eerie. Even so it was pleasant, if not warm. Not daring to look back, Barlow's hand scrabbled over the wall, searching for the light switches and turned them on. He gripped the butt of his pistol as he took in the number of hiding places behind settees and curtains, and of potential blunt instruments displayed on flat surfaces.

'He's very easily annoyed,' Mrs Collins said.

Barlow wondered why the woman put up with the man, he sounded like the greatest bully. It was her house for life, if he remembered the talk at the time of the husband's death. So there was no reason why she couldn't tell him to be gone.

Pistol drawn and handcuffs handy, Barlow walked around the back of the chairs and checked behind the curtains, and found no one.

'He's not here,' he said.

'He is, and he's in a good mood.'

Rather than argue with her, Barlow looked again. No one other than themselves stood or sat in the room. He shook his head. The old woman was beginning to dote.

Feeling safe, he pulled out his notebook and pencil. 'What's his full name and could you describe him for me?'

Mrs Collins pointed at a family portrait of a man in a naval uniform. ‘That’s him, Captain Alphonsus Collins.’

Barlow didn’t know whether to explode with rage at her constant lying or call for the men with straightjackets. ‘Are you telling me that Cattle Collins...?’

In an instant, the temperature of the room dropped until frost crackled underfoot at every step.

8

The cold of the room intensified until the mirror over the fireplace turned opaque. The last time Barlow had felt that cold he'd been carted off to hospital with hypothermia.

'Friggin' hell!' He grabbed Mrs Collins and hurried her out of the room. 'Sorry for my language, Missis.'

He kept them going until they found themselves back in the kitchen, with all the doors between them and the morning room safely closed. His heart pounded as if he'd run a race and his legs had a definite shake.

'He doesn't like being called that,' she said, patting her hair and clothes tidy after their rush through the house.

'What Cat…?' He choked back the word and collapsed onto a chair rather than risk his jelly legs giving way. 'You should move out,' he told Mrs Collins.

'Where would I go, son? Anyway, this is my home and the captain likes me around the place.'

She poured him a fresh cup of tea. He noted that her hand was absolutely steady.

'You should go back and apologise,' she said.

Hell would freeze over before he went anywhere near that room again.

He didn't dare sip the tea, knowing his shaking hand would spill half of it, so he sat and had a good think to himself. There'd always been rumours of ghosts in the house, Cattle Collins being the latest. Of vile goings on in earlier generations. Of screams in the night. Back in the day, he had invented a few stories of his own when friends heard that he did odd jobs around the place.

Meantime, half the Ballymena police force was heading for the house to hunt for a brutal killer. He could see himself telling Harvey that the murderer was Cattle Collins and to arrest the portrait. He'd be on a charge of insubordination, and they'd whisk the old dear off to the mental hospital.

'I'm thinking we should work on your statement,' he said.

'I'm not for telling any lies.'

'Not lies. Omissions.' He steadied a mind that wanted him to run in terror from the house. 'Something woke you up. You can't say what.' His finger had more of a shake to it than a warning wag. 'I can't say what, and keep saying that. I – can't – say – what. It's no lie.'

'I can't say what,' she repeated.

He wondered if the captain could blow hot as well as cold. Kept her feet warm these December nights. His feet were cold in bed now that he was on his own again, yet he didn't dare buy one of the new rubber hot-water bottles. His daughter, Vera, would laugh at him.

He continued. 'You crept downstairs and saw two men arguing in the great hall. The larger of the two men made to attack you. You ran back to your bedroom and stayed there until daylight…'

'I heard the milkman leave my pint,' she said.

'Even better. At which point you risked coming downstairs and phoning the police.'

He pointed a finger at her.

'I knew from the captain that it was safe to come down again,' she said.

He turned the point into a warning wag.

She corrected herself. 'More than that I can't say.'

'You're a born conspirator.'

Her old eyes blinked hard at him. 'Tell me, son, do you do this all the time, make people tell omissions?'

'You're lucky,' he said. 'I keep a rubber truncheon to beat confessions out of innocent people.'

In the distance, he could hear a medley of police bells approaching the house. Steady as she was, Mrs Collins would handle questions better if she was in some familiar routine.

'There's a lot of hungry men on the way,' he told her.

She bustled to her feet. 'John Barlow, you're angling for me to make you some wheaten bread.'

'Guilty as charged.' he said.

He needed something in his system to settle the shakes. He decided on Clove Rock, a sweet he could get his teeth into. He touched his mouth as if slipping in two Clove Rocks and imagined their strong taste seeping into his system.

'You're still at that trick,' Mrs Collins said.

'What trick?'

'Fooling yourself that you're eating something you can't afford to buy.'

'Now it's just meanness,' he said and went off to greet the new arrivals.

9

District Inspector Harvey was deep in conversation with Sergeant Thompson when Barlow came around the corner to the front of the house.

Harvey's sharp little voice echoed off the stone walls. 'Barlow, over here.'

Barlow took his time: not rushing but not dandering either. He acknowledged Harvey's rank with a two-finger salute. 'Sir, there goes our quiet run up to Christmas.'

'Why didn't you secure the premises?'

'Sir?'

'You should have positioned Sergeant Thompson and WPC Keane at the gable ends of the house. With you at the rear, the murderer couldn't possibly have got away without being seen.'

Barlow didn't even bother looking Thompson's way. 'In my opinion, the murderer has long departed the scene. Anyway, I doubt if any of those old windows could open that easily, though we'll do a double check when we search the house.'

'Not you, Barlow. I'll detail people I can depend on. If one of those windows is found unsecured, you will be disciplined.'

Harvey stumped off.

Thompson said, 'Barlow I didn't …' but Harvey shouted, 'Thompson, I told you to stay with me.' She went off without finishing what she wanted to say.

Next up was Detective Sergeant Leary. 'Barlow, your timing is way off. There I was busy interrogating a prime suspect from Trish's Pantry.'

Barlow brushed a coating of sugar off Leary's lapel. 'I see you gave it a good dusting.'

Leary grunted and headed off to examine the body. A detective constable dragged behind, hauling the murder bag.

Barlow drew easy breaths as he looked around him. The day looked like it would stay dry, if cold. And Harvey was in a good mood, merely flinging accusations instead of ordering him back to the station like a naughty schoolboy. Acting Sergeant Gillespie was bossing every spare constable into doing something useful, which gave Barlow time to have a good think to himself.

If the back gate was locked on the factory side, where were the dead man and his killer going? How did they get in, in the first place?

Starting at the front gate, Barlow walked the perimeter of the garden. He payed as much attention to the wall as to the ground, and especially any shrub that looked strong enough to bear a man's weight. The more than annoying ones slapped his face and dragged at his clothes.

He stopped near the back gate, having seen nothing of interest on the first half-circuit.

Leary was bending over the body. He levered himself upright and rubbed an aching back.

He scowled, daring Barlow to step onto the murder scene. 'I'll tell you one thing, Barlow. The killer didn't like the victim.'

'I'd never have guessed.'

Leary pointed. 'Look at the jacket. The match was still lit when it landed.'

Barlow arched forward to have a good look and did his own pointing at a smear of mud on the material. 'And kicked him in the ribs for good measure.'

He started to understand Cattle Collin's habit of sending out a chill when annoyed. He felt his own chill at what was out there, running around his town. 'Give me a name before that man kills again.'

'You've got to keep an open mind. It could be a woman,' Leary said.

'Don't you start with this feminism malarkey.'

At that Barlow took a wide curve around the murder scene, and carried on with his inspection of the boundary.

10

Barlow found nothing of interest along the boundary wall and soon found himself back at the front gate. He kept on going, out the gate, along the road and down the back drive leading to the old stables and staff quarters, now Lorrimers' furniture factory.

Like half the town, the two-storey building had been constructed of local lava stone. Normally it looked dull, but the damp of the day reflected the weak sun off the stones making the place appear homely.

Out of politeness, he knocked the door but let himself into the factory office without waiting for a reply.

'Sergeant Barlow,' he said to the three people sitting there: Mr Lorrimer, a tall thin man with sloppy grey hair; his son who was half-a-head shorter and bulky; and a young lady. The daughter, he guessed, because she had the family look about her. The room was wood panelled and heated by a paraffin burner. Wood dust layered every high surface. From the back of the building came the muffled grate of power saws and shouted voices. No laughter. From somewhere in that same direction a gate clanged open and a draft whistled around Barlow's ankles. He moved closer to the family to get away from the draft.

The young lady – 'Rose,' she said when he asked her name – was busy writing cheques. Wages envelopes sat stacked in a wooden tray at the side of the desk. The two men appeared content to act as supervisors.

Barlow already knew Mr Lorrimer from seeing him around the town. Patrick or Paddy or Patsy? He wasn't sure which.

'Mr R Shaw Lorrimer,' said the son when asked his name.

'I need an account of your movements last night,' Barlow said, just to annoy.

'We were here 'till late doing the wages,' R Shaw said.

There were upwards of fifty wage packets on a tray, together with statements from suppliers. The wages packets might be prepared, with the pay and deductions showing on the outside but they were unsealed, so the money had yet to go into them. A lot of work for someone. Eyeing the harassed looking Rose, Barlow could guess who.

R Shaw stood up, lifted a piece of paper off the desk and tore a blank cheque out of the cheque book. 'I'm off to the bank.'

Rose indicated a stack of suppliers' statements with cheques attached. 'Go easy.'

R Shaw laughed and attempted to leave.

Barlow blocked his way. 'As you may have noticed, Mr R Shaw Lorrimer, I am still wearing my cap, which makes this call official, which means that you can answer my questions either here or down at the station. The choice is yours.'

Lorrimer senior raged to his feet. 'I know District Inspector Harvey…'

'And so do I, sir, and I'm sure he'd agree with me that a chat here would be much more convenient for all concerned.'

Rose, he noted, looked startled at the confrontation, but didn't seem to mind her brother being forced to stomp back to his chair.

Barlow pulled up a chair for himself, took the cap off his head and placed it on the wage packets. A quiet hint that all work should stop until his questions were answered.

''Right now, young lady and gentlemen, about last night. Where were you and when, what you were doing and who with?'

11

The questioning of the Lorrimers didn't take long. Really all Barlow wanted to know – was the postern gate leading into Mrs Collins' back garden always kept locked?

'Never,' Rose said with a decided shake of her head. 'It's always on the push in case the old lady has an emergency.'

'And to collect her rent money on the due date,' Mr Lorrimer said with an edge of spite.

'Cash not cheque, if you would,' R Shaw added, holding out his hands as if begging.

Barlow didn't say anything or nod in case it was taken as agreeing with them. He eyed the top supplier's statement on the pile waiting to be paid. The attached cheque was for a rounded off figure, and considerably less than the balance showing on the statement. It was a payment on account so, maybe, Mrs Collins had good reason not to trust a Lorrimer cheque.

If the gateway between the two properties was always on the push, then the chances were that the murderer had closed it behind them when escaping out of Mrs Collins' garden. From the factory grounds, the murderer had a choice of clambering over a wall onto the laneway, or stepping over a rickety fence into the surrounding fields. Barlow made a mental note to send men to look but knew he was wasting their time. They'd find nothing.

It was going to be one of those cases, he decided. A man callous enough to flick a lit match onto the body of someone he'd just battered to death wasn't going to make any panic-induced mistakes.

He didn't tell the Lorrimers that there was a body lying on the far side of the boundary wall, but they asked all the right questions at the right time, and not liking people was no reason to suspect them. The Lorrimers stated that they'd worked late the previous night sorting the wages for the men. When finished, R Shaw called a taxi to take Rose home while the two men sat on and planned their work schedule over the Christmas holidays.

'The whole thing is a nuisance,' R Shaw said. 'It breaks the rhythm of work and makes the men unsettled for days afterwards.'

Barlow thought R Shaw an uppity little shite, but he never let that word, and many others like it, pass his lips. Not with a teenage daughter ready to say even worse.

As for Lorrimer senior? Peppermints might conceal the stale alcohol on the breath but the other signs were there: the veins stitching the cheeks, the hand to the mouth to change a burp into a cough, yesterday's shirt, or was it the day befores, roughly tucked into the trousers. He could hardly blame the man. He was struggling with a failing business.

Rose, he liked. Her body had still to mature fully, her lingering dumpiness emphasised by the sensible worsted and wool outfits beloved of certain Gospel Hall Brethren. Busy and all as she obviously was, she couldn't wait to go around to see Mrs Collins and make sure that she was all right.

'She's fine, she's making her famous wheaten bread,' he reassured her, and hoped the old lady was.

12

Barlow was in no rush to go back into the Collins' house, not with Cattle Collins gunning for him. In the end he had to go, if only to tell DS Leary to send a man to fingerprint the Lorrimers' side of the door. He took Rose with him. Without him there to vouch for her she'd never have got past the police cordon at the front gate.

People were coming and going by the front door and someone had lit a fire in the morning room. Barlow stayed in the grand hall rather than risk another confrontation with Cattle Collins.

'I'm daft,' he told himself. 'What harm can a dead man do me?'

All the same, he had no intention of finding out.

He was grateful when Inspector Foxwood appeared out of the morning room. Foxwood was an Englishman who had transferred to the RUC after he married a Northern Irish woman. Unlike Harvey, who was always trying to prove something, Foxwood was comfortable in his rank and, coming from an army background, knew the importance of an impeccable uniform and, even more importantly, how to treat his subordinates.

Barlow gave Foxwood a casual but respectful salute and told him about the Lorrimer side of the postern gate.

'Well done, Sergeant. I'll get someone on it straight away.'

Barlow pointed to the police van in the driveway. The back door was open. The taller, dark-haired WPC sat there with the dog's head resting on her knee. 'You brought the dog, sir?'

Foxwood rubbed thoughtfully at his chin. 'I know the regular handler is away on a course but WPC Milton seems competent enough.'

'If you say so, sir.'

'I do, Sergeant, and we'll send…'

'If I may suggest, young Wilson.'

Foxwood gave the smallest of frowns to indicate that he knew he was being maneuvered but was willing to let it pass. 'I'll leave it with you, Sergeant,' he said and walked off.

Barlow could see Wilson doing something in the morning room and indicated for the young constable to follow him. Junior ranks came to senior ranks, not the other way around, he reasoned. It also avoided him coming face to face with Cattle Collins' portrait.

Barlow led the way out of the house, down the steps and across to the police van. WPC Milton got to her feet and brushed self-consciously at her jacket lapels though no blemish showed. Her tongue worked at the gaps between her teeth.

'What are you chewing now?' he asked.

'A tube of your wine gums.'

'All of them at once?'

'Well nearly.' Her tongue worked again at her teeth. 'I'm going to throw the rest away. They're the devil for getting stuck in the gaps.'

'They are that.'

The dog raised its head and showed teeth. Barlow scowled back at it. 'That Towser's a nasty brute.'

'Rex,' Milton said in a 'here-we-go-again' tone.

Barlow gave the young officers their instructions to check along the roadway and the boundary fencing bordering Lorrimers' factory. He seemed unaware that his left hand was massaging the back of the dog's neck. Wilson and Milton watched with interest to see if the dog dared upgrade its rumbling snarl to an actual bite.

'What are we looking for, Sergeant?' Milton asked.

'Anything that catches your eye. The odd dead body.'

'Nothing too complicated then,' Milton said and made herself busy checking the dog's paws and exchanging his short lead for a longer one.

'Sarge,' said Wilson, who had been unusually quiet.

'What?'

'Why me?' His voice dropped to a hiss. 'You're not trying to do matchmaker or something?'

Barlow indicated for the young constable to come with him as he stepped away from the van. 'Two reasons, son. You have a keen eye and a sharp mind. That's important. Secondly.' He nodded to Milton who right then had a hand in her pocket. The hand came out empty. Even so Milton made a throwing gesture. 'You're a policeman and should be nosy about things. Milton eats too much of the wrong foods. It's more than a bad habit and I want to know why.'

'Oh. Right.' Wilson's shoulders squared. 'Leave it to me, Sarge.'

Barlow did leave it to him and went back into the house. Before he could escape to the comparative safety of the kitchen and the promised slice of wheaten, Harvey surfaced like a bad penny.

His usual creeping walk had a bounce to it. ‘Barlow, this case is easily solved. A burglary gone wrong and a fallout among crooks.’

Barlow eyed him warily. It wasn’t like Harvey to volunteer him information.

‘So what we do, Barlow, is arrest and interrogate every known burglar in the area.’ Harvey delivered the blow with the ease of a stiletto going in and twisted. ‘I want you and Sergeant Thompson to go and arrest your good friend, Geordie Dunlop.’

13

'Me, arrest Geordie?'

Barlow could have kicked himself for showing his upset. Harvey was out to annoy and he had succeeded. Burglary with violence was not Geordie's style.

'Get on with it, Sergeant,' DI Harvey said.

'With pleasure, sir. It must be three months since I last felt his collar.'

'This time he's going down. Hopefully with a rope around his neck.'

'And you're the man to do it, sir,' Barlow said giving Harvey a nod of approval.

He walked away, conveniently forgetting to salute first. Sergeant Thompson followed him.

WPC Keane stood posed against the police car. She chatted to every available officer that passed, and some that shouldn't have been.

Barlow jerked a thumb at her to come on.

Thompson said, 'That is no way…'

Barlow eyed Keane, now busy settling herself into the driver's seat. 'She wouldn't hear a police whistle if you blew it in her ear, but bring a car into the conversation and she'd hear a pin drop.'

The car was already crunching over the gravel towards them. Barlow went to meet it and swung himself into the front seat. 'Geordie's house.'

Keane crunched the engine into first gear as Thompson scrambled into the back.

Keane asked, 'You're not going to arrest Geordie for this?'

'Aye.'

'Sarge, when his wife starts throwing things, you're on your own.'

'Not me, Sergeant Thompson.'

With that he sank down in the seat and pulled his cap over his eyes. Geordie arrested when guilty, was bad enough, but when he was obviously innocent? There were bound to be ructions.

He selected a bitter sweet to suck on. Something acidy to build up his resentment of Harvey.

All too soon the car stopped outside Geordie's house, a temporary wartime prefab that would probably still be there when Geordie's grandsons were old and grey. The picket fence was fresh-painted, not a blade of grass out of place in the garden.

Connie Dunlop answered Barlow's thump on the front door. She was stout and homely and given to wearing black dresses to show off her colourful aprons. Today's apron was pink and green.

'Who's there?' she asked.

'Me,' Barlow said stepping back and motioning for Thompson to take the lead.

'Is that "me" the Sergeant Major or "me" that bastarding policeman?' Connie asked over Thompson's shoulder.

'Is Geordie in?'

'No, and he hasn't been out all night.'

She slammed the door shut in Thompson's face.

'I'll do her for assisting a suspect in evading arrest,' Thompson said.

'And I'll do you for not having your foot in the door-jam instead of standing there like a lump of clay.'

Barlow ordered Thompson out of the way and gave the door another thump. 'Connie.'

'He could be getting away out the back,' Thompson said.

'On you go then.'

He gave the door another thump. 'Connie.'

The neighbours started to gather: the unemployed men, the women coming or going from their shopping. They stood grouped, mostly silent. The odd remark or conversation among them rolled towards Barlow like distant thunder.

With the neighbours came the dogs. The friendliest looking was a Pit Bull Terrier, the most dangerous a little Yorkie. Barlow had closed the garden gate behind him and Thompson, so they were safe. Keane hopped smartly back into the car.

He gave the door another thump as Thompson came back.

'Well?' he asked.

'There's a trellis on both sides covered in climbing roses.'

'Lord preserve my nylons,' he said and reached under a flowerpot for a spare door key.

'You knew that was there all the time,' Thompson said, making it sound like the first line of another official complaint.

'It's polite to announce your arrival,' he said.

14

Barlow shouted, 'Connie, I'm coming in and swung Geordie's door open. He closed it even quicker when a plant pot shattered on the door-jam near his head. Soil splattered around him.

He brushed a spider plant off his shoulder. 'Connie!'

Something else slammed against the closed door.

'I'm coming in,' he repeated, and pushed the door wide open. The remains of a plant pot left an arc of dirt along the tiled floor.

Connie stood between them and the kitchen. Her face burning, hair awry, arm back for a third throw.

Thompson stood safely behind Barlow's bulk. 'You're under arrest,' she said.

Barlow could see the alleged murderer, Geordie, sitting at the kitchen table with an amused look on his face. He had this itch to grab Thompson and use her as a battering ram to get at Geordie.

Instead, he said, 'Connie, that's one of those miniature Japanese tree things. They cost a fortune.'

Connie looked at the plant, looked back at Barlow, and placed the miniature tree safely on a table. 'You're not welcome in this house.'

'It's both of us this time. The Sergeant Major and the policeman.'

Thompson shoved past him and placed a hand on Connie's arm. 'Connie Dunlop I am arresting you …'

'Oh shut up,' Barlow said.

'But she threw …'

'She hasn't hit anyone yet, and she's thrown plenty in my direction.'

Geordie laughed. 'She didn't miss the time she caught me with that wee blonde.'

Connie's face stayed stern. 'Well one of you come in.'

She took a good look at Thompson before she shook her arm free and fussed the plant onto the kitchen window.

'Meet Sergeant Sybil Eloise Thompson,' Barlow said as he followed them down the short hallway into the kitchen.

Geordie sat at the table in his trousers and vest, a heaped fry in front of him. 'I'm not going nowhere until I get my breakfast.'

'At this hour? It's near lunchtime,' Thompson said.

'Why do you think he's got a big family and a contented wife,' Barlow said. He took a seat across from Geordie. 'Where were you last night?'

'All night?' Thompson specified. She stood guarding the door into the hallway in case Geordie tried to bolt.

Somehow with his "last night" and Thompson's "all night" the atmosphere in the kitchen eased. Why, Barlow couldn't figure, especially when a more relaxed Connie said, 'He's innocent, and you'll take a bite.'

As Thompson had said, it was near lunchtime so Barlow nodded. 'He's always innocent and I wouldn't mind.'

He could sense Thompson seething before she even spoke. 'Sergeant Barlow, may I speak to you outside?'

'And leave a prisoner unguarded.' He pushed a spare chair out with his foot. 'Sit down.'

He waited until he had swallowed the first bite of food before he growled at Geordie. 'There's something up. It's not like you to be pleasant.'

'Now, Mr Barlow, you know me.'

'I do, and that's what's worrying me.' Barlow loaded a fork with fried bread, sausage, black pudding and egg, and slid it into his mouth. The mouthful swallowed, he gave a sigh. 'Connie, when you catch yourself on and divorce this man, I'll marry you myself.'

'I'll probably be doing time, Mr Barlow, because I'll murder him first.'

Thompson didn't look amused. Especially when Connie slid a fry in front of her. Thompson had refused even a cup of tea.

'So what were you doing last night? Barlow asked Geordie.

Connie rushed to stand by her man. 'He never left the house.'

Barlow nodded. 'Other than that, where did you go? Who did you meet?'

Geordie continued to chew thoughtfully for a moment. 'I want my solicitor.'

'But does he want you?'

'I'm his best customer.'

Thompson, Barlow noted, was nibbling at the edge of her bacon. Then a second nibble. After that she tucked in.

'Good on you,' Barlow said and continued to eat as Geordie

pushed himself back from the table. 'I'll go dress.'

Thompson went rigid as Geordie ambled out of the kitchen. 'Sergeant, shouldn't you go with him?'

'And let my fry go cold?' Barlow held out his cup for a refill. 'Don't you go worrying about him, Connie. He's in good hands.'

He didn't know why, but warning bells were ringing in his head. Geordie was coming too quietly and Connie had become too friendly, too quickly.

Geordie came back tucking in his shirt, his coat over his arm. He laughed when Thompson produced handcuffs. 'When it comes to handcuffs and women, love, my wife is particular that it's only her.'

'I'm Sergeant Thompson, not your love,' Thompson said.

Barlow thanked Connie for the meal and led the way out to the car. He saw Geordie into the back and blocked Thompson from getting into the front.

'I'm not sitting in the back with him,' she said.

Barlow settled himself in the front passenger seat. 'You should have handcuffed him when you had the chance.'

15

By the time they arrived at the station some of the steam had gone out of Geordie's humour. His old Sergeant Major might have come to arrest him, but once in cells he was out of Barlow's power.

Barlow found the Enquiry Office a shambles of officers, all of them waiting to log in their prisoners. Cigarette smoke, voices, and male testosterone choked the air. For once Sergeant Pierson smiled as Barlow came in the door.

'Now you're here,' he said.

Barlow kept his hand well clear of the proffered sheaf of papers. 'I'm on my lunch break.'

Harvey, with his typical bad timing, came steaming into the room. 'Barlow, this place ... How you expect Sergeant Pierson to cope on his own is beyond me.'

'I don't, sir.'

'Well sort it.' His eyes turned on Geordie. 'You're mine.'

'Don't let him goad you into doing something daft,' Barlow muttered to Geordie as Thompson led him away to an Interrogation Room.

All the same, he was glad that Harvey was concentrating on Geordie. That meant that Mrs Collins hadn't cracked under questioning and mentioned Cattle Collins. He reckoned it took more than a nosy policeman to intimidate an old District Nurse.

A good gulder brought silence to the room and a growl turned the shambles of officers and suspects into an orderly queue. Barlow went off for a sit down and a quiet cup of tea, and a good think to himself.

The dead man in Mrs Collins' garden was a stranger. Barlow knew all the local villains and would have recognised him, face down in the humus or not. Then there was the arm. He couldn't be sure, but was that the edge of a tattoo he'd seen under the jacket sleeve? Again, not a local thing, though some of the old army men had them. He'd all that to mull over before he even started to work out why the dead man and his accomplice had gone into the house in the first place.

He dismissed the possibility of a vengeful Cattle Collins pursuing the men into the garden. After all, if it was the captain, why bother hiding the murder weapon? It wasn't as if they could arrest a ghost.

With a second cup of tea in hand, he wandered into the detectives' office. DS Leary and his men had cleared their desks of everything except evidence from the crime scene. With Barlow's arrival the detective constables headed to the kitchen for a break. Leary sat on with a bemused look on his face.

Leary's hand made a welcoming sweep of the room. 'How is it, in your cases…?'

'It's hardly my case.'

'…that I have to make sense of loads of nothing?'

Barlow kept quiet. He might not like the detectives making a shambles of his station, and the crumpled suits they wore to work put his teeth on edge but, though he would never admit it, he admired Leary's professionalism.

'So?' he asked.

'Decent clothes but not the best.' Leary rolled his bulk off the chair. He went over to a desk and picked up a watch. 'Expensive but not reported as nicked.' Next he held up a wallet. 'We found this rather nice wallet in the inside pocket, but no money. Not so much as a ten-bob note.'

That made sense to Barlow. The killer was obviously someone with brains. A stolen watch could lead to the hangman's rope, but paper money was untraceable unless someone had made a record of the numbers.

'Cause of death?' he asked, though from what he'd seen it was pretty evident.

'Blunt force trauma,' Leary said. 'Long narrow breaks to the skin as opposed to circular depressions, so I'm guessing a long, heavy metal something.'

From what he'd seen of the dead man, that made sense to Barlow. 'What about fingerprints?'

'Only the dead man's and the smears of someone else who wore gloves.' Leary waved the torn cigarette packet under Barlow's nose. The remaining cigarettes tumbled about. 'The same here. Both the dead man's and smeared fingerprints.'

The little fat man's moans at finding nothing was leading to something. Barlow let Leary talk on. He owed him a few favours and recently they'd worked some cases in harmony. So much so that he trusted Leary not to spit on a pastry before handing it to him. Well almost!

'So you're stumped,' he said to speed things on a bit.

'Certainly not, a good detective is never beaten. The man had tattoos on his arms.'

'Did he now?'

'The haj knife, the union jack and the Star of David, which makes him a Protestant.'

'So you can ignore the Catholic community. That leaves only a million or so people to question. Half a million if you ignore the women.'

Leary gave a grunt of impatience. 'Tattoos are hardly common on the Malone Road, which takes us into East Belfast or the Shankhill. Soooo…' he paused for effect. 'Rather than let Headquarters take a month of Sundays tracing the dead man's fingerprints through Records, I contacted the detectives in Tennent Street and got a possible hit.'

'Well done,' Barlow said and meant it.

Leary rolled back to his own desk and picked up a note pad. 'Reginald Corkey, better known as Reg. Age forty-seven, height, weight and so on all tally with the Pathologist's initial survey of the body.'

'Undoubtedly he sang in the local church choir.'

'Hardly. Bully boy, professional bouncer, done time for GBH and aggravated burglary.'

Reg Corkey, wondered Barlow. Now what would bring a man like that to Ballymena?

For once Leary looked concerned. 'Listen to me Barlow. The late, unlamented Reg Corkey associated with a major piece of scum called Stan Holloway. You charge in with your usual flat-footed, ignorant attitude and you're likely to end up in trouble. The sort of trouble that puts people in a wooden box.'

16

The day wore on for Barlow. Prisoners sat doubled and trebled up in the cells, meals had to be sourced for them, and officers called in on their day off to guard them. Overtime had gone through the roof, and that would be his fault when it came to the monthly returns. Yet somehow in spite of the turmoil, he couldn't build enthusiasm for anything practical. About the only useful thing he did was to phone his daughter, Vera, and tell her not to expect him home for tea.

What a man like Reg Corkey was doing in Ballymena, had Barlow puzzled. He was hardly here to rob someone like Mrs Collins. It was well known about the town that her stepchildren had walked off with anything of value after their father died.

Sergeant Pierson went home at the end of his shift. He didn't look for any overtime and Barlow didn't offer it. Under Acting Sergeant Gillespie the aura of restlessness about the building eased. DI Harvey still grilled his main suspect, Geordie, but going by his face when he took the odd break, Geordie was more than holding his own.

The Hart twins, two old farmers from Slaght, were brought in. 'They were trying to organise a dance in the middle of Church Street,' the arresting constable informed Barlow. There was no spare cell so Barlow told Gillespie to pour tea and sandwiches down their throats and send them home by taxi.

Wilson and WPC Milton returned from their examination of the fields around the house. The detectives could take a look if they wanted, but there was nothing there of interest.

'Not so much as a footstep,' Wilson said in an aggrieved tone.

Finding clues leading to the arrest of a murder suspect was a quick way for an ambitious young constable to earn promotion.

Barlow nodded, not really interested in a negative report, his mind elsewhere. He himself hadn't missed anything either, but there were things there: things heard, things seen. Individually they didn't make sense. He only needed to figure out what those things were, then he could put them together and crack the case.

Gillespie stuck his head around the door of the room where Barlow had hidden himself. 'The DI's sent for Mrs Collins.'

He felt a twist of fear. 'What about?'

'An ID parade, and there'll be a big arrow sign over Geordie's head in case she doesn't recognise him.'

If Geordie or any of the other detainees hadn't confessed to the murder, then Harvey's idea of holding an identity parade wasn't such a bad idea. Mrs Collins might recognise someone in the line-up.

The line-up was the easiest Barlow ever organised. There was no need to scour the streets for volunteers. He just put all Harvey's detainees into a straight line and waited for Mrs Collins to arrive.

She came in all fidgety and nervous, wearing her Sunday best hat and coat. Barlow caught her eye and smiled a greeting. It seemed to settle her.

Seeing her out of her own environment, he was shocked at how shrunken and old she had become. Harvey kept a balancing hand on her arm as he led her into the room. Mrs Collins obviously appreciated his concern for her safety.

Barlow knew that once she'd identified Geordie as one of the burglars, she could go break her neck for all Harvey cared. Barlow stayed close enough to take over from Harvey.

'There's no rush, take your time,' Harvey told her. 'Have a good look at each man, and if you recognise anyone from last night raise your hand.'

She started down the line, peering upwards at some of Ballymena's worst citizens. She'd say no and Harvey would urge her on, closer to where Geordie stood.

Finally, she came to Geordie. Barlow felt himself tense as the head bobbed to the left and right and back again. Mrs Collins took Geordie's hand in both of hers. 'Why Mr Dunlop, this is an unexpected pleasure.'

'You're looking a picture yourself, missis,' Geordie said.

'He's such a gentleman,' Mrs Collins said to Harvey. 'When I got a puncture, Mr Dunlop changed the wheel and saw me safely home. Not only that, he took the punctured wheel away to be fixed and brought it back the next day.'

Harvey had gone six shades of puce from disappointment. Barlow had to close his own mouth. That big, fat, jammy…

'I take it that's a no?' Barlow said.

'Oh indeed,' Mrs Collins said. 'Not a penny would Mr Dunlop take, not even for having the puncture fixed.'

Geordie was smiling. Someone in the line-up snorted and the whole lot burst out laughing. So far as Harvey was concerned, the ID parade was over. He stalked out of the room.

Barlow took Mrs Collins' arm and guided her down the rest of the line.

At the end she told him. 'I might have smacked some of those bottoms in the Delivery Room, but other than that …' She shook her head.

'You didn't hit them half hard enough, missis.'

The line of men filed out. Geordie stood on. 'You'll give me a lift home?'

'Your house is barely around the corner.'

'I didn't see you walk when you came to arrest me.' Geordie smiled down at Mrs Collins. 'Thanks for speaking up for me.'

Her hand on his arm was like a fairy duster touching rock. 'I wanted these gentlemen to know that you're not all bad.'

'The exception proves the rule,' Barlow said.

17

Barlow found WPC Hughes in the kitchen where she was treating Mrs Collins to a cup of tea. Hughes had spent most of her shift in the armoury, cleaning weapons. 'You should be home,' he told her.

'I'm fine, Sarge, really. And there's half a dozen wives out there complaining about police victimisation.'

She felt up to the job. He'd have to take her word for it.

'I'll be ready for you in ten minutes,' he told Mrs Collins.

She smiled up at him. 'John, son, you're looking to get one of my wheatens.'

'It never occurred to me.'

'When did I ever send you home without one?'

Back those long years ago she had done just that. She and her husband had given him money for the work, a meal, a gentle education in table manners and a wheaten to tuck under his arm when heading home. Even now, he could remember the acrid-sweetness of her hot wheatens.

Barlow told Mrs Collins to take her time finishing the tea and went looking for Geordie. 'So where were you last night?' he demanded.

'Who's asking?'

'Geordie, it's been a long day and it's not over yet.'

Geordie tried to play the innocent maligned, Instead, he looked like he'd indigestion. 'Didn't the old bitch of a lorry break down in Londonderry, right outside the Strand Road Police Station.'

What Geordie was doing with a lorry was something Barlow didn't want to go into, not with other officers hanging around, so he asked. 'Strand Road will confirm that?'

'They'd need to. I bought the Duty Sergeant a fish supper and they gave me a bed for the night.' He developed a smirk. 'They left the cell door open. It was flaming draughty so I shut it myself.'

'Wait in the yard, not at the front door. I don't want the place getting a bad name.'

Geordie's retreating figure had a swagger in its step.

Before Barlow could take a quiet breath a hovering Sergeant Thompson went toe to toe with him. 'Barlow, when one of my woman constables has a period, I will deal with it.'

A dead body and Harvey on the warpath, Geordie feeling that he was ahead on points and now Thompson ready for another confrontation. Barlow had to take his frustrations out on someone. 'Is that right?'

'And it's not seemly for a man to know it's a lady's time of the month, let alone acknowledge it in any way.'

'So when did you notice it?' he asked. 'Certainly not this morning when you were sorting out lipsticks and makeup.'

'I was not!'

'No, you were too busy laying down the law according to the Goddess Thompson. Too busy to notice that Hughes' face looked like old parchment.'

'How dare you!'

He knew her building temper was for effect. He'd caught her out in a mistake and she didn't like it.

'You think I didn't see copies of your ten commandments, your ten "Thou shall nots" on the WPCs' desks?'

'I have every right ...'

'Not without my permission.'

'Mr Harvey...'

'I have already informed you, Sergeant Thompson, as to the chain of command in this station.' He seemed to be doing it a lot with Thompson, but he again stuck his face nearer hers. 'You have a reputation for being difficult to deal with, but when it comes to dealing with *my* Woman Police Constables, you had better be on the ball or I'll take *difficult* to a new level.'

18

Barlow knew he'd gone too far with Thompson. At the same time she had to learn her place in the station. He had trouble enough getting the men to look on the newly created Women's branch of the RUC as something to be taken seriously. The last thing he needed was Thompson giving them a chance to start muttering, 'Typical woman. Give them a bit of authority and they think they rule the world.'

He went into the yard where a couple of WPCs were seeing Mrs Collins safely into the car.

Geordie hovered. Barlow nodded him over. 'What were you doing with a lorry? What was in it and why weren't you arrested?'

'All honest and above board,' Geordie said. 'I want to get Connie something special for Christmas and the Lorrimers were advertising for a driver.'

He sounded embarrassed at being caught doing something legal.

Barlow caught his breath. 'The Lorrimers? You mean crookery doesn't pay, so you thought you'd try honesty for once?'

'Aye, thanks to you. You scuppered a couple of good wee schemes I had going.' It came as a reluctant admission.

'So, what were you doing in Londonderry?'

'Delivering stuff people had bought through a Christmas Savings scheme.'

'You were leaving it late enough.'

Barlow meant the time of delivery, but Geordie replied, 'The furniture shop people weren't too pleased either, being a Thursday evening and all. They were beginning to worry in case the stuff never came.'

With Mrs Collins waiting and it getting late, Barlow left it at that. Even so Geordie had given him a fair bit to think about. Either the Lorrimers were so busy that they could hardly keep up with orders. Or their credit so bad that they had trouble sourcing supplies to complete those orders.

He swung himself into the driver's seat beside Mrs Collins. Geordie's bulk crunched into the back and they set off. To please Mrs Collins, Barlow put on the blue light but not the bell. There were too many sleeping babies in the area for that.

He dropped Geordie off first. Geordie took a fond farewell off Mrs Collins, but only nodded at Barlow who nodded back.

Mrs Collins settled herself comfortably in the seat, handbag on her lap. 'I can see why you like Mr Dunlop. There's not a bad bone in his body.'

Barlow glanced her way in surprise. 'Generations of roguery are in his blood. It's like he can't help himself.'

'And don't the Collins know it,' she said.

He took his time driving out the Larne Line because he knew Mrs Collins was lonely and wanted to talk about the good old times: when she and her husband had a large circle of friends, and his children were happy to accept her as a presence.

Barlow was less sure of those "good" old times. Then he was on the run from the Workhouse and living hand to mouth. His good times were right now: a home he was happy for people to visit and a daughter any man would be proud of.

After the buzz of police earlier in the day, the Collins' house seemed brooding, as if leaning forward to frown at him. The chill from the morning room came back into his bones and he shivered. 'Missis, would you ever think of moving out? Get yourself a wee house with a bit of a garden and neighbours over the wall.'

'And leave the captain? And as for neighbours, better the devil you know.'

There was something in the way she said it and, earlier in the day, that remark about the captain keeping her warm on a cold night. Could there be more than hot-water bottling going on in that bed?

He almost apologised for that dirty thought. Mrs Collins was way past that sort of thing.

That remark about neighbours intrigued him as well, especially when the "neighbours" were the Lorrimers.

'You've had trouble with the Lorrimers off and on?'

'Not Rose, she's a wee pet, but that R Shaw one, you could never trust him from any age. Nothing you could put your finger on, but every time he was in the house something went missing. In the end, we told him not to come back.'

Barlow nodded. He trusted Mrs Collins' opinion, but the fact that neither of them liked R Shaw didn't make him a crook.

He drove around to the back of the house. The headlights swept across the yard and he noticed for the first time that it needed tidied. He knew Mrs Collins liked a place just so. Given good weather and a fair wind, he'd come out over the Christmas break and make things shipshape.

He almost laughed openly at himself for getting all nautical. It had to be from the Captain worrying his brain all day.

The night threatened damp, a fine mist already settling on the windscreen. He parked as close to the door as he could and turned off the engine and the lights. He left the blue light on to guide Mrs Collins into the house.

Rather than sit and have her continue to reminisce, he hopped smartly out of the car. As he did so the back door of the house swung open and a dark-clothed figure burst into the yard.

'Hey!' said the startled Barlow.

Something clanged as the figure ran straight into the side of the car. It stumbled back, which gave Barlow a chance to intercept. He ran at the figure, only to see it raise its arm. A huge extended arm.

'Frig!'

He flung himself sideways as the arm came down, but fire exploded in his head, then roared through him a second time when his shoulder hit the old cobbles.

He got onto his hands and knees. Mrs Collins was screaming. The dark figure stood over him, its arm raised for a second strike.

Barlow rolled sideways, trying to avoid the blow but immediately came up against the car bumper. The arm came down.

Another metal crash. The figure and the extended arm seemed to struggle over something. Then the figure ran off and cold metal thumped against Barlow.

19

Barlow's arm didn't flop about with both bones shattered. His head hurt with the pounding rhythm of a migraine, but no way did he feel on the verge of passing out.

Mrs Collins had stopped screaming, which also helped.

He flopped onto a sitting position and leaned against the car. The still warm headlight felt pleasant against the back of his neck.

Mrs Collins crouched over him. 'John, son, are you all right?' Her voice sounded weak from shock.

'Aye, maybe, aye.' His voice sounded even weaker.

'I'll fetch you a glass of water.'

'No don't…'

But she was already gone, into the dark house and potential danger from a second burglar. He tensed when he heard an internal door open, but seconds later light flared out through the kitchen window.

With the light coming into the yard he became aware of a hard shape near his shoulder. Turning slowly, so as not to flare the pain in his head, he took a good look at the shape. It was a wrench. One end was buried in the radiator grill of the car.

For his money, the same man and the same weapon had battered Reg Corkey to death. Barlow un-holstered his revolver and rested it on his thighs. Whoever it was might come back to finish the job.

His attacker, he supposed it was a man, was a good height and build, but definitely "wee" when compared to the late Reg Corkey.

Mrs Collins, he realised, was taking a long time fetching that glass of water. Too long. Anyway, he felt there was a bit of malingering, him sitting there waiting to be spoiled by her. With the help of the car bonnet he staggered to his feet. The movement increased the pain in his head to a hard pound, but at least it didn't fall off.

He walked to the house. The first steps were a stagger.

Almost before he could start worrying about Mrs Collins running into a second man, he heard her tapping footsteps in the inner hallway. She appeared in the doorway, her eyes widening at the sight of the revolver aimed in her direction.

'It fell out,' he said and re-holstered it, feeling a bit foolish. Even so he insisted on bolting the back door shut before agreeing to sit down and drink the water.

'John, son, you should have stayed where you were.'

'You were taking a while and I began to worry.'

She said, 'I rang 999 and spoke to that nice Sergeant Gillespie.'

'You don't know him,' he said.

He got the look he used to get when he wiped his nose with his sleeve.

Mrs Collins said, 'He sounded really concerned and said he'd be straight out.'

Barlow looked forward to Gillespie's arrival. Seeing the man's face when he saw the damage done to one of his beloved cars was nearly worth a clunk on the head.

Just about every policeman at the station answered Mrs Collins' emergency call. Inspector Foxwood and Gillespie arrived first. Gillespie checked that Barlow was alive and making sense, then he went off to grieve over his damaged car.

Foxwood pulled up a chair. 'Barlow, this is an old house with goodness-only-knows how many odd corners. Could we have missed the man when we searched the place earlier?'

'Mr Harvey took personal control of the search, sir.'

'An opportunist then, someone who spotted that Mrs Collins wasn't at home,' Foxwood said, straight-faced.

Leary came staggering in under the weight of his murder bag. 'I brought it along more in hope that expectation,' he said.

Barlow nodded to the window, then wished he hadn't. 'Take a look at that wrench buried in the radiator of the car.'

The police doctor came and an ambulance, which was sent away. No, Barlow hadn't passed out, not even for a second. He was sure of that. 'If I had, I'd be dead.'

'Good point,' the doctor said, eyeing the wrench which now lay bagged on the kitchen table. Leary stood drooling over it. The wrench had to be the murder weapon. He could see hair and coagulated blood on the larger end.

Barlow's head was sore and there was a growing lump under his hair, but no cuts. The doctor shrugged, apparently as disappointed as Leary at finding Barlow alive.

'I'm sorry for your trouble,' Barlow said in mock sympathy as the doctor departed for home and his interrupted night-time noggin.

With the area secured and the house scoured in case a second burglar skulked unseen, Foxwood allowed a WPC, in the shape of Sergeant Thompson, into the house. With her came Constable Wilson.

Thompson's task was to convince the now fading Mrs Collins to go to bed, with the assurance that two police officers, Thompson herself and Wilson, would spend the night in the house.

Barlow found his eyes closing from exhaustion. He forced them open again because he had one more task – no two – to perform before he could call it a night and head home. He found a wheaten-round lodged in his arms and had no idea how it had got there. The old woman had remembered a promise, even when she was shattered and heart-scared.

They'd get Mrs Collins to check in the morning but, again, nothing seemed to have been taken.

So what and why?

The old lady's life could depend on him getting it right.

20

Barlow forced himself to his feet. Stay sitting and he'd merely nod off.

Somehow the kitchen seemed wrong for what he needed to work out. He went into the back hallway and stood for a moment getting his bearings. To the right was the back door leading into the yard. To the left, the door separating the servants' quarters from the rest of the house. In front of him the narrow back stairs and two doors. From memory, the Laundry Room and the Butler's Pantry.

He borrowed a torch off a passing constable and checked the Laundry Room first. Clothes and bedding lay folded neatly on shelving. The only change he could see from those years a lifetime back, was the addition of a modern ironing board and a hanging rail painfully lacking the late Mr Collins' double-cuffed shirts.

The Butler's Pantry: as ever without a butler but full of neatly arranged items the Collins wanted to keep handy.

He went through the door into the great hall, and somehow managed to stop himself from doing a useless check of the house. Lights from the police cars glared through the windows, setting everything in cold shadow.

If he could see that, then the burglar would have seen the car turning in the gate, unless…

He turned a slow circle, facing each side of the house as he thought about it. Even in a back room or a room on the far side of the house there'd have been enough reflected light for the man to escape before they reached the back yard. Had the man waited, hoping to kill Mrs Collins? That didn't seem likely. Then was he somewhere in the house where he couldn't see the car lights and was reacting to the sound of the engine?

Where? He thought he knew and felt sick at the thought. Mrs Collins only had a life interest in the house. Was it possible that one of her stepchildren was trying to hasten her departure by an apparent accident?

He went back into the Butler's Pantry. Now he knew what he was looking for - the signs were obvious. The gas meter sat in an ancient recess, the coins for the meter lay scattered on a side table. He gritted his teeth in disgust. He should have seen that the first time he looked in. Mrs

Collins always kept her rows of coins stacked like soldiers on parade.

He sniffed, first gently then harder and got a smell of gas, more lingering than anything else. He shone the torch on the connection between the meter and the gas pipe. Brass from the nut gleamed through generations of old paint.

Barlow backed out of the Butler's Pantry. His heart pounded harder than his injured head as he went shouting for Leary and his murder bag.

21

Not for Barlow the now frenzied search by others through the house for the smell of gas or for signs of appliances tampered with. The Ballymena Gas Company took gas and safety around it very seriously. The thought of someone deliberately tampering with supplies and putting Mrs Collins at risk, had sent the company boss into shock. A platoon of engineers were on their way. In the meantime, would the police please switch off the gas at the meter and vacate the house.

Mrs Collins was in her dressing gown and slippers when Barlow chivvied her into a car and sent her to spend the night in the Castle Arms Hotel. Once the gas people declared the house safe, Sergeant Thompson would look her out a change of clothes for the morning.

Ignoring Foxwood's orders to stand well clear of the building, Barlow took his thumping head and equally busy heart into the morning room. He closed the door tight behind him so that no one could overhear and have him sectioned.

He stood before the portrait of Cattle Collins and felt a chill that was probably fear. 'Captain, you must have a good idea of what is going on in the house. There have been two attempts on the life of Mrs Collins. Why? I don't know. By whom? I don't know. But you do or you must have a good idea who is involved.'

He hardly expected the portrait to nod back at him. In fact, with no more than reflected light seeping in through the windows, he could hardly see the frame let alone the figure.

'My grief is with you, Captain. You're awfully grand. Too grand to go into the servants' quarters. Too grand to do more than sit in this room and think of what might have been, but, oh boy, are you quick to defend your domain in the great hall and beyond.

'Last night, you had to know that those men had broken in, but you did nothing until they came into *your* part of the house. Only then did you rouse Mrs Collins, putting her at risk. And then tonight, you had to know that someone was tampering with the gas, but again you did nothing.'

He wanted to shout and gulder but kept his voice down to a hiss that no one else could hear. 'Get off your high horse! Get into the servants' quarters and guard Mrs Collins with your… I was going to say life, but you know what I mean.'

He stopped with his hand on the handle of the door to let himself out. 'Next time I come in that back door, you had better announce your presence good and loud or I'll remind everyone why you're called Cattle Collins.

A frost came at Barlow, a frost even more bitterly cold than the one he'd felt earlier.

He gave the portrait a two-fingered salute, and called it a night.

Blank Page

Saturday
December 17th

22

The next morning, six-thirty on the button, Barlow came awake.

'Feckin' shift patterns.'

His snuggled-in-body told his mind to go back to sleep for another half hour, but worries and problems kept intruding. Finally, a restless arm lifted the bedclothes, letting cold air in, and a shudder turned into a reluctant crawl out of bed.

A wrap-around dressing gown and feet jammed into unlaced boots deflected much of the winter chill as he staggered towards the kitchen. Toby, their Jack Russell, lay on a mat, blocking the corridor leading from the bedrooms. He showed his teeth and lay on, forcing Barlow to step over him.

'Stubborn brute,' Barlow said, stooping to pat Toby in spite of the silent growls that vibrated his body. Toby followed Barlow into the kitchen and after a quick run around the back garden made himself comfortable on Barlow's favourite chair.

A glow still showed in the kitchen fire. Barlow stirred the embers, quietly so as not to disturb the sleeping Vera, and added fresh sticks and coal. He made a pot of tea. Rather than fight with Toby he sat at the kitchen table. 'Linfield are in town today. There'll be enough fighting without having a go at you.'

He decided to focus his mind by listing people involved in the murder investigation, and fetched pencil and paper out of the sideboard:

VICTIM — Reg Corkey
INTENDED VICTIM — Mrs Collins
SUSPECTS

He had no suspects and moved on from that. Then he paused and argued rational sense against what he knew. Finally he wrote:

Captain Collins

The "Captain" rather than "Cattle" because currently they were on the same side, or appeared to be.

INVOLVED? — Reg's mates in Belfast

AROUND Mr Lorrimer
R Shaw Lorrimer
Rose Lorrimer

He had another think while he sipped at his tea, then added:
Geordie Dunlop

He screwed the list into a ball. 'A flaming lot of nothing,' threw it into the now blazing fire and went off to get dressed. When he came out of the bathroom, Toby was back at his post at the end of the corridor.

Toby would remain there until Vera got up. Weekdays, he saw her safely to work in the Courthouse, even though it was barely across the road from where they lived. The rest of the day Toby spent lying in the outer hallway, waiting for them to come home. He'd even started to figure the times Vera would be heading home from work and go to meet her.

'Flaming dog,' Barlow muttered and gave Toby another pat before pulling on his jacket. He left even earlier than usual because it was going to be one of those days, with Linfield Football Club supporters in town, a dangerous murderer on the loose and Sergeant Thompson with her grudge against the world in general and him in particular.

23

That morning, Sergeant Thompson had the grace to turn up for Morning Parade with her buttons pointedly straight up and down.

'Mrs Collins?' Barlow asked Thompson immediately after the parade.

'Wilson's still there, and a Terry Esler turned up to improve her security. He said you called him last night.'

'That I did.'

Barlow wanted blocking pins put in every window so they could only be opened from the inside, and the back door needed replaced, the wood so rotten that it only took a good shake to get past the mortice lock.

The next problem was Harvey, Overtime Sheets in hand, breathing fire. 'Barlow, the amount of overtime you allowed the men yesterday was quite ridiculous. A complete overuse of manpower and resources. Have you any idea what this does to our budget?'

'No, sir,' lied Barlow who'd handled all the budgets in the years before Harvey's arrival.

'In future, Barlow, no one works so much as an hour's overtime without my express permission.'

'Very good, sir,' Barlow said, and called in with Inspector Foxwood to discuss the manpower required at the Ballymena United V Linfield football match. Sometimes the Linfield supporters came and went like lambs. Sometimes all hell was let loose.

The discussion didn't take long. Barlow tended to pile paperwork onto Foxwood. It kept the man tied to his desk and less likely to go snooping for trouble.

Trouble was in the corridor when he eventually left.

Harvey had Sergeant Thompson trapped in an alcove. 'Thompson, I'd like to discuss your future career prospects. However, I'm always under pressure of time during the day.'

Barlow stomped his feet to make sure that Harvey heard him coming, but Harvey merely glanced his way before moving closer, his uniform buttons all but touching Thompson's. 'What about some evening after work? Perhaps we could meet for a drink?'

Barlow said, loudly, 'Sir, I've been thinking about that budget thing of yours, and I'm not coming up with any ideas of how to reduce it.'

Harvey glared his way but stayed tight up to Thompson.

Barlow asked, 'For instance, today's football match, sir. Is that authorised or unauthorised overtime?'

'Clear off Barlow.'

Barlow couldn't see Thompson's face so he couldn't work out what she was thinking. Nothing good of Harvey, he reckoned. If the lady pressed back any further she'd crack the plasterwork.

'I'm only trying to get this new overtime thing sorted in my head, sir.'

Harvey stepped back from Thompson. 'I told you, Barlow, this does not concern you.'

'I was wondering if you had any ideas yourself, sir?'

'Barlow! Last chance!'

Just then Harvey's secretary came looking for him. 'The ACC's on the line.'

'Good morning, Miss Fetterland,' Barlow said, ever so politely.

She sniffed as if getting a bad smell. 'It's Fetterman. Miss Fetterman,' she said and walked off.

Harvey had already rushed ahead so as not to keep an ACC waiting. His voice carried back. 'You'll regret this, Barlow. You and your budgets.'

Barlow was more interested in the red-faced Thompson and the way she brushed at her uniform.

'Well?' he asked her

'A private discussion.'

Obviously, Thompson didn't intend to complain. Even so, he spelled it out for her. 'Any more trouble from Harvey, you let me know and I'll sort both it and him.'

24

With the arrival of the Linfield supporters, traffic in the town ground to a halt. The men who poured off the special trains filled the streets from pavement to pavement on their way to the Showgrounds.

As usual, the police station received a few straight-arm salutes and shouts of 'Nazi pigs.'

'It takes one to know one,' muttered Barlow.

He was standing at the railings of the Memorial Garden, elbows at the ready in case a supporter *accidentally* trod on his toes. His job was to assess the mood of the crowd, and right then it was worrying him. He'd never seen the Linfield supporters so sweet and nice. Some of the hardest men veered his way to say 'Afternoon, Sergeant.' It was like watching Albert Pierrepoint, the hangman, assessing him for the big drop.

The crowd flowed on, finally draining down to a trickle of stragglers. Barlow followed at their heels, calling in the officers manning junctions as he went, redeploying them to the Showgrounds where they could watch the match. Wilson stood with WPC Milton and the dog, manning the five ways at the Pentagon. Their specific task, as detailed by Harvey, was to detour the Linfield men through the centre of the town. Too much local money was involved for Harvey to risk Linfield supporters vandalising the newly refurbished Castle Arms Hotel on the Ballymoney Road.

Barlow took his time going through the town, popping occasionally into a shop to hear the owner's puff of relief that things had gone quietly so far. Crowd roars and tribal songs filled the air as battle commenced on the pitch.

It was nearing half time when he eased himself through a side gate into the Showgrounds. High metal railings and a cinder running track separated the crowd from the players on the field. But not so far that shouted threats and jibs couldn't find their mark.

Barlow walked along the back of the stand, let himself in at a private doorway and ran up the stairs leading to the Directors' Box: an open wooden structure at the top of the main stand.

He got startled looks that eased to nods of greeting when he smiled and took off his cap. "Cap off" meant that it wasn't an official visit and the collective guilty consciences could go back to sleep. The man he was looking for: Charles Denton, owner of the Ballymena Brewery Company and Chairman of the Local Policing Committee. Denton sat in the front row beside a man who definitely wasn't a member of the visiting dignitaries. The man nodded to Barlow but never took his eyes off the field. It was a mild day for December but the watchers were glad to huddle into their heavy overcoats.

Barlow pulled up a chair behind Denton. 'I'd like a word.'

'At half time, we're nearly there.'

Denton's voice was tight with tension as he watched the Linfield players surge towards the Ballymena goal. The goalkeeper caught a weak attempt at a goal and punted the ball way up field. Now the players surged in the opposite direction. They were led by the one man who had held back from defending his own goalmouth, R Shaw Lorrimer.

'So we're getting beat, as usual?'

'It's nil all, and what do you mean "as usual"? We've had eighteen straight home wins in a row.'

'Even so we only ran up the City Cup.'

From away over on the left, Ballymena's No 10 shimmied the ball around an opponent. He then ignored R Shaw's screams to pass the ball to him and fired in a shot that the Linfield goalie barely managed to fingertip over the bar.

Denton sucked air in disappointment.

'R Shaw Lorrimer?' asked Barlow. It was as good a place to start as any. Given a minute or two he would come up with No10's name. He'd recently seen him working on a building site.

'Our No 9, the Righteous R Shaw,' Denton said. 'Didn't make the rugby squad, let alone the first team, at the Academy so he takes up soccer. Other than the fact that he's unfit and doesn't train, he's a glory hunter instead of a team man. He'd hardly make the second squad if it wasn't for his father's badly needed sponsorship.'

'There has to be a fair bit of loose cash about the business then,' prompted Barlow, remembering the unpaid bills.

'They've started to export bespoke furniture,' Denton said.

As a Workhouse boy, Barlow never got a packed lunch to take to school but Denton's mother always gave her son extra sandwiches to share with him. He'd known then when Denton was being evasive and he knew it now, but let it go for the time being.

'At least they were doing rightly until Geordie took a job with them,' continued Denton. 'He wanted me to give him a reference. Me! The last thing that bloody man drove was a lorry load of whiskey stolen out of my yard.'

A hard-pressed Linfield defender punted the ball over his back line for a corner kick. The referee was looking at his watch, ready to blow the whistle for half-time.

R Shaw and No10 took up positions on opposite sides of the goalmouth.

Barlow remembered. 'No10, that's young Tom Rankin.' He wondered at the youth working as a labourer. 'I thought he had a junior management job at Lorrimers?'

Denton indicated the unknown man sitting beside him. 'He's a scout from Tottenham Hotspur. There's talk of them giving Rankin a trial.'

The corner kick came curving in near the goalmouth. Both Rankin and R Shaw went for it. R Shaw, in his greed for glory, knocked Rankin off balance and the defenders managed to scramble the ball clear.

Denton growled in frustration at the missed opportunity. 'Rankin has scored eighteen goals already this season, including a hat-trick last week against Glentoran.'

Again there was the sense of evasion. Barlow didn't let it pass. 'A building site is a dangerous place for a youth with those skills.'

'It is,' Denton said.

A Ballymena defender blocked a new Linfield surge and sent the ball flying up-field again. The referee had the whistle hovering near his lips.

Barlow nudged Denton and nodded at the football scout. 'A brewery would be a safer place to tide him over.'

Denton looked between Barlow and the scout. As he did so, a hope-and-a-prayer kick from a Ballymena player sent the ball sailing towards the Linfield goalmouth.

Denton held up his hand and made a rubbing sign with his thumb and forefinger. 'Sticky fingers,' he mouthed as both Rankin and R Shaw went for the ball.

Rankin was closer and better positioned. His kick drove the ball into the back of the net. R Shaw's kick powered into the side of Rankin's knee.

'I missed that goal, it's your fault,' Denton yelled at Barlow over the roar of the delighted Ballymena supporters.

Rankin was on the ground, clutching his knee. The referee blew his whistle for half time.

Barlow left. The football scout left with him.

25

Barlow saw the subdued Linfield supporters onto the train home and then went back to the station to sign off work for the day. Signing off was part habit and part example for the other officers. Harvey refused to pay him overtime regardless of the circumstances.

When he arrived at the station, Sergeant Pierson took great pleasure in pointing out the revised Duty Roster for Christmas and the New Year holidays. The number of men on duty had been cut to the bone to save on overtime rates. Worse than that, Harvey had Barlow down for a double shift on Christmas day. That meant Vera would spend Christmas on her own as they had no relations in the town that she could go to.

Barlow could cope with Harvey's spitefulness, but to get at him through Vera…

He nodded to Pierson as if he couldn't see anything unusual about the shift arrangements, and phoned Terry Esler, the builder. Terry confirmed that he had replaced Mrs Collins' back door and had made the house as secure as possible. The old lady had insisted on moving back into her home.

'Bless her stubborn old heart,' Barlow said and went on.

He arrived home to find a Christmas tree winking seasonal greetings at the sitting room window, their bungalow shining from its Saturday clean and Vera just back from giving Toby a long walk. In addition, she'd found the time to put up the Christmas decorations. Multi-coloured streamers criss-crossed the hall and the living room, and a Christmas wreath hung from the front door knocker.

'I like your idea of helping around here,' she said.

She looked weary and sweaty.

He felt guilty. 'Sorry love. Next week it's all on me.'

'Aye, Christmas Eve, aye. And every drunk in the town making merry.'

Which didn't make it a good time to mention Christmas Day and the double shift. Instead, he praised everything she had done, taking time to notice the small things, and dared ask how she'd managed to string the decorations into all the high corners, single handed.

'I hired a solicitor,' she said and ran for the bathroom before he could ask any more questions.

'I need a bath,' trailed behind her.

One thing he was sure of. The holly hanging from the central light in the hallway had been well tested.

He made the tea, giving her the more than her fair share of the braised meat but less of the onion gravy. Recently she had cut down on greasy food, trying to reduce her bulky figure. In his opinion, she'd never be slim and trim like those film stars, but he admired her for trying.

'Are you going anywhere tonight?' he asked.

She was wearing a dressing gown, with a towel wrapped around her hair.

'Ernie's taking me to see *Let's Make Love* at the State.'

'The what?'

'You'd love it, Dad. Marilyn Monroe's in it, and you've a *thing* for blondes.'

Barlow growled inwardly rather than get into an argument about what was suitable for his daughter and what wasn't. Vera's latest beau, Ernest T Potter, was one of a series of young solicitors she had met through her job in the courthouse. "Ernie" worked for the hated Moncrief firm and was already well on his way to being a ruthless, no holds barred, pain in the ass.

Vera kissed Barlow on the nose and went off to get ready for the evening.

He watched her bounce out of the room, proud of the daughter he had raised, and worried about her and this "Ernie." When it came to his daughter there had better be plenty of bars, and high ones at that, or this *Ernie* fellow would feel his wrath.

In rushing off to get ready, Vera had deliberately overlooked the rule that whoever ate the tea as opposed to making it, had to do the dishes. Like her stepping out with her Ernie, he was in no position to object. He had a sneaking suspicion that this new relationship was rapidly becoming serious.

26

The call came near pub closing time. Barlow was technically still in uniform, though his jacket hung over a chair and his bootless toes glowed close to the coal fire. He stuck his feet into unlaced boots and slithered into the tiled hallway to answer the phone.

The Duty Sergeant, Sergeant Pierson, said, 'Sarge.'

'Sergeant.'

'Sergeant there's trouble in the pubs.'

There would be. A Saturday night, with the remnants of the Linfield supporters still in town and them hurting from a 2:0 defeat.

Barlow said, 'Tell DI Harvey and round up all the officers on duty.'

'He's in Belfast, the wife doesn't know where.'

'Inspector Foxwood?'

'He can't be got.'

Barlow shook his head in despair as Pierson's voice rose in panic. This was the man Harvey kept angling to make Station Sergeant.

'Ring Gillespie then. Tell him to round up as many men as he can and report to the station.'

Pierson's voice went nearly falsetto. 'I can't. Mr Harvey said no overtime. Not without his permission.'

'Tell Gillespie to say I made the call.'

Barlow slammed down the receiver and quick-tied his boots, grabbed his jacket and was out the door in less than a minute. The fireguard wasn't up to protect the house if a burning coal fell out and he found Toby at his heels instead of in his chair.

'Pierson isn't the only one who's panicking,' he told the dog.

It was this feeling he'd had all day, of bad things happening. Sometimes during the war, when he detailed a man to defuse an unexploded bomb, he knew he would never see that man again. It was the same feeling.

He went on with Toby at his heels. Toby played hard-to-get when he didn't want to go back into the house, and Barlow hadn't the time to fight with him.

Policemen in uniform do not run unless in active pursuit of a fugitive, but Barlow's walking pace had his legs aching within a hundred yards. He kept it up until he reached the station.

Pierson was on his own, sweating with tension. 'The Raglin's wrecked and now there's trouble brewing in Bridge Bar...'

'Who did you send?'

'I don't have enough men for normal patrolling…'

'Who?' roared Barlow, because whatever the answer was, it had to be bad.

'You said "all officers" and Sergeant Thompson …'

Barlow all but ripped the door off its hinges as he tore out of the Enquiry Office and ran full pelt down the street. He'd kill them both, Pierson and Thompson. With Pierson's collusion, Thompson had taken the WPCs into a dangerous situation. WPCs who didn't carry nightsticks let alone guns. Which reminded him that his nightstick was still safely secured in his locker at the station.

'Bugger and blast.'

His lungs hurt already but he tried to run even faster. Toby ran ahead, barking with excitement.

He sprinted the length of North Street into Bridge Street. People stood, wide-eyed at him running, instead getting out of the way on the narrow footpaths. Outside the Bridge Bar he crashed to a halt and listened to the silence where there should have been voices raised in friendly arguments and laughter. Somewhere inside the bar, glass shattered against the stone floor.

He'd heard that sound before, of a bottle being made ready to shove into someone's face.

27

Barlow eased through the front door of the pub with Toby at his heels. Chairs and tables had been kicked aside. Men stood, lined up for the fight: visiting Linfield men to the left, the locals to the right. In the middle stood Thompson and her three subordinates. Thompson and Keane faced the locals. The other two WPCs and the dog faced the Linfield men. The WPCs had truncheons to protect themselves with. Thompson carried the WPC standard issue cosh.

Barlow ordered, 'Thompson and Keane – about face.'

Keane obeyed immediately, turning towards the Linfield men. Thompson stood on, looking like she wanted to argue the point. Right then a bottle flew and the warring parties surged towards each other.

The three WPCs stood shoulder to shoulder, but far enough apart to strike with truncheons they weren't supposed to possess. Milton stood in the centre with the Alsatian already on its toes, anxious to attack. Barlow tried to get to them but found his way blocked by a beefy Linfield man. They traded blows but the man had the weight of his friends behind him. Barlow found himself trapped against a wall until Toby sank his teeth into a couple of legs.

A shove and a leg hook sent Thompson to the floor. Barlow struggled to reach her. Geordie got there first. He grabbed Thompson by the scruff of the neck and hauled her onto her feet.

'Put me down,' Thompson said.

'On the floor again if you want,' Geordie said, and swung a fist at a man coming at them with a raised bottle.

The other three WPCs were doing better. No one wanted to be savaged by an Alsatian, which gave them space to their front. Any knee, elbow or shoulder that came close received a swipe from a truncheon. A man managed to grip WPC Hughes' truncheon and hauled. She let go of the truncheon and he stumbled back. Hughes had draped the loop around her thumb where it slid free, and not the wrist where it would have snagged and left her off balance and vulnerable.

A second man saw his opportunity and came in, stabbing at her face with a smashed bottle. She grabbed his fist, twisted his arm behind his back and, using his own momentum, sent him head first into the bar counter.

At that the fight was over. The Linfield men knew they were getting the worst of it and headed for the door. Any Linfield man on the floor was arrested. If they even attempted to get up Milton had the dog snarl in their face and they quickly subsided. Local men were helped to their feet and sat on a chair to recover. No one seemed to need an ambulance.

One of the prisoners had shouted "Nazi pig" at Barlow earlier in the day. 'Sieg Heil,' Barlow informed him.

The WPCs were unharmed and busy organising the locals to tidy up the place. He gave them a nod of approval. Really, he wanted to give them a big hug. Thompson had her back to him. The idea of his boot meeting her backside was tempting.

Geordie leaned on the bar counter, ordering a replacement beer from the barman. He blew on skinned knuckles. 'That was fun.'

'I'm glad you were here,' the barman said, pulling a complimentary pint for both men. 'I knew they'd be back and there would be trouble.'

'Who would be back?' asked Barlow. The pint went down like nectar, soothing a throat dry from exertion.

'Those Belfast men trying to sell me protection.'

Geordie beamed at an easy way of making money. 'You could pay me instead.'

'Don't you start,' the barman said.

Thompson came storming over. 'You're under arrest,' she informed Geordie. 'Assaulting a police officer in the lawful exercise of their duty…'

'Know your friends,' Barlow said.

'What do you mean by that?'

'All the locals came here for a quiet drink.' He stabbed a finger against her nose. 'And you turned your back on the ones who came looking for trouble.'

She went stiff with outrage. 'You have just assaulted me.'

'Oh, piss off! And, you can report me for that as well.'

28

The cells were full to bursting, two and three men to a single bed, and no one in the station caring too much one way or another. Gillespie was supervising the WPCs while they wrote up their reports and acting as a comforting big brother when the aftershock of the violence hit them.

The barman's remark about "protection" coupled with a coordinated attack on local pubs by hard men from Belfast, had Barlow worried. First thing Monday he'd get Wilson on it: how many pubs had been approached? When, and why oh why didn't the pub owners tell him? On the QT if necessary.

The Police Doctor was having a busy night. Every prisoner had to be examined, as had every officer, man or woman, involved in the fight. Harvey's budget for medical costs had just gone sky high. It brought a glow of warmth to Barlow's heart.

He caught up with the doctor in the corridor for a final report.

'No one for the hospital as such,' the Doctor said. 'However, those bones your Amazons battered will need X-rayed in the morning. As for yourself.' His voice took on a vague tone as if talking while he wrote down the words. 'A new scuff mark on your cheek.'

'A glancing blow, Doc.'

'Another headache?'

It came reluctantly. 'Yes.'

The blow and staggering back against the wall had reignited the previous day's headache. Nothing bad. A couple of aspirins and a good night's sleep and he'd be fine.

The Doctor stared into his eyes for a long moment. 'Ok, Barlow, but no more chances for a while. That's two head blows in two days.' He walked on.

WPC Milton came out of the kitchen. She developed a stagger when she saw Barlow. 'Sarge, I need something sweet to get me home. I'm gasping.'

He put his hand in his pocket. It came out empty, even so he pressed his fingers against hers. 'Cadbury's Fruit and Nut.'

She looked at her empty hand. 'Oh wow!'

She simulated unwrapping the chocolate bar, jammed half of what wasn't there into her mouth and chewed vigorously. 'Sarge, you are a life saver.'

She went off with a bounce in her step that hadn't been there before.

Thompson had appeared and stood watching. 'What was that all about?'

Barlow made it short and snappy, not inviting any more questions. 'Retraining Milton's eating habits.'

Thompson gave him one of her hard looks and headed off down the corridor.

'Where are you going?' he called after her.

'The Section House. It's been a long day.'

She did look weary but he hardened his heart. 'You're coming with me.'

'I've already signed off duty.'

'Around here, the fact that you don't get paid for overtime doesn't mean that you don't work it.'

He walked out of the station with Toby at his heels, and she had to follow. It was a good night, cold but not nippy. In spite of the street lighting, stars studded the sky. The person he sought should be about.

'Where are we going and why?' Thompson asked coming level with him.

He countered with. 'I've submitted a report about your actions tonight, and I can tell you it's a bad one.'

'Because I took my WPCs into that pub?'

He ignored the "my". 'Because you took unnecessary chances with them.'

Her voice was firm, schoolmarmish. 'Women police constables must only be employed in roles applicable to women unless and only when male colleagues are not available.'

He wondered how often she had quoted that section.

'Aye, try using that as an excuse if one of them had got a bottle in her face.'

'They didn't.'

'What do you know about my WPCs' The "my" was emphasised.

He listened to her as he led the way across Mill Street and Lower Linenhall Street and from there into Albert Place, which ran behind the court house.

She had read the WPCs' files before coming to Ballymena and could quote from them in detail. They were all still at the station when the call came through from the Bridge Bar. It was the first chance she'd had all day to talk to them as a group. Mr Harvey had graciously granted them the overtime.

'So you talked,' he said. 'On the Saturday before the Christmas weekend, when they had planned an evening together at the Flamingo to hear the Imperial All-Stars.'

'Exigency of service,' she said. Again well-rehearsed.

'But did you listen? Did you let the WPCs speak?'

She had to stop walking when he slammed to a halt.

'You didn't listen, did you? You were too busy laying down the law according to Sergeant Thompson.'

'So what did I miss?' she asked.

He counted the facts off on his fingers. 'Women cannot be pursuit drivers, but Gillespie, who is a qualified instructor, would give WPC Keane a full certificate tomorrow.' He touched the second finger. 'The normal dog handler, Constable McGinn, is currently at Hendon, where he is lecturing the experts on training police dogs. And while he is at Hendon, he happily left the best police dog in the force in the care of WPC Milton.' Barlow didn't bother with the third finger. 'As for our blue-eyed blonde, WPC Hughes. Again, women aren't allowed to bear arms but she is a crack shot with both pistol and rifle.'

He couldn't hold back his anger. '*My* WPCs didn't go into that dangerous situation tonight because you ordered them to. They went because that self-same Constable McGinn schools them in unarmed combat.'

'I didn't know that,' she said.

'And that, Sergeant Thompson, is the first sensible thing you said since you got here.'

29

While they walked and talked, Barlow became aware of a scurry of movement around them. By then they were in Clarence Street. Cars turning into the street, caught sight of the two police officers in their lights and turned into the car park of the now closed Castle Arms Hotel. Cars coming from the opposite direction reversed or speeded up and drove past them. The same thing with echoing footsteps in the otherwise empty street.

Near the top of Clarence Street, Barlow turned into the short, all but derelict John Street. John Street had a narrow entry into an abandoned courtyard. The high stone buildings were devoid of roof, floor and floor-joists. Even the wooden frames of the doors and windows were long gone.

A woman's voice carried out of the shadows. 'Clear off, Barlow. You're ruining business.'

'Ah now, is that the way to speak to an old friend?'

A woman in her late thirties stepped into the street lighting. She was tall and broad-shouldered and she matched Thompson, hard look for hard look.

'I'm Evon. Like the Avon Ladies, but with an E instead of an A,' she told Thompson. 'I carry enough weight to be comfortable but not a squishy lay.'

'How's business, Evon?' Barlow asked before Thompson could react to this blunt admission of prostitution.

'Better when you're not around, Mr Barlow.'

'A cold night's bad for business,' he replied, ignoring the cars and pedestrians who had turned away when they saw the police.

Evon's head jerked back towards the derelict courtyard and the darker shadows of other women staying out of sight. 'It's not all blow jobs back there. There's the odd job with a fire and a comfortable bed for the night.'

'When the wife's away…' Barlow said.

'That lot! They play among themselves. They have parties that not even I would get involved in.'

Thompson reached for her notebook. 'Names. Addresses.'

'You are kidding,' Evon said.

'Those fires and comfortable beds,' Barlow said, elbowing his way between the two women. 'Be careful, there's rather nasty men trying to get involved locally.'

'I will,' Evon said.

'Do, and goodnight.'

Barlow decided that a soft Clarendon Mint would be good company on the walk home. He turned to walk away but Thompson pulled him back. 'She should be arrested, she's just admitted to living off immoral means. Keep her and the rest here while I call out the Paddywagon.'

'When you do arrest them, where are you going to put them tonight – the Section House? The boys would love that.'

She stayed silent, trying to work her way through the impasse of the cells currently stuffed with Linfield supporters.

Thompson had worked all over Northern Ireland, and should have known the facts of a policeman's life when it came to dealing with the sex trade. Even so, he spelled it out for her. 'Evon makes sure that every customer is over sixteen and insists that the women get a monthly medical.'

Evon butted in. 'And if they don't I send them to the back of the Tower Cinema to service the policemen and policewomen coming off duty.' She stared Thompson straight in the eye. 'I could get you a special rate, especially if you wore your uniform.'

Barlow linked Thompson's arm and forced her back with him into Clarence Street.

Thompson's voice had a shake to it. 'That is Incitement to Prostitution, pure and simple. Offering me a job in the sex trade. She could get two years for that alone.'

Barlow pointed to his left. 'I head that way and downhill for home. You go back the way we came.'

He waited until he was sure she was walking back to the station before shouting after her. 'Friday night is the staff do. I'll pick you up at eight forty-five.' She spun around as he added. 'You don't want to be walking into that sort of party on your own.'

'I do it every year,' she called back.

'This is Ballymena. We know how to treat our women here.'

'I'm not your woman.'

‘Heaven forbid,’ he said, and went on.

30

Vera was waiting up for Barlow when he got home. She was in her dressing gown and slippers.

'What time of the night is this to be coming in?' she demanded.

He was tired and weary to the bone, but he played along. 'A few curlers in your hair, cream on your face and you could be any old vixen.'

He beat Toby to his chair and sat down. With Vera around, Toby was on his best behaviour. Rather than snarl at Barlow he went and sat next to Vera and rested his head on her leg.

'He'd take a biscuit if you offered him one,' Barlow said and told her of the trouble in the Bridge Bar while she made him a cup of tea.

Not that he particularly wanted tea at that time of night but he sensed that Vera had something to tell him.

She waited until they were both settled with freshly made tea and Toby crunching through Barlow's favourite ginger nut biscuits. 'Mum rang the other day.'

'Did she?' he said, making it sound casual, as if his wife, Maggie, rang the house regularly.

She never had before. Always, her sister, Daisy, rang and then Maggie would speak briefly on the phone.

'She's talking about me spending Christmas with them.'

'She'd like that?'

Maggie knew that Vera was her daughter but could never relate that to being married to him and to them sharing a bed for seventeen years.

'She would,' Vera said.

He could tell Vera would like that as well. She'd given up on her dream of them ever coming back together again as man and wife, but she needed quality time with her mother who had spent much of her youth in a mental institution.

'Why not then?' he asked.

There were tears in her eyes and wish in her voice. 'I can't leave you, Dad.'

'Aye you can.'

Without intending to, Harvey had done him a good turn putting him on double shift on Christmas day. But what about the rest of the holidays?

'You've got tickets for the pantomime,' she said.

'There's always someone who can use them.'

It was sort of decided then. He felt lonely, as if she had already gone.

'How are you going to get there and back?' he asked.

'I'm working on it.'

Now there was an evasion if ever there was one, but it was late and he was too tired to be bothered.

He gave her a hug and a kiss and assured her that she would enjoy Christmas in Donaghadee with her mother and aunt. Wished her a goodnight and headed off to bed.

'And if I hear a noise from either you or that blessed dog between now and midday,' he shouted back down the corridor.

'Yes Da, no Da.'

'I'll take the strap to the two of you.'

'Go on you aul rip you,' she shouted back.

Blank Page

Sunday December 18th

31

Sunday morning dawned bright, though a hard frost glittered the ground. Barlow stayed deep under the blankets until his conscience bothered him about Sunday lunch. Mainly because Vera was still a hit-or-miss cook and he'd bought a roast especially.

He staggered out of bed and under the shower. Hot water instead of the expected cold scalded him wide awake. Vera was up before him and had the immersion on.

He dressed in uniform shirt and trousers. There was just too much going on at the station for him not to put in a brief appearance.

'Morning,' Vera said, pointedly looking at the clock, which said twelve-twenty.

She also had a pot of tea waiting for him and had made a start peeling the potatoes. Onions were always his domain. The tears made her makeup run.

He ate a plate of Corn Flakes, gulped tea and took over in the kitchen. After all, Vera had spent the previous day doing all the weekly housework and put up the Christmas decorations. Vera retired to his chair, Toby hopped off for her, something he never did for him. She stretched her feet onto a pouffe and noisily turned the pages of a glossy magazine.

Barlow got the message, he was on the washing-up as well.

He had the roast prepped and ready for the oven, and was thinking about dessert when the doorbell rang.

'It's probably for me,' called Vera, so he could ignore it. Anyway, it probably was, like most of the phone calls into the house.

He decided on stewed apples and custard. He was on his hands and knees hunting through the vegetable tray for cooking apples, when he became aware of police regulation shoes and stockings, towering over him.

He looked up, knowing it was bad if they'd come looking for him, and recognised Thompson.

Her face was carefully bland at finding him on his knees and wearing an apron to protect his uniform.

'Sergeant, it's Evon. They've just found her body.

32

Evon's body lay on a stretch of land flanking the river.

WPC Keane could have taken the squad car down the slope to Curles Bridge and driven under a dry arch to reach the murder scene. Instead she parked on the road.

'Sorry, Sarge, DS Leary's orders.'

'Good call,' Barlow said and eased himself out of the car.

The news of Evon's death had added to his headache. He knew he should have taken the time to swallow an aspirin before he left the house.

He and Thompson walked down the slope to the river and along its bank until he came to the bridge itself.

The bridge had two dry arches. In one a detective was making plaster casts of selected tyre tracks. Instead of pouring plaster out of the bucket he stood scratching his head. 'Sarge, just how many people use this area for a shag?'

'You'd know that better than me, son.'

Barlow went through the second dry arch, the one nearest the river. It was partly blocked by a wooden hut, tarred and papered against damp. A scrawny, ageing man sat on a bench outside it. He wore a faded greatcoat against the cold and he looked shaken and upset. His eyes were red, the sure sign of a hangover.

The man said, 'I found her. She and the other dear ladies depend on me to protect them during their assignations, and I failed. I let her down.'

Barlow asked, 'When did you find Evon?'

Thompson butted in. 'I suppose you protect them and they pay you in kind?'

'Certainly not, Madam' the man said. 'One has one's standards to maintain.'

Barlow said, quickly, 'Thompson let me introduce you to Major the Honourable Edward Adair, George Cross, Military Cross. The last of *The Adairs* of Ballymena.'

'Unfortunately,' Edward said.

'Not necessarily,' Barlow said.

Edward stood and extended a hand to Thompson. 'How do you do.'

She checked it for cleanliness before she shook hands. ‘Sergeant Thompson,’ she said.

Barlow wanted to get on. Neither did he want Thompson questioning Edward as a potential suspect. He said, ‘When we finish here we’ll give you a lift to Mrs Anderson’s.’

Edward’s head barely moved but it was a definite no. ‘My esteemed fiancée will have taken exception to my missing Church and in addition …’

‘You’re still pissed.’

‘Really, my dear chap. One can only say that the survivors of the battle of the Raglan Bar were most generous when one called to offer ones’ commiserations and condolences.’

‘So that’s why you weren’t in the Bridge Bar.’ Barlow nudged Thompson to come on. ‘You’re for Mrs Anderson’s. This place will be crawling with police for the next few days.’

33

Barlow and Thompson slipped between the wooden hut and the river.

'One good flood could wash that away,' Thompson said.

'One can always hope,' Barlow said, his mouth on automatic because his whole being was focused on the rubber sheet that covered Evon's body.

DS Leary stepped forward. 'There's no need for you to look.'

'Aye, but I have to.'

Thompson said, 'We spoke to her just after midnight. She was fine then, and lippy.'

'A late customer turning nasty then,' Leary said.

Evon lay face down. Smears and spots of her blood stained the hoarfrost around the body. Barlow knelt beside her. 'I knew her as a kid. She kept wanting me to arrest her again.'

'Again, what did she do?' asked Thompson.

'We found the mother unconscious and kept the kid until Social Services could organise something for her. Fed her cream buns and cakes, things she wasn't used to, until she sicked them up.' He smiled at the memory of the waif with the clean face and grubby dress. 'Ten minutes later her little hand was back in the bun box.'

Evon's hair straggled out from beneath the sheet. Barlow tidied it with his hand. 'When I came back from the war she was on the game: abusive boyfriends of her mother, and other men who promised her the earth and then betrayed her.'

He turned the sheet down until he could see her head and neck. What he could see of her face was a dark purple, the hair matted with blood. Vivid bruises blotched her neck.

Leary made a play of checking his notes. He had to clear his throat before he could speak. 'It appears that she was strangled, but the eventual cause of death was a blow to the head with,' He pointed to a paper bag held by a detective constable, 'A nail-bar. We found it in the water, there's hair caught in the claw.'

Barlow made himself look carefully at the head. 'Just once?'

'It gets worse.'

Leary folded the rubber sheet down and held up Evon's dress so that Barlow could see her back. The surface of the skin was scraped and torn, ribs broken. The attacker had jumped on her body.

'I hope she was unconscious before he did that,' Barlow said.

Rather than answer Leary shook his head. Then he asked, as much of himself as Barlow. 'Could we be looking for a maniac?'

Thompson said, 'You go on the game, anything can happen.'

Barlow turned on her. 'Evon never lost her heart. Did you ever find yours?'

Annoyed at himself for the outburst, he got to his feet and brushed dust from his knees. A hearse waited on the road, the morticians coming down the slope.

Rather than watch Evon being bundled into their body bag he walked to the edge of the river. 'So where did you find the nail-bar?'

Leary lobbed a pebble not more than two feet from the bank. 'About there.'

'Where it could be found.'

'Or not caring.'

Barlow could hear the rubber sheet being removed and folded neatly and the grunt of the morticians as they eased Evon's body into the body bag. He tried to focus his attention on the lead coloured water flowing past.

He pointed across to the far bank. 'What's that?'

'What? Where?'

'Shoes, boots rather, half in and half out of the water.'

'Why didn't we see that?' asked Leary.

'Because you're only a detective.'

A detective constable was dispatched to collect the boots.

Barlow went over to Thompson. She stood on her own, hands behind her back. Her ramrod stiff stance deterring anyone from starting a casual conversation with her.

Barlow said, 'Thompson, I'd like to apologise. I spoke out of turn back then.'

'It's quite all right, Sergeant.'

'No it's not, and you know it.'

She said, 'I was being insensitive. You obviously thought a lot of Evon.'

The admission came with a sigh. 'I did that. There's always one that gets to you. In this case it was her.'

They stood in almost companionable silence until the detective arrived back with the boots.

'Football boots,' he announced. 'Old and battered football boots with the studs worn down to the nails.'

The boots were covered in mud, either from football or from lying on a muddy bank. Either way there was no chance of extracting a fingerprint. Barlow deferred to Leary as he examined the boots inside and out.

Leary said, 'That could be skin attached to the studs and there are initials on the inside of the tongues. They're a bit faded but I think it's a T and an R.'

'Thomas Rankin,' Barlow said.

A young man, who having been fired from his junior management post through theft, and the loss of a career in football through injury, now faced a lifetime in prison, if he was lucky.

People had been hung for less.

Barlow looked at where Evon's body had lain. Right then, he'd have happily stood in for Pierrepoint and pulled the lever.

34

Barlow accompanied the detectives as the "uniform" when they went to arrest Tom Rankin. This was personal with him, something he had to do. At the same time, he wanted to be sure that no mistakes were made, some technical slipup that could have the case thrown out of court.

Tom lived in digs in Hill Street, a short run of tight little houses dating from the turn of the century. Hill Street wasn't that far from John Street where Evon and her *ladies* plied their trade.

'I'll bet he was a regular with the prostitutes,' Leary said.

'We'll find out soon enough,' Barlow said.

They pulled up in Hill Street. Barlow led the way to the house. 'I know the owner. A bit serious about her religion but decent enough.'

He tapped the door gently and the landlady answered, still in her Sunday best hat and coat, with her bible pointedly in hand.

'Is Tom in?' asked Barlow, keeping his voice down.

'In bed asleep.' She sniffed. 'He didn't even attempt to go to church this morning, though I called him twice.' Another sniff. 'The time he got in at, and him smelling of alcohol.' Her voice rose in pitch and Barlow had to shush her down. 'I told him right at the start. I won't have this house associated with alcohol in any way.'

'We'll go up then,' Barlow said and eased past her before indignation gave way to curiosity.

They went up the linoleum covered stairs, not on tiptoe but trying to keep the noise of their footsteps down. Barlow guessed that Tom would have the small room at the back and opened the door.

Tom lay on top of his bed, still wearing shirt and trousers. A heavy book, the size of a small encyclopaedia lay open on his chest.

He came blearily awake and struggled onto an elbow. 'Wha?'

Barlow deferred to Leary who said, 'Thomas Rankin, we would like you to accompany us to the station.'

And there it was on his face, that flicker by someone who knew they'd been caught.

Tom opened his mouth to protest and was smart enough to close it again without speaking.

Barlow rubbed his hands against his trouser legs to keep them busy. Better that than take Tom by the throat and let him feel something of what he'd put Evon through. When he had control of his hands again, he hauled Tom off the bed and snapped on handcuffs. Forced himself to ensure that they weren't too tight.

Leary read Tom his rights. 'Do you understand?'

'Yes,' Tom said, and nothing else.

A detective picked up the book which had fallen to the floor. 'Biology, are you planning on poisoning someone next?'

'Shut it,' Barlow said.

Tom had to know why they were there, but why tell him.

They made Tom walk in his socks because his shoes could be evidence. Barlow went ahead of him on the stairs and listened to his shuffling step as he protected his bad knee.

Barlow wished the bad knee would go septic. Then he decided not, because a one legged man could gain a jury's sympathy.

He also kept a hand handy to the bannisters in case one of the men coming behind gave Tom a push.

35

At the station Tom was stripped of his clothes and given a boiler suit to wear. His hands and nails appeared spotless but samples were taken anyway for analysis. There were no scratches on his body but several fresh bruises. Chances were, he'd got those playing against Linfield, but he'd say that anyway.

All this time Tom remained silent which, in Barlow's opinion, was a major mistake. An innocent man or an experienced criminal would be full of questions and protestations of innocence.

Technically and operationally Barlow should have left the questioning to the detectives but he backed into a corner of the Interview Room and made it plain that he intended to stay. Leary was good at his job but still… And Barlow didn't want any mistakes made. Evon's killing had been a dirty, vicious attack. She must have gone through hell before she died.

In his mind's eye he couldn't see the woman Evon had become. Only the little girl with the clean hands and face and the filthy dress.

'Where were you last night?' Leary asked Tom.

It came out pat. 'I'd had a bad day. I went out in the evening and had a few drinks. I'm not used to drinking and it went to my head. I wandered about until I sobered up enough to go back to my digs.'

Where he had wandered he didn't know. Who he saw and spoke to during the early part of the evening he could remember, and supplied names and details to back up his story. From about ten o'clock onwards was a complete blank.

After a while of stonewalling he said quickly, 'Look, if this is about me threatening to kick R Shaw's head in, it was all talk. She wouldn't …'

'Who's she?' asked the detective constable present to take notes.

At that Tom caught hold of himself and went silent.

It was the same mouthy detective who had suggested poisoning in the digs. From the look on Leary's face, Barlow reckoned the New Year would see him back in uniform.

Someone knocked the door. Leary suspended the questioning and went out. Almost immediately he put his head around the door again and asked Barlow to step out as well.

It was a second detective constable, backed up by Wilson, who had a list of negative reports.

They had gone through Tom's room. It hadn't taken long because he hadn't much by way of worldly goods other than a batch of technical books.

'Define "technical",' asked Barlow.

'Chemistry and biological science,' said Wilson.

Barlow nodded. Wilson would know, he had been to college and university. Barlow's formal education had stopped at age twelve when he ran away from the Workhouse. He had a general idea of the differences between the sciences but wouldn't like to be pushed to explain them.

'And a well-thumbed *Gray's Anatomy*,' said the detective constable.

Leary sighed. 'So he knows how to poison people, and where best to stab, shoot or bludgeon to kill.'

'And there was this,' Wilson said producing a thin item wrapped in tissue paper. He unwrapped it and opened out a handmade tapestry about eighteen inches by fifteen. The tapestry had a cobalt blue background with the words "To Serve all your Days" stitched across it in white.

Barlow refused to be diverted from the business in hand. 'The night before last, when Reg Corkey was killed. Did you ask his landlady about that?'

'We did,' Wilson said, consulting his notebook. 'Tom Rankin arrived back from work, had his tea and went to his room. According to the landlady, he never left it again until the next morning.'

Which meant they were looking for two killers and not one.

Leary gave another sigh. 'Let's go sort this one anyway.'

He fetched the football boots from his office and stomped into the Interview Room. 'Do you recognise these?'

The thump of the boots on the table made Tom start. He looked at them puzzled. 'They're mine. So what?'

Both solving the case and Tom's very life could hinge on this identification. Barlow strove to keep his voice sounding unconcerned. 'Take your time. Have a careful look. Be absolutely sure.'

'I am. Look, on the underside of the tongues you'll find my initials

TR.'

'When did you last see these boots?' asked Leary, giving Barlow a look as if to say, 'Shut up, this is my case,'

'I dumped them in the bin on the way out the door,' Tom said. Anger flushed his cheeks. 'The Lorrimers blackened my name and then crippled me to stop me from playing in the English League. But that's not enough for them. They want me in court, ground down to a nobody when I had a chance…'

His voice cracked. He went silent.

'So you were angry at being injured by R Shaw?' asked Barlow. 'Angry enough to take it out on anyone who annoyed you, especially R Shaw?'

He thought of what had been done to Evon, the sheer brutality of the rage inflicted on her. If Tom had just killed Evon in a fit of anger, that he might have understood, but not a brutal, senseless attack.

'Wouldn't you after what that bastard did to me,' Tom said.

'What exactly did he do?' asked Leary.

'He kicked me on the lateral aspect of my knee. This caused a second degree sprain to the medial collateral ligament. As a result of which, I am experiencing an acute joint effusion, rendering my knee joint unstable. Possibly chronically unstable.'

'So you were mad,' Barlow said, ignoring all the hardly-understood big words and getting back to the crux of the interrogation. 'Raging mad and ready to take it out on anyone.'

Leary held the boots up so Tom could see the studs. 'That's the flesh and blood of a woman who deserved better from you.'

'I didn't do her any harm. Is she all right? Tell me she's all right.'

'Give the woman the dignity of her name. Evon, Evon Flinton.' roared Barlow. 'You kicked her to death with those boots.'

Tom's mouth froze open. His face developed the pallor of a corpse. 'I didn't. No, no I didn't do that. I thought you meant something had happened to …'

Again he clamped his mouth shut. The next time he spoke was for a glass of water. The only time he spoke after that was to ask for a solicitor.

36

Leary let Tom Rankin cool his heels in a cell for two hours before he agreed that Barlow could send for the Duty Solicitor. It was the turn of Solicitor Moncrief's firm and Moncrief sent Ernest T Potter. Moncrief only came himself when there was a chance of having Barlow jailed.

Ernest was as serious as his name and lanky, with a frame still to bulk out.

'Good afternoon, Mr Barlow,' he said in a deliberately relaxed voice.

'Good afternoon, Mr Potter,' Barlow said back.

Ernie had been in the police station often enough to know the way to the detectives' office but Barlow made a point of escorting him. There Ernie sat and listened and took notes but made no comment as Leary summarised the case against Tom.

When Leary had finished Ernie asked, 'At what time did my client request that a solicitor be present?

His lips pursed at hearing of the two-hour delay.

'I am currently running two murder investigations,' Leary said by way of excuse.

'And after my client made that request, what subsequent questioning took place?'

Barlow said, 'We confirmed that he wanted a solicitor present, then we put him in a cell to await your arrival.'

'Nothing else?'

'No,' Barlow said, noting that Ernie recorded every answer.

Ernie stood up. 'I will now speak to my client.'

Barlow gave orders for Tom to be brought to an Interview Room then he went back to the Enquiry Office. He should feel happy – if that was the right word – that Evon's killer had been caught and there was already enough evidence against him to ensure a conviction.

And yet?

After a long time Ernie appeared in the Enquiry Office.

'First of all, Mr Barlow, my client confirms the timing of the events. He further confirms that after he requested that a solicitor be present the interview was immediately terminated.' Ernie gave a dry cough. ‘However, no mention was made by either yourself or by Detective Sergeant Leary about further questioning that took place subsequently in the cellblock.’

‘What questioning?’

‘A potentially serious omission by the officers concerned with this case, which has been duly noted and affirmed by my client,’ continued Ernie.

‘What questioning.’

‘What did he want for lunch? Did he take sugar in his tea?’

‘You can’t be serious?’

Ernie smiled. ‘However, on this occasion, one is willing to overlook the matter.’

‘One appreciates your forbearance, Mr Potter,’ Barlow said.

And yet Ernie was right. Sometimes the man in charge of the cells got nosy, asking questions that he shouldn’t. Something Barlow would have to check on.

Barlow picked up a pencil as if busy and wanting to get on with his work. ‘Anything else, Mr Potter?’

‘I gave Detective Sergeant Leary my client’s written statement. However, I see no harm in informing you that my client states that he is more than willing to facilitate the enquiry into the untimely and unnatural death of Evon Flinton. Unfortunately, my client is so shaken and upset at even being thought capable of hurting anyone, let alone murdering them, that he cannot, as he previously stated, remember where he went and to whom he spoke during the relevant hours. As his memory returns we will be more than pleased to supply that information to the police for verification.

‘Right.’ Barlow flicked the pencil to and fro while he thought this statement through. Tom was even giving his solicitor the run-around.

He focused in on the one hard fact supplied by Tom. ‘He said that he dumped his football boots in a waste bin. Can he remember where?’

Ernie consulted his copy of Tom’s statement and quoted from it. “After I was helped off the field I spent an hour with the physio. Then I changed into my street clothes and left. I knew I would never be able to play football again so, on the way out, I threw my football boots into a waste bin in the corridor. I was not aware of anyone seeing me do this.”

Barlow could only think that Harvey’s budget for overtime was going to take another hammering. Every man who had been in the

Players' area of the stand that day would have to be traced and a statement taken from them. The players themselves, the management and support team, the directors and their guests, the cleaners, the sweeper-uppers, the men on the gates, the programme sellers. Even the police on duty.

'No problem, we'll get onto it right away,' he said.

Ernie nodded and made as if to leave. Then he paused, no longer the cool solicitor. 'About Vera staying over in my house for the party…'

Whatever he saw on Barlow's face shut him up fast. He disappeared out the door.

37

Vera was waiting for Barlow when he got home. The table set, with even the seldom utilised tablecloth put to use, and the tea steaming in the scullery. She stood defiant in front of the fire with Toby curled tight against her legs.

'So you know,' he said.

'And so do you,' she said.

He found his hands bunched into fists. 'And when did you intend to tell me?'

'When are you ever here to listen?'

He stretched his fingers straight and sat down in his chair. 'Tell me now.'

She stood on, still defiant. 'Ernie is going to pick me up from work on Friday evening and run me to Donaghadee.'

'That's a fair distance.'

'He lives in Belfast anyway.'

'And Donaghadee is as far away again on the other side.'

'Then on Boxing Day afternoon, he's going to pick me up in time for the party.' Her voice raised. 'In his parents' house. You know, families, get-togethers.'

That hurt. It hit parts of him that had been closed off for decades. He hadn't listened, taken time. Assumed everything was okay between them, when she wanted a bit of attention.

He knew it was an excuse but he used it. 'It's the job, and it's particularly bad this week.'

'It always is "the job".'

He could be angry too, he found. 'It's personal this time. Evon …'

'A prostitute! Don't say she was one of your women.'

It would be easier to slap Vera and keep slapping her into submission. No one had a good word to say about Evon. A prostitute. Got what she deserved. The judgment of God on a fallen woman.

Evon deserved better than that.

He said, 'There was a time when things were bad, real bad. You weren't much more than a baby and your mother spent more time in hospital than out. You were being shipped around from pillar to post, to whomever would take care of you that day. Police hours are long and then there was you.'

He was making his daughter seem like some sort of imposition. 'Not that way, not the way it sounds. Somehow you made the exhaustion and the long hours and the lack of sleep worthwhile. And yet…'

How could he tell her and yet he had to. He couldn't look her way, see her disappointment at his failure. 'In the end I was done, beat. Not sleeping, hardly making sense of anything. Then one night Evon came across me. I was on patrol, or supposed to be, but I was shambling about not even aware of what street I was on.'

Still he couldn't look at her. 'That day I had given up. I'd gone to Social Services and begged them to get you a good home.' He had to say it, let no doubt linger in her mind. 'Be adopted.'

'Oh,' was all she said.

'As I said, Evon came across me. She grabbed my hand and led me to her place.' This was embarrassing but easier to say than "adoption." She undressed me and lay with me.'

'You had sex, with a prostitute?'

He didn't know what to make of her tone. More disbelieving than judgemental.

'I cried for every hurt in my life. I cried for my marriage that never was.' He looked her way but couldn't see clearly for the moisture in his eyes. 'Mostly I cried for you, for the horrible upbringing you were suffering. For my failures. For gratitude to Evon who was giving me something without forbearance or out of Christian duty.'

'Then you had sex,' she said.

'When I finished crying I got up and dressed and went back on patrol. That whole time I never spoke to Evon nor she to me.' He wanted to make three things quite plain. 'No we didn't have sex. No, I didn't pay her and, not once in all the years since, did she ever refer to it.'

Vera was at his leg, kneeling against him in the old way. He hadn't seen her come.

'But the adoption?' she asked.

He put a hand on her head and felt the silk of her hair. Toby was against the other leg. He put a hand on him as well. 'You're here because that hour with Evon gave me the strength to keep going.'

He wiped at moisture that had somehow got on his face and gave her his handkerchief to wipe away her tears.

'All I want for you, Love, is the best. I don't want you to *have* to get married or bring up a child on your own the way I had to. I want you to meet the man of your dreams, to fall in love and get married and have children in your own good time.'

An admission tore out of him. 'With all my heart, I want you to enjoy a normal family life. Whatever that is.'

38

The doorbell chimed at near eight o'clock. Tea was over, the dirty dishes and the pots jointly washed and put away. Barlow sat in his chair waiting for the promised cup of tea. Vera had insisted on making it and it was good to have her bullying him again, though things were still quiet between them.

'It's bound to be for you,' called Vera from the scullery.

'And I'm sick answering the phone, only to find it's for you,' he shouted back.

Toby was already heading for the door, raised heckles forming a ridge down his neck.

'The kettle's just on the boil,' she said, so he had to go.

A tall, thin shape showed through the stippled glass of the inner door. Not a shape he recognised so it couldn't be someone for him. He opened the door and found himself face to face with Ernest T Potter.

'Mr Barlow.'

'Mr… um Ernest.'

'This afternoon at the station …'

'You'd better come in.'

If he was going to chew out this would-be Lothario better to do it in private than have the neighbours hear.

Behind him he heard Vera say, 'Wait, wait, wait,' and the sound of her feet fleeing towards her bedroom.

The sitting room was cold, the fire set but unlit. Vera would probably *kill* him for taking Ernest into the kitchen with its mishmash of furniture, but it was warm there.

He stopped himself from thinking about the bad old days. His experiences of bare concrete and upturned orange boxes that, praise the Lord, weren't Vera's.

Ernest followed Barlow in. He took a seat at the table, facing Barlow's chair and the little settee where Vera normally sat.

Ernest cleared his throat. 'This afternoon at the station I presumed…'

'I thought solicitors never presumed. Never asked a question where they didn't know the answer first?'

'That's counsel. Mere solicitors put their foot in it all the time.'

Barlow liked that answer. The lad was not for intimidating.

Ernest cleared his throat a second time. 'Well anyway, I'm sorry, and I'm here to assure you that... that, well it's my parents' house and they have a family party every Boxing Day. It's only for one night and she would sleep in the spare bed in my sister's room.'

At long last they heard Vera's footsteps as she returned. Ernest stopped talking and Barlow had a chance to think.

A family party? Like Ernest was holding up Vera for inspection and approval.

Vera came in saying, 'Dad, don't go bullying poor Ernie.'

She had brushed her hair and freshened her lipstick and she wafted spray perfume Barlow's way as she passed him to sit on the settee. Toby went over and sat tight against her.

Vera was his daughter. He wanted to wrap her in cotton wool until she was old and sensible and in control of her passions. He wanted her to go out into the world and live a full, meaningful life.

When did he dare let go? And how?

The gleam off Toby's teeth caught his eye. Toby's stare was fixed hard on Ernest, his lip rolled back to show his dislike.

Barlow said, 'I'm working a double shift on Christmas Day.'

'You never told me that,' Vera said.

'Didn't I? Well anyway, I can't have the dog lying out in the porch all that time.'

A straight lie. He could take Toby to work and let him spend the day in the Enquiry Office, lying in front of the coal fire.

'So you'll have to take the dog with you to Donaghadee,' he told Vera.

'Dad, I can't. I've never met Mr and Mrs Potter, and to arrive with a dog? You wouldn't do that on me.'

He could see her point of view and began to waver. Maybe he didn't need Toby there to guard her honour. She had been reared decent and knew about things.

'Toby's no problem,' Ernest said, eying the dog doubtfully. 'My father's old mutt will probably die of apoplexy, but other than that.' He shrugged.

Vera changed in an instant to the young lover playing hard-to-get. 'Ernie, I must warn you that after my father, Toby is the number one man in my life.'

She put her hand on Toby's head. He rumbled a growl, his eyes still fixed on Ernest.

'Does that mean I can never hope to be more than number three?' asked Ernest.

'I'm afraid so,' Vera said.

There was something about her face. Heightened colour, yes, and a look of peace and confidence that Barlow had never seen before.

It mightn't be Earnest in the end, but his daughter was fast leaving him.

Blank Page

Monday
December 19th

39

Barlow went to bed convinced that he wouldn't sleep. He closed his eyes more out of habit than belief and when they snapped open again it was seven o'clock. He felt well rested and fit for another day.

His morning prayer was a grateful, 'Thank goodness I've only got one daughter. Three or four and I'd be grey as a badger.'

He cycled into work, sucking an imaginary Polo Mint on the way. He liked a bit of heat in his tongue when it came to sorting out sloppy uniforms during Morning Parade.

All three WPCs were there. Thompson, as befitted a sergeant, stood a step in front of them, her chest pushed out to show off her straight up and down buttons. Barlow pointedly paid more attention to her nylons, confirming that the back seam ran straight.

Wilson was there as well.

'You again?' asked Barlow, though he knew what the boy was up to.

'Swopped shifts, Sergeant.'

'Well tonight swop a shift with someone off duty.'

Detailing the multiple tasks to be undertaken that day was almost a pleasure. With ongoing enquiries into two murders just about every man was on duty. The overtime budget had to be through the roof.

Harvey could hardly blame him for that. There again…

Miss Fetterman came looking for him. 'Sergeant Barlow, you and Sergeant Thompson are to report to Mr Harvey. At once please, he's waiting for you.'

'Be advised, we're on our way, Miss Fetterbane,' Barlow said.

He checked his buttons and looked over at Thompson. Her mouth was set tight with anxiety. He said nothing to comfort her on the way to Harvey's office.

Harvey waited behind his desk, spine stiff, a sniff of disdain on his face.

'Really, Barlow, this report criticising Sergeant Thompson for quelling that riot in the Bridge Bar.'

Harvey hesitated, reluctant to show a weakness, especially a physical weakness, in front of Thompson. In the end he reached for his glasses.

'Exceeded her authority. Acted without first obtaining approval from a superior officer.' He removed his glasses to give Barlow his full glare of disapproval. 'Would you wait for permission from me to throw a bucket of water on a fire?'

'No, sir,' Barlow said very truthfully.

Harvey smiled at Thompson, replaced his glasses and continued to read. 'Exceeded duties and responsibilities of a Woman Police Officer as laid down in the regulations relating to the formation of the Women's Police Service.'

The glasses came off again. 'Really, Barlow, what century do you belong to? Things are changing, women are taking a larger say in world affairs. We already have a woman inspector in Miss Macmillan and, no doubt, more will follow in due course.' He looked at Thompson as if her promotion to Inspector was all but guaranteed. 'Also, do I again have to remind you that from the ninth of January the duties of a woman constable will be extended into what is currently a male preserve?'

'No, sir,' Barlow said, again truthfully.

For all his voiced enthusiasm Harvey didn't look too pleased about the change.

Harvey smiled at Thompson. 'In fact, Sergeant Thompson, I completely reject Sargent Barlow's criticisms of your action and I will append a report of my own to that effect.'

'Thank you, sir, and please remember to mention the brave actions of the WPCs who accompanied me,' Thompson said.

Harvey scribbled something on a pad. 'Of course, of course.'

At that they could leave.

Thompson waited until they were through Miss Fetterman's office and in the corridor before she spoke. 'That's not the report you said you were putting in.'

'It's on the second page. Harvey is a slow reader,' Barlow said, and walked on.

Thompson had to follow because they were due in the detectives' office.

Barlow stopped with his hand on the handle of the door. 'A word of warning. If Harvey was being as nice to me, I'd be doubly careful.'

40

Leary's office was crowded with detectives and uniform branch officers waiting for their instructions. Inspector Foxton had the floor.

'Now we're all here,' he said as Barlow and Thompson entered. 'Firstly, the questioning of Tom Rankin will recommence once his solicitor has arrived. DS Leary leading.' He nodded to Leary to add something.

Leary said, 'Rankin is still claiming memory loss occasioned by an excessive use of alcohol. Or to put it another way, he was pissed out of his mind.'

That raised a titter of laughter.

Foxwood frowned everyone silent again. 'Rankin claims that he threw his boots into a waste bin in the Ballymena Showgrounds. Again, no witnesses that Rankin can remember.' He held up sheaves of foolscap paper. We have the names of every man we know of who may have seen Rankin dump the football boots as he claimed. There may be others. This is a murder inquiry, Rankin potentially could hang, so I don't want any shortcuts taken. Every man on these lists will be spoken to and every man will make a statement in writing as to what they did or didn't see. Is that understood?'

Heads nodded. 'Yes, sir.'

'Now the victim's friends.' He looked at Thompson.

She shook her head. 'In accordance with DI Harvey's instructions, yesterday evening WPC Keane and I went to John Street. Most of the prostitutes had stayed away and those that were there claimed they saw nothing and knew even less.'

Barlow caught Foxwood's eye.

'Barlow,' Foxwood said.

'Perhaps I could help there, sir.'

'If you would.'

After that Foxwood moved on to the parallel enquiry into the death of Reg Corkey. Barlow left them to it and slipped out of the room.

Thompson followed him, her face burning with anger. 'You might have said.'

'Said what?'

'That you had contacts who could help trace Evon's friends.'

'You didn't ask,' he said and didn't try to keep the irritation out of his voice. 'I told you before, Thompson. In this station, you start with me and work up the chain of command. Not the other way around.' He resisted the temptation to go nose to nose with her. 'Don't ever make that mistake again.'

He went off chewing an imaginary Jelly Baby, the sort of sweet he could get his teeth into and shred.

All the cars were needed for the policemen driving from pillar to post trying to trace potential witnesses. Barlow decided to take his bike. On his way, he detoured by the Enquiry Office where Sergeant Pierson looked comfortable and settled.

'No one's getting any tea breaks today,' Barlow told him. 'So, there's a lot of sandwiches needed for lunchtime.'

'That's the women's job,' Pierson said.

'Foxwood wants them out on the street doing the normal patrols.'

'So who?'

'Guess,' Barlow said.

He went into the yard and retrieved his bike from the bike shed. Someone had cleaned and oiled it, pumped the tyres hard and tightened the brakes.

'Gillespie would do anything to avoid foot patrols,' Barlow said.

'It was me,' WPC Keane said. She was giving her car a final polish before trusting it into the hands of a man who, hopefully, wouldn't damage it.

'Well, thank you,' said Barlow, surprising himself by giving Keane a big smile.

The day was dry even if the wind was bitter, and he had the morning if not the whole day to himself.

41

Major Edward Adair was "in" and "receiving".

That meant he sat on a bench in front of his old wooden hut, experiencing the weak winter sun on his face. His old army greatcoat protected his wasted body from the cold air.

'I told you to stay at Mrs Anderson's,' Barlow said by way of greeting.

He had already tried Mrs Anderson's house in Farm Lodge Lane without success. And that had meant a steady cycle uphill, using legs grown tired from late nights and busy days.

Edward gave a nod both of greeting and apology. 'One regrets to inform you, Mr Barlow, that the good lady and I had words. Or rather, Mrs Anderson verbalised her feelings while I listened.'

'Okay, so you got a bollocking. It's not the end of the world.'

'The world, no, but our engagement, yes.' He searched in his pocket and produced a diamond ring in a "H Samuel, the Jewellers" box. 'Evidence of her determined intent.'

'Ooops, I think a bit of crawling is needed there,' Barlow said.

'Worse than crawling, my dear chap. One is required to present oneself at the Anderson household on Christmas Morning. Not only fully sober but also able to swear that one has not allowed the demon drink pass one's lips since the good lady and oneself last met.'

Really tough conditions, since Edward habitually spent the Christmas fortnight celebrating the end of one year and drinking toasts to the hope of the new. It was only the first day of Edward being *dry* and he was already suffering withdrawal symptoms.

Barlow sat down beside him. 'I've a job for you that might take your mind off things for a while.'

Edward smiled. 'My dear chap, anything to oblige an old comrade.'

'Evon's friends. Any that we can find won't talk to the police. They trust you. I don't need names but I do need to know what's going on out there.'

Edward looked worried. 'One associating with certain young ladies when one's own good lady is already on the offensive…'

'Is dangerous,' agreed Barlow.

He sat on for a time, enjoying the sun in spite of the cold.

Edward caught his arm as he got up to go. 'Thomas Rankin.'

Barlow sat down again, this could be important. People told Edward things they wouldn't tell their confessor. 'You know him?'

'When out with his comrades, Thomas obliges one with a complimentary beer.'

Tom claimed that he never drank. If they could challenge that lie then Leary might be able to crack his stubborn silence. 'How often did you see him in a pub?'

'Occasionally.' Edward paused searching for exactitude. 'Very occasionally and only when celebrating some special event with friends. Thomas invariably drinks Britvic.'

Edward shuddered at having to vocalise "Britvic", the leading brand in quality non-alcoholic drinks.

Barlow cycled away, his mind busy with denials. Thomas Rankin had killed Evon, there was no doubt about that. No matter how drunk, he should be able to remember something of what happened between ten o'clock and the time he got back to his digs. It was just a matter of Leary tying up loose ends before sending the file to the Public Prosecutor.

Catching a criminal out in a lie could make a case. But what about discovering a truth, no matter how immaterial?

42

The cycle ride back to the station along the river should have been a pleasure for Barlow. However, Edward confirming that Tom Rankin wasn't normally, if ever, a drinker worked like a canker in his conviction of his guilt. The police needed something to convince a jury that he was a bad one.

And Barlow himself, though he would never admit it.

There was one thing, the hint by Charles Denton that Tom had been let go by the Lorrimers because he had *sticky fingers*.

Barlow headed for the lower end of Ballymena and the Ballymena Brewing Company.

'Is the Captain about?' he asked the gatekeeper, an old soldier like himself, who had come back from the war with damaged lungs and a shortened leg.

'In the Loading Bay,' said the gatekeeper and grinned.

Barlow left his bike against the hut. 'Keep an eye on that.'

'I remember it well from Catterick Camp,' the gatekeeper said.

'It deserted near the end of the war,' Barlow said.

'And the army's still looking.'

Barlow nodded and went on, following the echoing crash of crates from the cavernous Loading Bay. He found Denton there, as the gatekeeper had said.

The Loading Bay had room for two lorries at a time, with raised platforms extending the length and height of the lorry beds. Beyond that, a carousel carried a stream of rattling bottles out of the dryer, turned sharply back and disappeared them into the bottling area where they would be filled, capped, hand loaded – four at a time – into crates and stacked for immediate shipment.

Denton was in his shirt sleeves, tie gone and top button undone, hiking crates of beer onto the lorry where men stacked and secured them. Denton worked fast, forcing the men around him to keep up the same pace of work.

Barlow gave a casual salute. 'Captain Denton, sir, if I could have a word.'

Denton stopped, crate in hand, his face flushed and sweating from effort. He looked pleased with life. 'Can it wait?'

He'd given Denton one "sir" and that was all he was getting. 'I'd rather not.'

Denton lobbed the final crate to the man on the lorry. 'Okay, take ten, boys. Have a cuppa.'

The foreman, another old soldier said, sotto voce, 'Barlow, you couldn't arrest the Captain, keep him locked up until we've the Christmas orders dispatched?'

'He's killing us,' another of the men said.

'Lazy, shiftless lot,' muttered Denton as he picked up his jacket and walked off. He was still smiling.

Barlow followed Denton up a steel stairwell into the offices on the first floor. Mrs Anderson was Denton's main bookkeeper and office manageress.

Barlow paused at her desk. 'Edward?'

'If he ever comes around me again with drink on him, I'll wring his neck then I'll kill him.'

'You've got him well shook, this time,' Barlow said. He followed Denton into his office and pulled up a chair across from Denton. 'Charlie, you said a couple of things the other day that puzzled me.'

'What?' asked Denton. He had his jacket on and was busy straightening his tie.

'Tom Rankin and sticky fingers.'

Denton paused with the tie still at half-mast. 'Him?'

'A man is helping us with our enquiries,' intoned Barlow.

'That's fine as a press release, but him? Rankin? You're kidding? One of his problems as a footballer is that he plays like a gentleman instead of someone whose next meal depends on him winning that ball.'

Barlow wished with all his heart that Denton hadn't said that.

43

'Sticky fingers,' Barlow reminded Denton, as much to get his own mind back on the subject as anything else.

'I know nothing. That's as much as I could get out of Paddy Lorrimer. That's R Shaw's father.'

'No details at all?' Barlow pressed, knowing that Denton valued any information that might affect either him personally or his businesses.

'He wouldn't even discuss it.'

Barlow looked at the wall for a moment, at the calendar with a big red circle around Christmas Day. He now faced a long cycle out the Larne Line to Lorrimers' factory.

Which brought him back to the second question.

'You said the Lorrimers now made bespoke furniture. That it had turned the business around?'

Denton stared at Barlow for a long time. 'By the holy heavens you miss nothing.'

He got up and checked that the office door was shut tight. He closed the window looking down on the loading bays, even though they were twenty feet below and echoed with their own clatter of noise.

He sat down again and kept his voice low. 'John, this is between us.'

'As ever Charlie.'

'And I'm only telling you because we're talking about a hanging here and you wouldn't ask if you didn't think it relevant somehow.'

Barlow let his surprise come out as a question. 'Okay?'

'The thing is, John, in my businesses there is a lot of cash floating about.' Denton did a visual check to make sure the door into the General Office remained closed. 'And not all of it has to go through the books.'

'Right,' Barlow said, knowing that his idea of a "lot of cash" and Denton's were of completely different worlds.

'Now I'm not talking about money needed for the business or for day to day personal expenses.' Again he had a look at the door. 'If I need a couple of hundred for, say, a trip to London, it's a couple of hundred slipped out. But if the tax is paid first and, bearing in mind that the

Higher Rate of Income Tax is in the eighties, then I have to take a thousand pounds, pay the tax and have the two hundred I need left over.'

'That's the government for you,' Barlow said.

He never expected to get anywhere near Higher Rate Tax himself but he could see the problem. At the same time he knew that Denton's admission of "two hundred" slipped out was a major understatement.

'So what has this got to do with the Lorrimers?' he asked.

'I've an account in a bank in Jersey. The only way to get money there without leaving a paper trail is to take cash.'

That made sense to Barlow, but then the cash itself set up its own problems. It was illegal under Exchange Control Regulations to take large sums of money out of the country, so a man flying to Jersey was likely to have his luggage examined by Customs & Excise.

'And if they found cash all hell would be let loose,' he said.

'It happened to a friend.'

'So, you came up with this idea of hidden compartments shipping the stuff out to…?'

'A business acquaintance.'

'And you told some of your friends and they told some of their friends.'

Denton looked uneasy. 'Something like that.'

Barlow nodded. That circle of friends telling friends had to lead, in a roundabout way, to hard men from Belfast. People like Stan Holloway.

He stood up to go.

'John?' asked Denton.

'You always give a couple of bottles of whiskey for the raffle at our Christmas do. I was just in confirming that.'

'I owe you one,' Denton said.

'Forget it.'

Denton's phone rang. Barlow was at the door when Denton held the receiver out. 'It's for you.'

The voice at the other end was that of Acting Sergeant Gillespie's. No other man at the station would have guessed where he'd gone.

'Sarge, they've found another body, a man's, at the town dump.'

44

The town dump was at Ballee, on the road to Antrim and Belfast. A long cycle for a man in a hurry. Barlow put his bike in the boot of Denton's car, grateful for the offered lift. It did him a power of good to appear blasé as he stepped out of a Rolls Royce at the murder scene.

He retrieved his bike and gave Denton a formal salute. 'Thank you, sir, much appreciated.'

'My pleasure, Sergeant,' Denton said. His eyes were busy taking in the scene. DS Leary and his detectives stood deep in the dump, near a tipper lorry with its half-unloaded cargo. The whole area reeked of rancid food and foosty materials.

Denton drove off. Barlow ignored the amazed stares of junior officers manning the perimeter of the crime scene and trudged through a sea of awfulness to join DS Leary.

'Three murders in the mouth of Christmas,' moaned Leary.

'Solve them all sharp-like, and you can take the New Year off,' Barlow said.

He stepped forward to look at the body. A man in his forties, from the look of him, and no one Barlow knew or recognised, which was a relief.

'The doctor's already confirmed death,' Leary said.

'That must have been difficult.'

The man's throat was cut right through to the bone, and that had happened in the dump because the head lay in a sea of blood. Fingers were missing or had their nails ripped out. The bare toes battered flat by something like a hammer.

There was something about the desecration of the body that drained Barlow.

'Have we got a name?' he asked.

'No, but according to the label on the jacket the suit was bought in the same shop as the late Reg Corkey's.'

Barlow sensed that Leary felt the same chill of apprehension as himself. Now they had two dead hard men from Belfast, organised riots, and the start of a protection racket. What else?

'Anything I can do here?' he asked Leary.

'We could always do without your smart alec remarks.'

'Fine,' Barlow said.

Acting Sergeant Gillespie was in attendance to direct the uniform branch until Inspector Foxwood arrived.

Barlow stopped with Gillespie on his way back to his bike. 'Where's Pierson?'

Gillespie wrinkled his nose, either against the pungent smell or at the thought of a superior who avoided all the worst duties. 'He decided to stay on and man the Enquiry Office.'

'Spoil his lunch,' Barlow said.

'I will. Every gory detail and some I'll make up.'

'A pint if you make him go white, and a chaser if he's sick.'

Barlow swung his leg over the bike. At Ballee he was more or less half way to Lorrimers' factory. All he had to do was go further out the Antrim Road and turn left near Cromkill Orange Hall.

He decided to chew on an imaginary Fisherman's Friend to burn the smell of death out of his head.

45

Barlow called with Mrs Collins before going to see the Lorrimers. It took her a bit of fumbling at all the locks and bolts on the new back door before it opened.

'John, son.'

'You're looking well,' he said as he stepped into the house.

And she did. He always wondered how old people could get over shocks and fears more easily that the young.

A waft of chill air hit him. Air much colder than the day outside. Then the cold faded into the welcome heat given off the old stove in the kitchen.

'And the Captain's with you now too,' he said.

'Yes, funny that. He never used to come into the servants' quarters. Now he's always around.'

'As long as he doesn't get under your feet,' Barlow said, satisfied that the old woman was as safe as he could make her until things were sorted out.

He accepted a quick cup of tea and left to see the Lorrimers, promising to be straight back for a bite of lunch. Whatever she had on the stove had to be good. His mouth watered in expectation the whole way down the back path, through the back gate and across the yard to the General Office.

Mr Lorrimer and Rose were in the General Office that never seemed to heat up. However, there was no sign of R Shaw. Barlow didn't know if that was a good thing or not. He tucked his cap under his arm and tried his best to look casual and relaxed about the visit. The best way, he thought, was to be wordy and impersonal: "We" instead of "I".

'I'm sorry for bothering you, sir, but it's a question that's come up. Are we right in thinking that Tom Rankin worked here at a time?'

At the mention of Tom's name both Mr Lorrimer and Rose jumped in their seats.

Rose put a hand to her mouth. 'Is Tom in trouble? Surely you don't think he had anything to do with…' Her hand left her mouth and gestured in the vague direction of Mrs Collins' garden.

'Over Reg Corkey's death? Certainly not,' Barlow, said making himself sound surprised that she would even ask that question. 'This is routine, making general enquiries about people associated with the area in any way.'

Wishing to ask questions rather than answer them he turned quickly to Mr Lorrimer. 'So Tom did work here?

'He did,' Mr Lorrimer said, halfway between a cough and a choke.

'And would you mind telling us the circumstances leading to the said Thomas Rankin leaving your employment?'

'He stole some goods.'

Rose jumped to her feet. 'Daddy, it wasn't like that at all, and you know it.'

'He took stuff without permission. A sackable offence in any employment,' Mr Lorrimer said.

He sounded more stubborn than self-righteous.

'You know that wasn't the real reason.'

Rose was yelling now. As if by instinct her hand veered towards a bundle of addressed envelopes awaiting postage stamps. The cheques on account for monies long overdue had yet to go out.

Mr Lorrimer shouted back at her. 'Be quiet. You are dishonouring your father with your outrageous behaviour.'

Rose dissolved into tears and ran from the room. Barlow heard her feet on stairs and the slam of a door. Mr Lorrimer would say no more about the circumstances leading to Tom leaving the firm so Barlow went back to Mrs Collins for his lunch.

He wondered what Rose thought was the real reason for Tom being dismissed. Had it anything to do with money? Like those unpaid bills and Rose telling R Shaw to "go easy" when he took a blank cheque for his own use.

Had the Lorrimers sacked Tom for telling them that they were idiots for running a good-going wee business into the ground?

46

Lunch was ready when Barlow got back to Mrs Collins' house: thick vegetable soup and even thicker wedges of her wheaten bread liberally spread with butter.

'My goodness,' Barlow said when he saw the table. She had spread a damask tablecloth over its worn surface and set out the best china and sterling silver cutlery.

He also observed that she had set three places. 'You're expecting company. Are you sure I won't be in the way?'

'It's for the Captain,' she said. 'It may be the servants' quarters but he insists on standards being maintained.'

'Missis, if anyone sees us eating with a ghost, they'll lockup the two of us.'

'John, son, your imagination is bigger than the Pacific ocean.'

She busied herself ladling the soup into bowls and bringing them over. The Captain's bowl she left empty but she carried it over anyway and put it down in the third place.

She talked as she ate. 'It's great having him all over the house now. It gives me someone to talk to. Nearly as good as talking to my late husband, he didn't say much either.'

'Sure the poor man never got a word in edgeways,' Barlow said, which earned him a slap on the arm.

'He can be grumpy at times and a bit particular.' She looked fondly at the empty place setting and her voice took on a teasing note. 'But when he gets out of hand I tell him I might just accept that offer from Mr Lorrimer.'

Barlow wished she would keep on talking and not expect him to reply. He didn't know which was best: the soup, the wheaten, or the soup and wheaten together.

He swallowed the food in his mouth and asked out of politeness while he readied the next mouthful. 'What offer was that then?'

'He wants to buy the house: lock, stock,' She made a face in the Captain's supposed direction. 'And ghosts.'

Barlow forgot about the next mouthful. 'Buy?' This was a man who couldn't even meet his current bills.

Mrs Collins rattled on. 'Cash, he said. Cold cash in hand. Enough to afford a wee house of my own and give the stepchildren an early inheritance.'

'Cold cash?'

Barlow knew that Paddy Lorrimer had a drinking problem but he didn't think he'd lost all his marbles.

47

Barlow slipped into the station by the back door and all but tiptoed through the building, anxious not to run into anyone. He ducked into the WPCs' office. It should have been empty but Keane sat curled into a chair.

She jumped to her feet. 'Sarge.'

He put a finger to his lips. 'I'm not here.'

'While you're not here, do you want a cuppa?'

'Thanks.'

He watched her go, knowing he should be irritated at catching her skiving. Keane he reckoned the smartest of the three WPCs but she bored easily. She only became really alive when dealing with non-routine work or when cars were involved.

He was looking up the number of the Tennent Street Police Station when she came back with a mug of tea. Not his own mug with the Royal Ulster Rifles Crest, he noted, but a plain day to day one. If anyone noticed his mug missing from the rack they'd know that he was somewhere in the building. The last thing he needed was for Pierson to box him in with a set of whines or Miss Fetterman telling Harvey that he was back.

At one time, someone had regularly used his mug when he was off duty. Worse they always put it back unwashed. Then a person or persons unknown swopped Pierson's lunchtime bar of chocolate for a chocolate laxative. After that his mug remained unsullied.

Keane tried to slip away, with a muttered excuse. He pointed her back to her chair as the telephone operator in Tennent Street picked up.

Barlow quickly established that the Station Sergeant at Tennent Street was in and would talk to him. Barlow sipped his tea while the sergeant transferred the call to another office where they could talk without being overheard.

'Barlow, you're doing a great job down there getting rid of our troublemakers.'

'Our pleasure,' Barlow said.

'Reg Corkey and his brother, Shorty Corkey, both dead as doornails. The DI danced a jig when he heard.'

Two brothers?

The Corkey brothers' deaths had to be linked in some way. 'Why would your scum float our way?' he asked.

'Don't you culchies ever read the papers?'

'Only as far as page three in the *Mirror*.'

The sergeant became serious. 'This month alone, the Forth River Mills announced they are closing with the loss of a thousand jobs, and Harland and Wolff have laid off a thousand men with another ten thousand to go by June.'

Barlow said, 'Tell me about it. A couple of our big mills are on their last legs.'

All the same he'd got the message. The men dealing in prostitution and drugs were seeing their existing markets collapse, so they were expanding, looking for new markets.

Ballymena had plenty of crime. However, it was a backwater when it came to really serious offences. The nearest thing they had to organised crime was the Dunlops. Now they had three deaths in one week. He shuddered at what was still to come.

The sergeant reeled off the names and descriptions of men the late Corkey brothers had associated with. Barlow told Keane to listen in on a second phone and take down the details.

When the sergeant had finished, Barlow told Keane to type it up and distribute copies to all the officers on duty. Now she was energised and typed away furiously.

Before he hung up the sergeant said, 'One other thing, Barlow. Pardon me if I'm teaching my granny to suck eggs, but, warn the banks and big firms in your area to tighten their security. Wages thefts and violent crime is on the increase up here.'

'Aye, it would be.'

It would be, because the loss in income from, say, prostitution had to be made up quickly otherwise the standard of living of the crime bosses would fall.

The sergeant added, 'There was a bad jewellery robbery here last Wednesday. A shop assistant, a schoolgirl earning a bit of money for Christmas, was badly injured.'

48

With the phone call to Tennent Street finished, Barlow decided that enough was enough for the day. He'd worked the weekend, had a double shift coming up on Christmas day and Harvey didn't pay him overtime. Anyway, that headache was bothering him again.

'Feck this for a game of soldiers,' he said as he made two cups of tea in the kitchen. One in his own mug and a second that he took down to the cells.

Thomas Rankin was sitting up in his bed, trousers off while he massaged his damaged knee. The air in the tight little room was rank because Tom hadn't been offered a bath or a shower since he'd been arrested. The knee itself didn't look too bad, Barlow had seen worse, but the injury had created a weakness that would bother Tom for the rest of his life.

Barlow handed Tom the second mug of tea and leaned against the door-jam while he sipped at his own. According to everyone he'd spoken to so far, with the exception of Mr Lorrimer, Tom was a model citizen. The sort who helped old people across the street and was good to cats. Was it all an act or did something trigger a homicidal rage?

Tom acted normal and sounded normal. His total lack of recall for that night was exceptional. He had never been in trouble before and wasn't used to the legal system. By now even a hardened criminal would have worked out some sort of alibi, no matter how vague.

'What?' asked Tom after a while.

It was the first time either man had spoken.

'Nothing.'

'You ask one question and I'll make an official complaint through my solicitor.'

'I'm not asking anything. I'm not saying anything.'

No way would he give Ernest T Potter an opportunity to claim unfair police tactics.

Barlow drank his tea, wondering what he was there for, other than seeking something in Tom's manner that would reinforce his certainty of the young man's guilt. Finished, he collected Tom's mug and was closing the cell door when Tom finally spoke.

'I didn't do it, you know, kill that woman.'

He sounded desperate, panicked even.

Barlow stopped the heavy metal door from closing over. 'When you're ready to tell us, son, we'll get your solicitor here.'

'If I was going to kill anyone it would be R Shaw Lorrimer.'

'And why would you do that?'

Tom pointed at his knee. 'He did that deliberately.'

'Why do you think it was deliberate?'

But Tom had control of himself again, and turned away.

Barlow shut the door and made sure it was secure, slipped out the way he had come and went home.

49

Lamb chops were Vera's favourite meal but expensive to buy so they seldom had them. Barlow had four lamb chops on the verge of being perfectly cooked when Toby escorted Vera in the door. From the restless bounce of the dog it was hard to believe that Barlow had given him four fast miles out the new Ballymoney Line and in by the old road.

'Heavens, what's all this?' Vera asked. She looked jaded.

Burning the candle at both ends, he thought, but didn't say. Instead he indicated the pot of floury potatoes and the baked beans on simmer. 'I mitched this afternoon, so…'

'Dad, you're a marvel.'

She was mashing the last of the potatoes into the gravy when she stopped and gave him a look he knew only too well. This was truth time.

'Dad, I said something very unfair the other day when I were arguing.'

'Did you?' Her eyes were hard on him, not accepting the evasion so he added. 'What did you say exactly?'

'That I came second to your job.'

He found himself looking into an exact copy of his wife's eyes, right down to the little fleck of yellow on the iris. He used to think that he could read his wife's every thought and discovered too late that he was heart-breakingly wrong.

'You were right, and I'm sorry for it,' he said, determined to be truthful with Vera.

'You're busy with those terrible murders and it's been an awful year anyway.'

'It's not just this year, love. It's all those years when you were shipped from pillar to post.'

'I used to think it fun. Who was I going to get playing with today?'

He wondered if she was being completely honest with him. 'Did you?'

'And you should hear Camilla Denton when Uncle Charlie breezes in at all hours. "At least John Barlow knows when to come home".'

A weight lifted off Barlow's heart. 'So I can stop feeling guilty?'

'No, not yet,' she said, suddenly all anxious. 'You did make a dessert?'

'Of course.'

They finished their tea. He washed up and tidied away while she put up the ironing-board. 'I'm in for the night,' she declared as if that was something unusual. Anyway, as it turned out, her Ernie was busy in the office catching up on paperwork.

She made herself busy packing for her holiday, which kept her running into the kitchen to hold up something in front of Barlow.

'What do you think of this, Dad? I mean this old thing.'

He put down his newspaper for the fiftieth time, one he'd pinched out of the station, probably Pierson's. 'That's lovely. I always liked that on you.'

'That's what I mean. I've had it for years.'

She fled back to her bedroom.

She needed three outfits for travelling. 'You can't wear the same thing twice.' Chaste outfits for the days she stayed with her mother and aunt, and something to impress her – possibly, maybe, future in-laws.

The electric iron, coupled with the coal fire, made the kitchen like an oven. Things draped around the kitchen offended Barlow's sense of neatness and Toby insisted on fighting him for every inch of his chair. Barlow didn't care. He sat with the radio turned on low, enjoying Vera's buzz of excitement.

Nearing ten o'clock, he headed off to bed. He couldn't have felt more content if he'd tried. Well almost.

The only thing Vera hadn't mentioned needing for her trip was nightwear.

Blank Page

Tuesday December 20th

50

Outside a frost hung in the air and swirled in the headlights of cars driving past the house. Barlow woke reluctantly, his brain soggy from a restless night of chasing maniacal ghosts. Now he was awake, he thought the town bad enough with three deaths to deal with, without dreaming up more trouble.

He crawled his reluctant body out of bed and staggered into the kitchen, put on a two-bar electric heater and made himself a large pot of tea. That done, he sat at the kitchen table, pencil in hand, not knowing where to start his long overdue list.

It seemed logical to start with the Corkeys and Evon. Murders were infrequent in Ballymena. Now all of a sudden they had three murders – all apparently separate and totally unconnected. That he didn't believe! In his mind, one death had led to the next and to the next, and he needed some sort of connection to make sense of things.

He thought he could basically ignore the circumstances of Shorty Corkey's death. The man had been killed in Ballymena, the blood around the body made that obvious, but none of the missing fingers had been found there. Now assuming the killers were normal ruthless psychopaths, who wouldn't want to keep them as trophies, then the missing body parts had to be near where the torturing took place. And that obviously – presumably? – had to be Belfast. Which begged two questions:

One. What information were Stan Holloway and his men trying to extract from the unfortunate Shorty?

And two. There was a huge city dump in Belfast, so why bring him as far as Ballymena before killing him?

Unless the killing and the dumping of the body had to do with warning a local or locals that the Belfast men were out to get them, unless…

That took him back to Reg, so he started there, working on a double list looking for connections between Reg and Evon.

Victim		**Reg Corkey**
Manner of death	Violent attack	

Location	Mrs Collins' back garden
Victim	**Evon Flinton**
Manner of death	Brutal
Location	Curles Bridge
Suspects	Tom Rankin
Known Associates	Tennent Street gang Fellow prostitutes Customers
Involved / in area	Mrs Collins Paddy Lorrimer R Shaw Lorrimer Rose Lorrimer
Idiots and drunks	Geordie Dunlop Edward Adair
Unknowns	Something the gang thought Shorty would know about. Coal fires.

As an afterthought, he put Tom Rankin's name in the Reg Corkey column – The Involved / in Area section. It was the only tenuous connection that he had to go on.

The killing of Reg Corkey had taken place late at night. Late enough for Tom to slip out of the house once the landlady was asleep. So could he have killed both Reg and Evon?

Which brought him back to motive, which brought him back to …

'Nout, Nothing, Bugger all,' said the frustrated Barlow and went off to get the real day started.

51

Inspector Foxwood had called for an early meeting between himself, Leary and Barlow. 'To dovetail our findings before we report to Mr Harvey,' he'd said. Which was a polite way of saying that he wanted things sorted between themselves before Harvey could interfere.

They met in Foxwood's office. A tight enough little room at the best of times and even less so with Barlow and Leary taking up much of the spare space.

'So what have we got?' asked Foxwood.

Leary detailed the forensics which gave plenty of information but absolutely nothing that could tie Tom Rankin into Evon's death. He finished by saying, 'If it wasn't for the boots and Rankin's lack of an alibi, we'd have nothing.'

Barlow said, 'The uniform branch have traced his pub crawl, from Agnews on Broughshane Street, to Kearneys in William Street, to Bobby DeLargys in Ballymoney Street and finally, near closing time, the Farmers' Rest in Mill Street. People remember him but can't remember if he was carrying his boots or not.'

Leary said, 'It's the same at the Showgrounds. Rankin's kitbag is still in the Changing Room and the masseur *thinks* Rankin took his boots with him but can't be sure. Anyone who actually remembers seeing him leave the grounds hasn't a clue as to what he was carrying, if anything.'

As for Reg and Shorty Corkey. That investigation had effectively moved to Tennent Street. The police there were trying to find out where and when the brothers had last been seen in Belfast, and who with. Leary was to catch a mid-morning train to Belfast to help co-ordinate the investigation while Foxwood took a turn at questioning Tom.

Barlow's own report about what he had discovered the previous day about Tom Rankin didn't help. Up until the time of the murder no one, other than the Lorrimers, had a bad word to say about the youth.

Foxwood grimaced. 'We're getting to the point where we'll have to charge him or let him go.'

Leary stated the obvious. 'Mr Harvey won't be pleased.'

Foxwood looked worried. Harvey would blame all three of them for failing to prosecute Tom. Barlow and probably Leary would be willing to take the kicks and suffer an adverse Periodic Report, but Foxwood had an ambitious wife.

The meeting with Harvey over, Barlow headed into the kitchen for a couple of hours of routine paperwork. The overtime returns were wonderful, fantastic, out of this world. With any luck they'd give Harvey a stroke.

It also gave Barlow a chance to plan his day. Edward he could ignore for another day. After a busy weekend, the ladies around John Street tended to take the Monday night off.

Geordie would be at work and it would be useless trying to talk to him there, even if he wasn't away in the lorry. That odd offer from Mr Lorrimer to buy Mrs Collins' house for "cold cash" had Barlow puzzled, so the more he could find out about the Lorrimers' business the better.

He swung himself onto the old bike and creaked his way up the Antrim Road and into Victory Park and Geordie's house.

Connie appeared, duster in hand as she gave the house its daily spring clean. 'He isn't here, and even if he was, he didn't do it.'

'Tell Geordie to meet me in the pub tonight. At about nine.'

'I don't want him drinking when he's driving.'

'One pint, Connie. You have my word.'

'And I don't want him involved in all this killing.'

That Barlow found interesting. Connie had an instinct about things. It made him feel that he was on the right track.

He refused the offer of a cup of tea and swung back onto the bike. 'Don't forget, Connie. When you're a widow...'

'I'll be in jail.'

'Then after they release you, I'm on the lookout for a first class cook.'

'Mr Barlow, I'm nearly too much for Geordie. What chance have you got?'

'I'd die happy finding out.'

52

Up the Antrim road again and across country to the Larne Line, with the whole way unremittingly uphill. Barlow got off the bike at Mrs Collins' house pleased with himself. His pedal-legs were definitely coming back.

Mrs Collins was in and delighted to see him. 'John, son, this is like the old times. You popping in at odd hours.'

He let her put on the kettle but said, 'Before we get to the cuppa, it's business first.'

'More trouble?'

She looked concerned and he felt a draft at his neck as if the Captain has come too close. Barlow didn't feel safe, not the way the Captain could throw a brass platter at a burglar.

'Not trouble, but while Terry Esler is a great builder, he thinks honest while I have a devious mind.'

'So you want to look around?'

'Please, to check things for myself.'

She wet the tea and left it to draw while she accompanied Barlow. He preferred it that way in case anything should ever be found missing from the house.

Terry had put catches on all the downstairs windows and, as a double security, had replaced the catches on the shutters so they could only be opened from the inside. The windows on the first floor and the attic were equally secure and the skylights on the roof nailed shut with long screws into the supporting trusses. The front door would need a sledgehammer to open it, equally the new back door.

Barlow made a point of praising everything to give Mrs Collins a sense of security. A sense of security that he thought misplaced. If anyone wanted to do her harm they could be in and out of the house, and long gone before the police got there. He had a feeling about things. In the old days he'd have parked an officer permanently in the house until things had settled, but with Harvey fussing about overtime? Not a chance.

He deliberately left her bedroom to last because it was on a corner, with one window over looking Lorrimers' factory. The ground floor windows were obscured by the boundary wall but he could see the first floor windows.

He remembered Rose running upstairs when she disagreed with her father over Tom Rankin's dismissal. There had to be a rest room or something.

'Do they use much of the upstairs?' he asked

'I'm not one for gossip,' Mrs Collins said.

That caught his attention.

'And anyway, John son, you never asked.'

'I'm asking now.' He edged her downstairs, knowing that she'd talk more freely if her hands were busy doing something. 'Mrs Collins, there's something happening in Ballymena that doesn't make sense. The only chance I have of getting things sorted is to have the whole picture.'

He was right, she talked more freely with her hands busy pouring the tea and laying out a plate of homemade pastries. Three settings as usual. Barlow found he was getting used to having the Captain sitting across from him.

'Now you know I'm not one to be nosy.' She wanted that to be clear before she started.

'But people tell you things and you have a quick eye.'

'Aye, and a good ear some nights when my sleep is disturbed. Especially by car doors banging and the shouts and gehaws of men with no consideration of a body trying to sleep.' She paused again while she put a pastry on his plate, an apple square, without being asked.

'You still remember which one is my favourite,' he said.

'Ough, son, I could tell you how many spoonfuls of sugar my granny used to put in her tea.'

'And?' he asked through a mouthful of apple square.

'Mostly it's just the men, boys really, and their drinking. Sometimes men and women, and that's the noisy nights with their high-pitched squealing and music blaring. As for the other thing, it never seems to occur to them that they've lights on and no curtains on the windows.'

Methodist and all as she was, she made a minuscule sign of the cross on her chest against evil.

'Did you ever complain?' he asked, hurrying to finish his tea and apple square because it was after twelve and he wanted to get to the factory before it closed for lunch.

'Complain? Never, but I told R Shaw once that I didn't think much of that Elvis singer and his *Wooden Heart*.'

'What did he say to that?'

'Not so much as a blush for the night before. Him and another man and a woman, and all three naked as Jaybirds.'

'When was that?' he asked and prodded for the answer he wanted. 'Last Thursday night?'

The night Reg Corkey was killed in her garden. Which would have put R Shaw and friends in the area.

She cleared away his empty cup and plate. 'Thursday night? No, and not a thing all week. But Saturday now, there was a car and a light came on for a minute or two.'

That he guessed was R Shaw celebrating the win over Linfield with a lady friend.

Mrs Collins was putting things away, making it plain that she had no more to say on the subject. Which made him remember what he had come about in the first place.

'This offer by Mr Lorrimer to buy the house. When did that come up?'

'The first of November, rent day.' He felt her relief at getting away from goings-on that shouldn't be mentioned in polite company. 'Normally I have to go looking for the rent, but that day he was at the door with the money and me barely out of bed.'

'And that was it?'

'Oh no, it came up again with the December rent, him saying it would be a welcome release of money to my late husband's children. With children of their own, he was sure they could be doing with it.'

She was an old softie so he knew the answer before he asked. 'So you told them about the offer?'

'Well I did, I felt I ought to, and they want me up on Saturday to give us time to discuss the offer before Christmas proper starts.'

She looked pleased at that. Not only being away from the house over the Christmas period instead of the begrudged one night, but for once she'd be made properly welcome instead of a shared-around forbearance.

The chance of getting a lump of money had the late Mr Collins' family being nice to her. It also solved some of Barlow's problems. This was Tuesday, Mrs Collins would be collected sometime on Saturday, which left four nights when she needed protection.

Acting Sergeant Gillespie was on night duty that night. He could arrange for Wilson to stay with Mrs Collins. At the same time, it would allow the young officer to clock up the overtime that he needed for an extended Christmas break. But what about the other nights? He'd come up with something. Do it himself if necessary.

Meanwhile.

'Tell me, have you mentioned this trip to anyone?'

He got an indignant sniff. 'My business is my business.'

'Keep it that way, missis.'

53

Barlow opened the door into Lorrimers' General Office without knocking and stepped in.

Mr Lorrimer was there and Rose and, this time, R Shaw. All of them at their separate desks.

'What do you want?' asked R Shaw.

'A few questions answered, straight this time.'

R Shaw snapped to his feet, which still made him four inches shorter than Barlow. He gasped a breath before saying, 'How dare you! You are aware that my father is a personal friend of Mr Harvey, your boss?'

'Is he now?'

R Shaw clicked his fingers at Mr Lorrimer who had remained sitting. 'Father, ring Mr Harvey and complain about this man's behaviour.'

Mr Lorrimer's hand touched the receiver, but didn't lift it.

Barlow said, 'Call Mr Harvey if you wish, sir, but don't be surprised if he reminds you that he is dealing with three murders in the teeth of Christmas. Stressed out the man is, and he's not in the mood to listen to complaints from people withholding information.'

Barlow had nodded firmly when he said "stressed" and "not in the mood". The "stressed" part was true but Harvey would drive to hell and back to hear a complaint against his Station Sergeant.

Still blustering, R Shaw subsided into his chair, his back arched and stiff.

'What information?' asked Rose. She sounded concerned.

Her desk was, as usual, covered in stacks of paper. From the colour of the sheets: blue, yellow and white, Barlow reckoned she was matching invoices with delivery dockets and order notes. The other two desks didn't hold anything requiring more than notional work.

'The names of friends and acquaintances who might know things, or have seen people hanging around at odd times.'

'This is a place for work, not social entertaining,' Mr Lorrimer said. Yet he shot an anxious look at R Shaw.

Barlow took off his cap and watched them watch him as he put the cap on again and adjusted it to regulation slope. 'Sir, we have information to the contrary.'

'That nosy old bitch, Collins.' R Shaw all but spat the words.

Not the way he had intended the thinking to go and R Shaw was the type to take it out on the old lady.

'Actually, sir, you'd be surprised whom we've talked to in the last few days.' He raised an eyebrow as if savouring the malicious gossip. 'Quite illuminating it was.'

Now doubt showed in R Shaw's face.

'In fact, sir, we warned the people we've already spoken to, to keep quiet about being interviewed.' He gave R Shaw what he hoped was a keen look. 'Even so, surely one of your friends tipped you off?'

Now that he had R Shaw on the back foot, he went for the information he needed. 'I want you to write down the names, addresses and telephone numbers of everyone involved, and if anyone we've already spoken to isn't on that list, then we will charge you with withholding information.'

He liked that final bit. R Shaw couldn't know whom he'd allegedly spoken to so the list would have to be complete.

R Shaw made a show of being willing to cooperate. 'For all the good it will do.' He pulled a pad towards him. 'It was mostly myself and friends sharing a few beer.'

Rose said, 'He knows, R Shaw.' She snorted her contempt. 'A place to sleep it off rather than drive when you've been drinking? Ha! Do you think I came up the Bann in a bubble? You and those awful friends of yours and the whores you go about with.'

Mr Lorrimer came erect in his seat. 'Rose, wash your mouth out. Using words like that. It says in the good book...'

Rose talked over him. 'He who condones evil is equally as guilty as the man who perpetrates it.' Temper flared in her face. 'I'm fed up with your self-righteous disapproval of people who have the same failings as yourself.' Her head and her wrath turned R Shaw's way. 'As for your whoring, you're disgusting.'

Barlow expected a repeat of tears from the last visit. This time she scooped up a set of keys from R Shaw's desk.

'Hey! He said.

'Go play with yourself.'

Boy does that temper go with that red hair, thought Barlow. It was like watching the runt of a litter bite back.

Rose stopped beside him as if needing the assurance of his presence to deliver her last piece of revenge. ‘And in case you haven’t got the message. On Saturday, after I give the men their holiday pay, I’m out of here. I quit. Finished. I’ve applied for a job that pays me more than the cleaner gets.

She turned on her foot and slammed the door behind her.

Mr Lorrimer shouted, ‘Don’t forget to call with Solicitor Moncrief.’ He turned to R Shaw. ‘And you too. Take my car.’

They heard a high-powered engine start up and the squeal of tyres as Rose gunned R Shaw’s car out of the yard. Barlow hoped she calmed down before she hit traffic.

He put his hands on his hips and looked from one man to the other. ‘Now, who is going to show me around upstairs?’

54

R Shaw pointedly made himself busy preparing a list of men and women who had been *guests* of his upstairs, so it fell to Mr Lorrimer to show Barlow around.

Not a bad idea, in Barlow's opinion, as he followed the waft of Paddy Lorrimer's alcoholic breath up the stairs. Mr Lorrimer would be less likely to object if he did any serious searching without a warrant.

The stairs were bare wood and shiny from generations of feet, as were the floorboards on the first floor. There was no second floor because there was no ceiling and the space stretched to the wood-pinned trusses and beyond that to the bare tiles of the roof.

It seemed so typical of staff quarters built all those generations back. A byre of a place with truckle beds laid out in rows. No privacy. Some of the beds were still there.

One section of the floor had been closed off. Presumably for the Butler or the Housekeeper. Ladies in one wing of the outbuilding, men in the other and impossible to tell which gender had slept where he stood.

He opened the door into the private room. The first thing he noticed was the ceiling, it had one, and a fireplace choked with burnt coals.

Evon had talked about somewhere with a fireplace.

He should have felt elated but he instead felt sad for her.

'Rather nice,' he told Mr Lorrimer, playing it slightly sarcastic but also casual.

'Sometimes we put business guests up for the night.'

The room had been painted white in the near past, and mats thrown down to take away the starkness of the bare boards. A double bed, well-endowed with plumped up pillows and a heavy bedspread, took up much of the room.

Barlow walked across and had a good look at a safe in the corner. It was the size of two large suitcases roped together, and was opened and shut by means of a sequence of numbers rather than a key.

'In case they have any valuables,' Mr Lorrimer said, trying not to make a big deal of its presence in a guest room.

Barlow could imagine what sort of guest. The sort that needed the

Lorrimers' bespoke service but thought the Lorrimers as untrustworthy as themselves.

The memory of Evon was still in his head as he looked at the fireplace. On top of the burnt coals lay a slip of cardboard, well singed by heat but still intact. A top of a cigarette packet if he guessed correctly.

His heart lurched as much from fear as excitement. Someone had killed Reg Corkey, possibly either Mr Lorrimer or R Shaw or the two of them. He didn't want to betray his suspicions of their guilt but he had no intention of leaving without that bit of cardboard.

He sat on the edge of the bed and took his cap off and felt around the inside of the brim as if something was annoying him. Then he put the cap on the bed, slightly behind him, and bounced up and down. 'You're good to your guests, Mr Lorrimer. That is some mattress.'

'It's a Slumberland, and well worth the money,' Mr Lorrimer said.

'Is it now?' Barlow said and wanted to know where he had bought it – McKinneys of Broadway Avenue – and if he didn't mind telling, the cost.

Mr Lorrimer was restless, obviously wanting the inspection to be over. Once Mr Lorrimer moved near the door, Barlow stood up, keeping himself between Mr Lorrimer and the cap on the bed.

'I need to be getting on,' Barlow said, and resisted the temptation to look at his watch and declare it was near lunchtime.

His body blocked Mr Lorrimer and he had his hand on the door handle when he noticed something. The window of the room looked straight across to Mrs Collins' bedroom, and Mrs Collins, he remembered belatedly, had a boxed set of Swiss binoculars on her bedside table.

The dirty old biddy.

He couldn't hold back a laugh. Mr Lorrimer jumped at the sudden noise.

'Sorry, I suddenly remembered a joke Gillespie told me this morning.'

He led the way through the dormitory, occasionally peering out of a window to give the impression of being interested in what people could see from there. About halfway down the stairs, Barlow ran fingers through his hair as if searching for something. 'My cap.' He pushed past Mr Lorrimer and raced back up, calling, 'Wait there, I'll be straight back.'

He pushed into the bedroom, letting the door swing to behind him. The piece of cardboard was definitely something torn off a cigarette packet. How to retrieve it was a problem, because it was carbonised in all but one corner.

A handkerchief.

There was one in his pocket, lovingly ironed and folded by Vera and still unused. He opened up the first fold, crouched over the fire and gripped the cardboard by its good corner. He teased it away from the clutching cinders. Mr Lorrimer's voice was raised, querying, 'Mr Barlow?'

Yet he daren't rush.

There was something on the cardboard, the white of numbers on the carbon. Finally the cardboard was clear and he could ease it onto the handkerchief. Mr Lorrimer was calling up the stairs, wanting to know what was keeping him. Barlow folded the handkerchief over the cardboard and slid it into a breast pocket.

He scooped up his cap, clattered briskly down the stairs and thanked Mr Lorrimer for his kindness. R Shaw had come to the General Office, wondering what was going on.

Barlow held out his cap by way of explanation. 'If my head wasn't screwed on, I'd forget it.'

He told R Shaw to leave the list of names into the station immediately after lunch and was on his bike and gone before either of the Lorrimers reached the front door.

Barlow didn't believe in ghosts, except for the Captain, but something about that room upstairs gave him the shivers. Evon had been there, had been abused by rough trade in that room. The woman who had given him a future had been denied hers by a series of men.

55

At eight forty-five that evening, Barlow pulled a sports coat on over his uniform trousers. 'I'm off,' he called up the corridor.

Vera popped her head out of her bedroom. 'Abandoned again.'

'I'm away to see a man about a dog.' He looked back into the kitchen where Toby was stretched out comfortably. 'One that can't get up on my chair.'

Toby snored on.

Vera disappeared back into her bedroom, shouting, 'Be good. Don't do anything I wouldn't do.'

The Bridge Bar was normally quiet on a Tuesday night. This Tuesday night was even quieter than usual, with men saving their pennies for the coming holiday. Geordie leaned on the bar counter, adding his own ring of damage to its surface with a pint. Barlow caught his eye and nodded across the clutter of small tables and chairs to the far corner where Edward usually sat.

'A pint for the sergeant and apparently I'm paying,' Geordie told the barman.

Barlow settled himself in a chair and looked at an infinite number of reflections of himself as they bounced from wall mirror to wall mirror and back again. He wished one of those selves knew what was going on in Ballymena.

Geordie appeared with the pint and sat across from him. 'Who am I talking to?'

'The Sergeant Major wants you to have a word with the policeman.'

'I'm no tout.'

'Touts get paid. You're paying.'

'You're getting as bad as the Major.' Geordie sipped at his own drink. 'Try me.'

Barlow lowered his voice. 'Tom – Thomas Rankin.'

'Before my time,' Geordie said.

'You've been at Lorrimers long enough. There has to be gossip.'

Geordie rubbed at a day's whiskers on his chin. 'I've been stitched up often enough'

'Oh aye?'

'But this was a bad one.'

Rose – Miss Rose to Geordie and the men in the factory – was complaining about her feet being frozen by a draught whistling under the door. Barlow remembered that draft and how he'd stepped smartly aside to avoid it.

Tom came up with the simple idea of making her a footstool to lift her feet off the ground and he asked his landlady to embroider a little tapestry to go on top. The problem was Rose herself. Rose had an instinct for things. Hide something under a bundle of rubbish that hadn't been moved in years, that was the day she'd want the whole lot shifted. To keep the footstool a secret until it was ready Tom said he would take it home.

R Shaw stood and watched Tom walk out of the factory gate before he called him back and challenged him, accusing him of theft. Tom was fired on the spot.

'But didn't anyone say something? The foreman for instance, he had to know what was going on?'

'He tried but they had Tom on the catchall "Nothing to leave the premises without the Lorrimers' prior approval."

'There has to be more to it than that' Barlow said.

'A few days before, Tom and R Shaw argued about the money he was taking out of the business.' Geordie shrugged. 'Money needed to pay the bills.'

'Not that you would do a thing like that,' Barlow said.

He didn't register Geordie's reply because the door opened and Edward walked into the bar.

56

Barlow thought that it couldn't be good, Edward in the bar, and him on a last chance with Mrs Anderson.

'Ooops,' Geordie said, spotting Edward as well.

Edward stood, his head turned towards Barlow, his heart and soul over the counter, pulling his first pint.

Barlow was on his feet without realising it, his chair clattering back.

'I'll stand the Major a pint,' an old soldier shouted at the barman.

Barlow reached Edward. 'Go and sit down,' he told him, indicating Geordie in the corner. 'I'll bring it over.'

Edward's eyes were burning with need. 'My dear chap.'

The barman had a fresh pint glass in his hand.

Barlow whispered, 'Fill it with ginger ale, I'll make up the difference later.'

'It's on the house,' said the Barman.

He popped the tops of two bottles of ginger ale and filled the glass. Barlow carried it over to the table and set it in front of Edward. Edward looked suspiciously at the glass, examined the colour of its contents, held it to his nose and sniffed.

He glared at Barlow. 'Sergeant Major, your humour is ill placed.' Then he held the glass up to the man who'd offered to pay and bowed graciously. 'My dear chap, one is most obliged.'

He put the glass down again with a determined finality.

'You're not supposed to be drinking,' Barlow said.

'Having been to John Street, one felt obliged to call at your house. There one wished to impart the knowledge obtained from the charming Ladies of the Night. At the house one was informed by your delightful daughter that you had, in her words, gone to see a man about a dog, and one…'

'Okay, okay, I've got the picture,' Barlow said and was grateful that he was in the pub when Edward came in because he wouldn't have left it sober.

He remembered the unshed tears in Mrs Anderson's eyes when she said she'd kill Edward if he took another drop before Christmas and knew he'd been lax there as well.

Barlow let Edward's circumlocutions and big words pass him by as he made sense of what Edward had found out. In recent weeks Evon had enjoyed a few all-nighters with new clients. Some of these men were into rough trade, leaving her bruised and, on one occasion, a split lip.

'But the emoluments were substantial,' Edward assured Barlow.

'And then?' prompted a fascinated Geordie.

'And then, my dear chap, our conversation was temporarily interrupted by a wayfarer seeking sexual gratification.'

'He meant about Evon,' Barlow said.

'Not really,' Geordie said.

Evon wouldn't say who her new clients were. The other prostitutes only knew that she was picked up by a car near the Courthouse. However, she had talked about a coal fire and the hope that some of the other women could become involved in a lucrative quality trade.

The Belfast men and their organised prostitution.

The very thought gave Barlow the shivers.

57

Being in a bar, with a glass of something in front of him, Edward's old habits took over and he began to sip its contents. Poison would have gone down easier but he turned every so often to the old soldier who had stood him the drink and smiled his gracious thanks.

Barlow said to Geordie, 'Lorrimers.'

'What about them?'

'Who gave you a reference?'

Edward swallowed a vile taste out of his mouth. 'Rifleman Dunlop gave one his word.'

'I get the picture,' Barlow said.

Geordie looked ashamed, not only at taking an honest job but getting it solely on the undertaking that he would refrain from doing anything dishonest in that employment. 'I told you before, Barlow, it's your fault. I could have been a millionaire by now.'

'Rubbish. By now, you'd be broke and doing ten years hard.'

Barlow asked, to get his thoughts away from Geordie spending his last days in jail. 'So you do the lorry work for the Lorrimers?'

'Here, there and everywhere. All sorts of hours and to the oddest places.'

Barlow played it casual. 'Oh really?'

'Especially when it comes to those fancy bits of furniture.'

Exactly what Barlow wanted to hear.

He played bland ignorance. 'What fancy bits of furniture?'

'Things people want special like, for a gift or something.'

'Bespoke,' Edward said, surfacing for a moment from his humped misery.

'What about them?' asked Barlow.

'Well I take them to the house and leave it for the people to look at. Then a day or two later I collect it again, and bring it back to the factory to be re-wrapped and sent somewhere foreign. Places like the Isle of Man and Jersey. Even Switzerland once.'

Barlow was intrigued. At a guess, the furniture with the hidden compartment was sent to the tax evader to be filled with money, then sent back to the Lorrimers for sending off to a contact in a tax haven. Getting

Lorrimers to send the furniture was clever. As a recognised firm, Customs and Excise were unlikely to query what was being sent abroad and why.

'Are there many like that?'

'Nah, but January's going to be busy.'

'Aye, it would be.'

The answer to the next question frightened Barlow because it could involve Geordie in something nasty, and who was going to believe that a serial criminal wasn't knowingly involved.

'Any special run like that last Wednesday?' he asked.

According to Barlow, Geordie had a small brain and only used half of it. At the same time he wasn't stupid. His eyes gleamed. 'Barlow, am I missing something here?'

'Just tell me.'

'Wednesday?' Geordie pretended to think back while he tried to figure out what Barlow was on to. 'Hi! If the Lorrimers are up to something shady, I mean with my experience…'

'Of being caught? Get on with it.'

'Okay, keep your shirt on.' Geordie threw his arms out in a peace offering. 'There was this pickup in Belfast, in a wee place near the Albert Bridge. The customer hadn't seen the item or something and they told me I'd have to wait a couple of hours.

'We're busy at the minute and I'd a lot on that day so I rang the Lorrimers. I thought they'd tell me to collect it the next time I was in Belfast but they said to hang on and not to worry about the overtime. They even told me to have a bite somewhere while I waited and charge them for it. That's why I ended up doing that late run to Londonderry on Thursday.'

'So what did you do while you were hanging around Belfast? Where did you go?'

Geordie leaned over the table, getting closer to Barlow. 'Come on, Barlow, what am I missing here?'

'Tell me, Geordie, it's important.'

Geordie's look was something between embarrassment and a glare of annoyance. 'I spent it with my family, the ones you put in the Crumlin Road jail. I wanted to leave them in sweets and tobacco for Christmas.'

The jewellery robbery had taken place on the Wednesday afternoon when Geordie was visiting his relations in jail. Of all places, Barlow thought. There again, Geordie always was a jammy bugger.

According to last night's late news, the schoolgirl injured during the jewellery robbery had died.

Barlow said, 'You've just talked yourself out of a charge of Accessory to Murder.'

58

By then Edward had nearly finished the pint of ginger ale. Barlow nodded meaningfully at Geordie who slipped off to get Edward a pint of water to keep his hands busy. Barlow concentrated on diverting Edward's thoughts.

He asked, 'So tell me, did the women say anything about Tom Rankin?'

'Oh yes, he's known to them.' Edward paused to drain the rest of the ginger ale and seemed relieved when he could finally put the glass aside. 'Known to them, not in your police way but as a gentleman of courtesy and consideration.'

Again Barlow syphoned off the big words and circumlocutions to get down to the story.

A certain "Lady of the Night" going by the name of Ophelia was on her way to work one evening when she broke her heel in a street grating. Worse, in falling she had twisted her ankle and couldn't walk. She lay bleeding and pleading for help from passers-by but everyone rushed on, afraid to be seen associating with a known prostitute. Then Tom Rankin happened along. Tom retrieved her broken shoe and helped her to her digs which, fortunately, were close by.

Having seen her safely to her room, Tom ran to the nearest chemist shop and came back with ointment for the cuts and bandages for the ankle. He examined the ankle, which by then was very tender and swollen. He didn't think it was broken but advised her to see her doctor the next day. Having cleaned and soothed the scrapes and cuts, and bandaged her ankle, he left, refusing to let her pay for the stuff he'd got at the chemists.

Geordie was arriving back with the pint of water when Edward said, 'He even refused the offer of a free…' He hesitated, not wanting to come out with it direct. 'Some sort of job.'

Geordie snorted, amused. 'You mean a blow job.'

The murmur of background conversation in the room stopped. Every head turned their way.

Edward said, 'That's it, my dear chap, a blow job. But what has the weather got to do with it?'

Edward's joke caused a ripple of laughter around the bar. Barlow laughed with the rest but at the same time his mind was busy recasting the list he'd made that morning. Under "Reg Corkey" Tom had worked for a time at Lorrimers and under "Evon" he was known as a sort of Boy Scout by the prostitutes in John Street.

Finally he had made a connection, no matter how tenuous, between Reg Corkey's death and Evon's.

What he couldn't understand was why he felt worried when he should have been elated.

Wednesday
December 21st

59

Barlow stood in the Enquiry Office and watched the minute hand on the clock click past one o'clock in the morning. If Harvey paid him overtime he'd be earning more than the Chief Constable.

But he didn't and right then home and bed seemed enticing.

'Now about this car?' he asked the Duty Sergeant, Acting Sergeant Gillespie, who was busy doing the crossword in an old newspaper, even as he played awkward.

Gillespie didn't even lift his head. 'Regulations, Station Sergeant. Resources have to be kept available to meet emergencies, not act as taxies.'

Barlow fetched a sheaf of papers from his "IN" tray and dumped them on top of the newspaper. 'If you oblige me, I'll let you start pulling information together for the Monthly Returns.'

Gillespie handed over the keys. 'An offer like that, how can I refuse?' He also folded the newspaper away and sighed at the stack of forms waiting to be filled in.

'Let them walk,' said WPC Hughes, who was there as well.

She was sour with Barlow because she had planned to spend the night shift making up to Wilson. Instead, Wilson was at Mrs Collins' with instructions to go to bed and sleep. If anything happened Wilson would know about it. Vague instructions maybe, but Barlow could imagine the young officer's face if he told him that that the ghost of Captain Collins would sound the alarm if anyone tried to break in.

He decided to give Hughes a ray of hope. 'Gillespie, would you arrange shifts so that Wilson can get to the Staff do for a couple of hours.'

Gillespie flicked a look at the unhappy Hughes. 'I'll see to it, Sarge.'

'Good man.'

Barlow's body ached with tiredness, but at least he'd finally coaxed a smile out of WPC Hughes.

Once he'd left Edward and Geordie home he could call it a night. Their statements and his report were already on Inspector Foxwood's desk, together with the piece of carbonised cardboard, still wrapped in his handkerchief.

For all the good it's likely to do.

He fetched Edward and Geordie out of the kitchen, where Geordie was busy eating someone's supper, Gillespie's with any luck. They followed him into the yard and got into the car. Edward sat in the back.

Barlow was busy accelerating through the gears when Geordie picked up the microphone. 'Kilo #1 to Control. Exiting station for a bumpy ride.'

'Put that down,' Barlow said.

Control in the form of WPC Hughes replied, 'Control to Kilo #1. Geordie, go away and give my head peace.'

'Who ate your wee bun?' asked Geordie and hung up.

The town was quiet, the pubs closed and their customers long in bed. The streets shone with damp but the evening rain had stopped. Geordie had work in the morning, but Edward looked absolutely wiped. Barlow ran him home first, taking the slope down to the river's edge and stopping right at the hut door.

His headlights illuminated the spot where Evon's body had been found. He paused for a moment before turning and driving out. Tom Rankin had killed Evon. There should be no doubt about that in his mind.

Evon had talked about a coal fire and being out of the cold. Not just herself but for other women, and on a regular basis. Which spoke of someone intending to pimp the local prostitutes, and no one in Ballymena had that capability. Maybe the odd wife or girlfriend shoved onto the streets to earn some money, but Evon was always quick to pass on the word and have that stopped.

Which meant Belfast.

Geordie said, 'I'd like to get home before I have to get up for work.'

'Can you even spell the word?'

'M O N E Y,' spelled Geordie. 'And if you ever tell anyone that I've been helping the police, I'll… I'll…'

'Go straight?' asked Barlow as he turned the car and drove back onto the road.

The wheels had barely touched black tarmac when the radio crackled into life. 'Control to Kilo #1.'

It was Gillespie.

Barlow's hand beat Geordie's to the microphone. 'Kilo #1.'

'Control. The Old Galgorm Road. Lorrimer's house is on fire.

There's people trapped and the Duty Fire Crew are out on a call.'

'Kilo #1. On our way.'

Barlow flicked on the blue strobe light but left off the bells because there was no traffic about. From deep in the town the wail of the fire siren called men from their beds.

He said to Geordie, 'I'll drop you as close as I can to your house.'

Geordie looked at him, wide-eyed at the distance he'd have to walk. 'I'll sleep in the car until you've finished playing cops and robbers.

60

At least Barlow and Geordie were south of the river and didn't have to go looking for a bridge to cross. Barlow gave thanks for that as they sped back into town and did a skid-turn onto the Old Galgorm Road. The Lorrimer house was easy spotted with flames roaring out of ground floor windows.

Barlow parked the police car outside on the road, well clear of the front gate. The firemen, when they arrived, would need full access.

Neighbours dotted the lawn, doing nothing other than exclaim their horror. One man was trying to fight the fire with buckets of water thrown from twenty feet back. Barlow couldn't blame him. The man, with his pyjama-top tucked inside his trousers, risked being burnt even at that distance.

He spotted a body lying on the front lawn. There was still no sign of the fire engine, not even the distant sound of its bell.

He aimed Geordie at the onlookers and the fire bucket hero. 'Get them out of here,' and went over to the body on the ground. As he suspected, it was R Shaw. R Shaw was busy telling anyone who would listen that he couldn't get near the stairs to rouse his father and Rose. He choked the words out, as if his lungs were still full of smoke.

Barlow didn't bother to be polite. 'Which bedrooms are they in?'

R Shaw's voice went high-pitched. 'Oh please help them.'

'Which bedrooms?'

'Father's there.' R Shaw pointed at a front bedroom.

Barlow's eyes followed the point. Smoke was already stacked up inside the windows. An apparatus job if there ever was one.

'And Rose?'

'The back.' His arm wobbled a point to the right side of the house. Now he was sobbing. 'I don't want her to die, and us not speaking.'

Barlow took to his heels across the lawn. Houses had bathrooms at the back. Bathrooms had downpipes.

Geordie kept pace with him.

'Where do you think you're going?' asked Barlow.

'If anything happens to you I don't get my lift home.'

They burst through an unlocked side gate into the back yard. The windows of the downstairs rooms reflected the glow of the fire, but not upstairs. Rose's bedroom door had to be shut, blocking much of the smoke from getting in, which gave her a chance.

'Shout,' Barlow told Geordie and shouted himself while he ran to the coal shed and grabbed an armful of coal.

They stood and shouted Rose's name while they flung coals at the window. Some hit solid and bounced off, others went straight through.

No Rose appeared. Smoke seeped through the broken glass.

Barlow ran to the downpipe, yelling at Geordie. 'Give me a hike up.'

'Hold on, I'm the professional burglar here,' Geordie said.

'With a gut that would buckle an elephant.'

Barlow threw down his cap, unbuckled his gun belt and shed his jacket. 'As soon as I start climbing the drainpipe, break that window near the catch.'

He stuck his truncheon into his trouser belt, stepped on Geordie's locked hands and then onto his shoulders.

'Those size twelves of yours don't half hurt,' Geordie said as he straightened up with a jerk, giving Barlow another six inches up the pipe.

Barlow found himself gripping cold metal on a chill December night, his feet scrabbling against the wall for purchase. A piece of coal bounced off the wall near his head.

'Hey!'

'Sorry,' Geordie said. He didn't sound particularly sorry.

His next thrown coal went straight through the bathroom window. And the next and the next.

Barlow's arms burned with effort he clawed his way upwards, his breath coming in rags.

A toe finally found purchase on a wall tie, allowing him to hang onto the downpipe with one hand while he drew his truncheon. He battered at the remaining glass in the bathroom window until he could put his hand in and release the catch. The window swung open, heavy smoke poured out.

'It's easy from there,' Geordie called up.

'Who got stuck in the pantry window the last time they were on a job?'

Barlow used the truncheon to sweep away shards of broken glass from the sill and the inside ledge. He ignored Geordie's, 'Wait for the fire brigade.'

Putting his faith in long forgotten army training, he stretched for the window frame, dug his toes into the gap between aged bricks and leapfrogged upwards until he could rest his elbows on the sill. From there, he gripped the hot and cold taps of the sink and hauled himself into the bathroom.

Stupidly enough he took a gasp of relief and nearly passed out from the smoke sucked into his lungs. He collapsed to the floor, his eyes running rivulets of tears. There was always two inches of air beneath the smoke. Someone had told him that years back. He hoped they were right.

After a few breaths, he began to believe it when his head cleared and he dared move on. The only way he could figure it, was to head out the bathroom door and not even think of breathing again until he was in Rose's room.

With that he took a deep breath, slowly so as not to drag smoke in as well, scrambled to his feet and found the bathroom door by walking into it.

Even before he opened the door the heat was intense. Once open, it was like standing in a roast spit. His eyes watered so hard that he had to keep them screwed shut. He turned left, away from the bright flames.

A door jam, a door. His hand searched for the handle. He gripped a round thing at waist height. Turned the handle and opened the door, and sensed the rush of smoke accompanying him in.

Something soft caught his feet. He kicked it away and felt a lump in the bed that had to be Rose. He hauled off the bedspread and used his toes to jam it tight against the bottom of the door. Found his way to the window and opened it. Heard Geordie shout something, but not what. He was too busy choking on nearly pure air.

He went back to the bed, found Rose's shoulders and shook her.

She didn't move. With his own coughing he couldn't hear if she was breathing or not.

He used one hand to trace her lips and nose and smacked her cheek.

'Rose. Get up.'

Still no movement.

61

Barlow sobbed with fear for Rose. It didn't seem fair to die, not at her age. Not when she had finally decided to make a life for herself, well away from her family and the factory. He thought to feel along the wall for the switch and the light came on. Not that he could see much out of eyes that burned and watered.

He pulled the bedclothes back and felt for Rose's heart. There was a pulse. Not much, but something at least.

He had to get Rose out of the house, put fresh air into her, and he needed time to achieve all that with his own energy fast disappearing.

He made it to the window again for a fresh breath of air. Two shapes stood in the yard. One of them had to be a fireman.

'Oxygen, quick,' shouted Barlow.

'Catch,' shouted the shape that wasn't Geordie.

Barlow grabbed at the heavy cylinder as it came flying up. It banged into his head and he staggered back.

Head reeling, he wobbled his way to the bed, turned on the oxygen and took a huge breath for himself before placing the mask over Rose's mouth and nose.

By the time he had the restraining straps secured around her head, a ladder had banged against the outside wall. A faceless figure appeared at the window.

Barlow helped him in.

The fireman gave him his buddy mask to suck oxygen while he assessed the situation. Then he grabbed Barlow by the shoulder and pushed him towards the window where a second faceless figure waited. 'You, out,' the fireman said.

Barlow went. The firemen were trained for the job and, anyway, his head was spinning from all the smoke.

'I can get myself down,' he told the fireman waiting on the wooden ladder.

But he couldn't and Geordie helped break his sliding fall.

Barlow's chest hurt, his face and hands burned from exposure to the flames and his head pounded. Yet he lay, content, stretched out on the cold concrete yard. After what he had been through, anything that came with fresh air had to be comfortable.

Geordie slipped Barlow's uniform jacket under his head for comfort and put his gun belt beside him.

Geordie said, 'I took the car keys out of your pocket. I'll see myself home.'

'Don't you dare,' Barlow said.

Geordie disappeared into the night.

Barlow lay on and listened to more and more emergency bells honing in on Lorrimers' house. People shouted and the fire roared louder as the centre of the house turned into a vortex of flame.

He decided to get up.

Someone crouching over him, a fireman, shoved him flat again. 'Don't even think about it.'

He subsided knowing that the man was right. Even that slight movement had his head spinning like a top.

His throat burned from the smoke but he managed to croak, 'Rose, the daughter?'

The Fireman pointed. Barlow looked and saw a fireman and an Ambulance man working on someone. He hadn't even seen them bring Rose out of the house.

'She's going to be fine, but I can't say the same for the father,' the Fireman said.

Barlow lay on. He was going to ask for a blanket when he realised he already had one tucked around him.

Eventually they eased him onto a stretcher and loaded him into an ambulance. The ambulance man put a mask over his face. With oxygen flooding his system his head started to clear and the pounding headache eased.

Before the ambulance could move off a leading fireman appeared at the door. 'Barlow, my report will say that you acted in the highest traditions of the Royal Ulster Constabulary, but you ever do a thing like that again on my watch and I'll kick you from here to Connaught.'

Barlow eased up the oxygen mask to allow his words out. 'My daughter is going to give me hell for this.'

Anger and tears from Vera were worth it. Rose would live.

He lifted the facemask again. 'Home, James,' he told the ambulance man.

62

Barlow's nemesis in the shape of Sister O'Hara, was waiting for him at the entrance to the Emergency Ward.

'They told us a policeman had been injured and I just knew it would be you,' she said.

'I love your bedside manner,' he said.

She produced a large pair of scissors and snapped them in front of his eyes.

'You don't have to cut off my clothes,' he said.

'It's not your clothes I'm thinking of.'

The oxygen had cleared his head so he was able to transfer himself from the stretcher to a bed in a curtained off cubicle. Somewhere nearby he could hear R Shaw's continuing moan about not being able to save his family and the sobs of Rose. From another cubicle came the clatter of instruments and the muttered concerns of the staff working on Mr Lorrimer.

With Sister's help, Barlow got his shirt off but held grimly onto his trousers. 'There's nothing wrong down there.'

He felt a lot better, even so it was good to lie back, while Sister used wipes to clean the cuts and scrapes on his hands and arms. He sucked air and coughed again when she started on his forehead.

'Where did you get that bump?' she asked.

'An oxygen cylinder.'

'Have you a headache?'

'Only when you're around.'

'That's a yes then. I'll get a doctor to look at it.'

She covered him with a light blanket to keep him warm and put pads of cooling ointment on his eyes.

He searched in the blackness for her hand and trapped it against his face. For someone who spent much of her life handling chemicals it was surprisingly soft. Neither did it pull away. 'Sister, tell me about Rose and Mr Lorrimer.'

'Huh! and I thought I was going to get the famous Barlow chat-up line.'

'Please.'

'Rose, we're keeping in until the specialist sees her in the morning. Mr Lorrimer…' He sensed her shake her head. 'Blood pressure, smoking, drink, lifestyle. He should make it this time but his life expectancy won't be great.'

She pulled her hand free, put the oxygen mask over his face to keep him quiet, and left.

With nothing better to do, he lay and listened to the sounds around him. Rose was transferred to a ward on a trolley with a creaking wheel, and the medical team continued to work on Mr Lorrimer. With increasing hope going by the tone of their voices.

R Shaw's voice continued to carry through the ward. According to him, he was in the sitting room asleep in the chair and woke up when he started to choke on the smoke. The hallway was on fire. He tried to warn his father and Rose but a sea of flames reached the stairs before he could. He jumped out of a window and ran to a neighbours to sound the alarm.

Barlow reckoned that by the time R Shaw came to make an official statement it wouldn't be a sea of flames, it would be an ocean.

Sister came back with a doctor and removed the pads from his eyes. Once she'd wiped off the remaining ointment Barlow found that he could see more or less properly again.

He took off his mask. 'What's R Shaw's injuries?'

'I can't answer that, most unprofessional,' the doctor said.

Barlow's jacket hung over a chair. He pointed to the three chevrons on the sleeve. 'Those trump your indignation.'

Sister said, 'Some smoke inhalation. The sleeve of his shirt isn't even scorched.'

'Surprise, surprise,' Barlow said.

He looked from Sister to the doctor. 'And?'

The doctor shrugged his acceptance at having to come completely clean. 'There are abrasions and contusions on Mr R Shaw's torso, along the ribs in particular, and he displays a significant tenderness in the lower midriff section. There also appears to be blood in his urine, but that has still to be confirmed.'

Sister said, 'In English, someone duffed him up, but not where it would show.'

Barlow asked, 'What about tonight? I mean the fire.'

'Older than that,' the Doctor said. 'Going by the bruising, two days ago, three at the most.'

'You're sure of that?'

'I play rugby,' the Doctor said and pointedly changed the subject by asking Barlow searching questions about the bang on the head.

Barlow admitted to seeing stars and, yes, he had a headache but the oxygen had brought it down to manageable proportions.

The doctor stepped back and away when Vera came flying in: no makeup, hair uncombed, her jacket wrongly buttoned so that it hung awkwardly. Behind her came Ernest T Potter, the suave solicitor but minus his tie.

She'll die when she next looks in the mirror, Barlow decided but said, 'A bit of smoke, Love, and some stupid fireman clunked me with his oxygen cylinder.'

He hurt for her. This was a wife's job, coming to dig him out of hospital. Not a daughter's.

He shook Ernest's hand. 'Ernie, thank you for bringing her.'

'It's a pleasure, Mr Barlow.'

Vera linked Barlow's arm and smiled at their unspoken acceptance of each other. He knew that his daughter might be clinging to him, but she was pulling away at the same time.

'John, if you like.'

'John, then.'

Inspector Foxwood and Gillespie arrived, Gillespie breathing fire as fierce as the one in the Lorrimers' house. 'I'll kill whoever brought the car back? They left it in the yard with the keys in the ignition and the lights on full. The battery's as flat as a pancake.'

Thursday December 22nd

63

Vera shook Barlow awake. She had taken the day off work to care for him. 'Manacles are the only thing that will keep him from work,' Sister had warned. Barlow was in bed and ordered not to put so much as a toe to the floor before lunchtime.

Barlow came out of a deep doze. 'Another cup of tea? You're spoiling me.'

'You're wanted on the phone.'

'If it's Harvey, tell him I'm dead. No flowers.'

She stopped him from rolling back under the blankets. 'It's somebody called Michael Sinclair. He says he's an old friend.'

If Sinclair had introduced himself by rank, that would have been business and Barlow could have safely ignored him. But calling himself Michael, and saying that he was a friend, made it personal. Michael was calling in an old favour or building up one for the future, and that was good enough for Barlow. 'Tell him I'll be straight down.'

'Dad?'

'I think I know what it's about, love, and he needs to talk to me.'

Saying he'd take the call and getting there, were two different things. His feet wanted to go one way, his knees another. If Vera hadn't been standing in the hall waiting for him he'd have used the wall for balance. Finally he made it and tried not to collapse into the hall chair.

He took the receiver from Vera. 'Michael, long time.'

He saw himself in the hallstand mirror and couldn't believe his appearance. He could pass as one of the weary old men ending their days in the Braid Valley Hospital. The livid bruise on his forehead was typical of an old fool who wouldn't use his stick and kept falling over, and his voice sounded weak and husky. He cleared his throat and made motions of drinking a cup of tea. Vera nodded and disappeared into the kitchen.

Michael said, 'John, I'm on "Conference" here so that everyone can listen in.'

He'd said "John" so nobody was taking offence at a mere sergeant calling a Detective Chief Inspector by his first name. Still it didn't hurt to do a bit of the *culchie*, make them bigwigs think that he was a man you could take out of the country but couldn't take the country out of the man.

His voice took on the cadence of a hill farmer. 'Michael, I hear great things of you these days. But you'll always be a disappointment to me, abandoning the uniform, and for Special Branch of all things.'

He heard a ripple of laughter from the men on the other side. There was also, he was sure, a spluttered, 'Really! Barlow,' from DI Harvey.

Michael said, 'John, no man made a greater mess of directing traffic at the Chapel Corner than me.'

'We're still trying to sort it out.'

And more laughter.

With credentials established on both sides they got down to business. Rather than second-guess what the call was about, Barlow let Michael take the lead.

'John, we've spent the morning coordinating things with your colleagues there in Ballymena. The information you uncovered about the jewellery raid is great. However, we would like to interview Geordie Dunlop, there must be more that he can tell us. And we need him to go through our rogues' gallery to identify the people he met and talked to. However…'

Barlow butted in. 'Is there a suspicion that he might actually be involved in the theft?'

'Mr Harvey has expressed doubts.'

Barlow bit back a "he would". 'Let me put it this way, Michael. When you were stationed here, did you ever know Geordie to do anything vicious?'

'No.'

'Geordie might be a bit of an idiot and he might try and bluff the Station Sergeant, but he gave both Major Edward Adair and his Sergeant Major his word that he had nothing to do with the robbery.'

They were at opposite ends of a telephone line but he sensed Michael nod. 'That's good enough for me, John.'

Michael put his hand over the receiver while he talked to the other men in the room. Vera timed it nicely bringing Barlow his cup of tea. It was hot and sweet.

She had added sugar, something normally he disliked. All the same it went down easily.

'You're looking better, Dad,' she said.

He examined himself in the mirror. He did look better, even with his hair standing on end and a day's stubble on his chin. His head hurt and his throat and chest still burned from the smoke but, yes, this old man would give the Braid Valley a miss a while longer.

Michael came back on the line. 'Okay, we're going with your opinion. So, what's the best way for us to approach Geordie?'

Barlow had been thinking about that. Geordie would be a reluctant witness, anxious about his street cred and not wanting to be seen cooperating with the police.

He said, 'Give Connie a ring and invite yourself to tea.'

'Would she remember me?'

'Michael she still talks about the day she knocked the cap off your head with a potato.'

He laughed at the memory. 'I never did get the dent out.'

'After that, take Geordie down to the pub, buy him a pint and tell him he's a bollocks.'

'Done,' said Michael. Then his tone changed, became officious. 'Station Sergeant at a meeting today, chaired by an ACC, it was agreed that the deaths of Reginald Corkey and his brother, Shorty, formed part of an ongoing investigation by Special Branch into organised crime in Belfast.'

Barlow kept his tone level. 'Yes, Detective Chief Inspector.'

'Therefore, the investigation into the deaths of the Corkey brothers has been transferred to Special Branch.'

Barlow nodded. Leary would like that. It would give him Christmas off.

'And there will be no, repeat no ongoing investigation into the deaths carried out at local level. Is that understood?'

There was a pause. Barlow could feel all the listeners-in waiting for his submissive. 'Yes, Detective Chief Inspector.' But he and Michael had always played it straight with each other since the day Michael had first arrived in Ballymena with his new sergeant's stripes.

'Michael, I'm concerned with only two things. First, to bring the killer of Evon Flinton to justice and, secondly, to protect Mrs Collins.'

'Why do you think Mrs Collins is in danger?'

'Reg was in her house, someone tampered with the gas supply and Reg was found dead in her garden. Would you like to take bets she's not?'

There was a pause at the other end, voices muffled and distorted by Michael's hand over the receiver. He came on again. 'Don't worry about Mrs Collins. I am authorised to tell you that the main players in the gang are under constant observation.'

With Special Branch tracking every move of the Belfast gang, Barlow felt he could stop worrying about Mrs Collins. He had intended to spend the night there himself, ghost and all, if he'd been fit. Unfortunately, there was no way he could slip Wilson up there for another night, not with Pierson being Duty Sergeant.

'Okay,' he said, feeling a reluctance at trusting Mrs Collins' safety to a bunch of Special Branch men with their own agenda.

'So, John, you'll remember, no interference?'

'Michael, when my foot comes down on the people I'm looking for, Special Branch toes had better not be in the way.'

64

The telephone call finished, Barlow sat on in the hall. Something about the call worried him. Not the call itself. The tone? Something said?

Geordie's crimes had always been stupid. Crimes that usually gave everyone, other than the victim, a laugh. So why would anyone think that he had changed?

He wanted to yell, he wanted to break that mirror with the old man image. Instead he sat on and drank his tea and repeated the mantra. Tom Rankin is guilty. Repeat: guilty.

Vera popped out of the kitchen. 'Dad, are you okay?'

'Dammit! I've been too busy hanging the man to do my job properly.'

He needed time to think. Time with a pencil and paper and an hour of quiet. An hour that he didn't have. He reached for the phone again.

'Dad, you're sick. You're not to get involved.'

He held out his hand to her. She took it reluctantly, still annoyed. 'I know I never get it right between you and duty, but this time…' He didn't want to say it, to admit to being wrong. 'I think we could be hanging an innocent man.'

She pulled clear of him. 'I'll look out clean clothes for you.'

'It's just a phone call. I didn't say I was going anywhere.'

She smiled and walked out of sight. He heard her go into his bedroom, heard drawers opening and closing.

He rang the station and asked to be put through to Inspector Foxwood.

'Sir, what is the position regarding Thomas Rankin?'

Foxwood sounded apologetic, as if he had let Barlow down personally. 'We were held up this morning by Special Branch, but we are now about to formally charge Thomas Rankin with the wilful murder of Evon Flinton.'

'How's Tom taking it?'

'He's extremely restless, pacing the cell: up down, up down. It never stops.'

Barlow had been expecting that. 'Aye, being charged with a capital crime tends to do that.'

He wished he had taken time to select a sweet, anything that would take away the bitter taste of being a fool.

'The thing is, sir, everything we discovered about Tom makes him a nice guy who for once acted out of character.'

'Okay.'

'What if his silence, his refusal to clear his name, is him acting very much in character?'

'Barlow don't you go complicating things.'

'Sir, I'd rather complicate things that have us all look like complete idiots.'

There was a static flow as the receiver changed hands.

'Look, Sergeant Barlow, what are you up to?'

It was Ernie, and being strictly formal.

'Mr Potter, I'm asking you to trust me for half an hour.'

'My Principle, Mr Moncrief, warned me never to trust you. Not ever, not for one second. Never.'

All the same Ernie sounded doubtful.

If Barlow told them what he had in mind it would take forever to convince them that he might be right. He decided to remain vague. 'The thing is, Ernie, lack of trust goes two ways. If I tell you, you might tip off your client as to what's expected of him.'

The receiver changed hands a second time. Foxwood came on sounding definitely doubtful. 'Barlow?'

'Sir, if I'm wrong District Inspector Harvey will enjoy throwing the book at me. A high-level case like this? It could cost me my stripes. But if I'm right…'

'I should run this past Mr Harvey first.' Foxwood sounded even more unsure.

'You should, sir.'

Foxwood, who never dared cross Harvey and took all the unfair kicks without complaint.

A muffled bang came down the line as Foxwood thumped his desk. 'Barlow, I trust your instincts. We'll do it.'

Barlow thought, another couple of decisions like that, son, and I'll speak to someone about promoting you to Chief Inspector.

65

Barlow was waiting at the gate when the two police cars pulled up. Foxwood was in the lead car. He sat in the back with the handcuffed Tom Rankin between him and Leary. Ernie sat in the front with WPC Keane, the driver.

Foxwood wound down his window.

Barlow spoke first. 'Follow the other car. I'll give Gillespie the directions.'

He hopped into the second car before Foxwood could start voicing his worries.

Gillespie drove the second car. He was all but panting with curiosity. 'Sarge, when you lose your job, can I have your stripes?'

Barlow put his cap on his knees and settled his gun belt comfortably. 'The Chapel Corner. I'll direct you from there.'

'But if you die in the meantime?'

Thompson sat in the back. She added, 'One can always hope.'

'She's human, she made a joke,' Barlow said.

'Is that's what it was?'

At the Chapel Corner, he found his heart beating hard when he told Gillespie to go to the hospital. He told himself that he was right, that he had to be right. Nothing else made sense.

At the hospital he led the way along the corridor and up the stairs. He had phoned ahead so he knew which private room to go to. The door was shut. He stopped dead. Everyone concertinaed to a halt behind him.

He pointed to Tom's handcuffs. 'Sir, please remove them.'

'Wait a minute,' Foxwood said.

Barlow drew his gun, cocked it and pointed it at Tom. 'One false move and I'll kill you myself.'

'I must protest in the strongest terms,' Ernie said.

Foxwood said, 'Mr Harvey will go mad.' and to Leary. 'Take them off.'

Leary nodded to Gillespie to do it. Removing handcuffs was for lesser Uniform beings.

The handcuffs came off. Tom stood rubbing his wrists.

Barlow pushed Tom forward. 'On you go, Son.'

Hesitantly, Tom knocked the door. The faintest touch that became lost in the hubbub of a general hospital at work.

'Go,' Barlow said.

Tom pushed the door open. A young woman lay in the bed. She saw only one person in the people crowding the doorway. 'Tom!'

'Rose.'

He rush-limped to her, she reached for him. Their hug had her half out of the bed.

Barlow pointed his pistol at the ceiling and pulled the trigger. There was a metallic click but no bang. 'Darn, no bullets.' He smiled at Ernie standing with his mouth open. 'You didn't really thing I was going to shoot your client?'

He had seen enough. Ernie and Foxwood could take it from there. He pushed through the onlookers into the corridor, dragging Thompson along with him.

'It's a gut feeling that there's more to it.'

66

It was as if the Emergency Ward sister, Sister O'Hara, was expecting them. She stood facing the door: arms folded, lips tight with annoyance.

She turned to nearby staff. 'Doctor, I want this man's hearing checked. And you, Nurse, ring the Psychiatric ward and see if they have a bed available.'

'Ah now, Sister, it's the only way I get to see you.'

'Barlow you're not well and you're supposed to be off duty. Do you ever do what you're told?'

He tried to look apologetic. Really, being back in uniform and right about Tom and Rose had re-energised him. All the same, he was getting to the point where a couple of aspirins and a sit down with a cup of tea would not go amiss.

He said, 'A few questions and we'll be gone and, I promise you, I'll go straight home.' Her lips went tighter. 'Please, it's important.' He watched the tension go out of her stance. 'Somewhere quiet.'

She led them into her office, hardly larger than a closed off cubicle. He'd seen bigger school desks than the one Sister O'Hara sat behind. He took the second chair. Thompson parked herself against a locked cupboard.

'Rose Lorrimer,' he said.

Sister might have relented but the annoyance was still there. 'A full report has been made to the appropriate authorities.'

'Aye, relevant to the fire, but what else did you come across?'

'Sergeant Barlow, may I remind you that confidentiality between a patient and the hospital is paramount.'

He asked, 'Did you examine her between her legs?'

She went silent and looked uncomfortable. He felt uncomfortable himself and didn't know what to say next.

Surprisingly Thompson intervened. 'Sister, in the next few minutes, maybe even as we speak, Rose will be making a statement to the police which will clear a person of a serious charge. A very serious charge.'

She nodded at Barlow to take over.

He said, 'We need, we must have confirmation that she is telling the truth.'

He could see Sister relent. She locked her fingers together and rested her hands on the desk. 'When Rose came in we did the usual tests, made sure her airways were clear and that she hadn't suffered any internal damage to the lungs. We also checked her thoroughly for burns or scorch marks. There was blood on the gusset of her panties. Not much, but we thought we should make a closer examination.'

'Go on,' Barlow said when she hesitated.

'Her hymen was broken and there were still traces of blood in that area.'

'Badly, I mean rough. I mean…'

'Had she been raped?' asked Thompson.

'She said no,' Sister said. 'And if it hadn't been for the bruising I'd have believed her.'

'What bruising?' asked Barlow and felt disappointment at Tom. It was the first time and he got carried away. All the same?

Sister said, 'It was as if someone had put their hand right up her skirt and gripped really hard. She said it had been an accident and that it wasn't him, the boy'

'What boy?' asked Thompson. She looked ready to grab Tom Rankin by the throat.

'She wouldn't say.'

Barlow wanted this particular interview over, and fast. Sister O'Hara and the doctor involved could prepare detailed statements later. 'We need the timing of the – let us say – injuries.'

Sister unlocked her hands and tapped fingers as if counting back. 'Rose came in last night, this morning really. Going by the blood and the rawness around the hymen, it had been broken sometime over the weekend.'

'And the bruising you talked about?'

'They were turning yellow so that happened a day or two before the hymen breach.'

Poor Rose, thought Barlow. She dreamt of being a virgin bride and now this mess.

Sister stood up. 'Frankly, Barlow...'

'I know, I know. You've work to do and I'm holding you back.'

Anyway, he'd everything they needed so they left. What he wanted now was time to sit and think.

They were walking down the corridor to the front door when Thompson said, 'You should ask her what's she's doing New Year's Eve.'

'Who?'

'The Sister.'

'What for?'

'She fancies you.'

'Don't be daft.'

All the same, all that talk about sex, he had never seen her flustered before. He felt his face flush.

67

Barlow and Thompson emerged out of the hospital into the bracing chill of the December day. Keane was standing by the cars. She made to join them but Barlow shook his head 'no' and guided Thompson to a summer seat well away from any flapping ears.

He stretched his legs out and wriggled himself comfortable. 'You've seen Rose and Tom together and you've heard what Sister had to say. Tell me what you think.'

Thompson said, 'He's been looking to get his wicked way for a long time. He tried earlier in the week but Rose managed to fight him off. Come Saturday night and drink taken, she hadn't a chance.'

He looked at her. She stared him back just as steady.

Finally he said, 'I didn't ask for a feminist rant. I asked for your opinion.'

'Okay, looking at it from Tom's point of view. Start with the earlier bruising, I think there was a bit of hard snogging going on. Things nearly got out of hand but both of them managed to stop in time.' She gave a false smile as she pretended impartiality. 'It would be interesting to check Tom for equivalent bruising.'

'And Saturday night?'

'He'd just been semi-crippled, he's drunk and she's the sympathetic girlfriend giving him comforting hugs and kisses. This time he didn't draw back and she didn't like to say no.'

'You're a harsh woman,' he said.

'So, you think different?'

He sucked at a Mint Imperial while he worked out the scenario in his head.

'Are you not going to offer me a sweet?' she asked.

'I keep them in my head, it's cheaper that way.'

Things started to come together in his head.

Satisfied that he had finally made sense of this part of the recent goings-on, he said, 'Tom was a Junior Manager at Lorrimers working closely with Rose because, frankly, she seems to be the only one of the family who does any work around there. They fall in love or at least they have a notion for each other. Rose's feet are constantly cold because of the draught. Tom comes up with the bright idea of making her a footstool to keep her feet off the floor. He's taking the nearly completed footstool out of the factory to hide it from Rose when R Shaw catches him and fires him on the spot.'

'Logical so far,' she agreed, 'and, may I remind you, R Shaw was operating strictly within the terms of the employee contract.'

'Yes, but management are usually given more leeway than blue-collar workers when it comes to the rules. So let's say R Shaw wanted rid of Tom and this was a golden opportunity.'

'It seems stupid to fire someone who did much of the work about the place.'

'Unless of course that someone had challenged R Shaw about being a lazy spendthrift and, worse than that, had the stated intention of moving to England as a professional footballer.'

'That gets rid of Tom without firing him.'

'Not if R Shaw suspected that Rose would go with him.' He felt sympathy for the young couple and all they'd been through. 'Remember the tapestry for the footstool, *To Serve all your days.* That wasn't a prayer, that was a declaration of love.'

His lips formed a spit of disgust that he held back. 'So, R Shaw fires Tom and blackens his name by rumour so that he can't get a decent job. However, there's still the possibility of him becoming a professional footballer, and if that happens then Rose still leaves.'

'Hold on,' Thompson said in a tone more thoughtful than disbelieving. 'Are you saying that honourable Tom won't marry Rose until he can keep her in some sort of comfort? When that hope is taken from him, he gets drunk because now he must tell Rose to find someone else. Someone who will give her all the good things in life.'

'I'm saying exactly that.'

Thompson snorted. 'Barlow, you're a romantic.'

Barlow blinked in surprise. No one had ever accused him of that before.

'Anyway,' he said pulling himself back to the present problem. 'Rose hears about Tom being hurt, maybe R Shaw boasts about it. She goes looking for Tom and takes him somewhere to sober up, I'm guessing the factory, and one thing leads to another.'

He went silent, envying Tom – and Rose's determination to hold onto him. Once she had gifted him her virginity he was hers for life.

All of Barlow's own life, one way or another, the women had walked away from him.

'What about the bruising?' asked Thompson.

'I'm working on that.' He jerked upright in the seat. 'Flipping heck!'

'What'

'I've gone about this the hard way. Mrs Collins told me that she saw the lights go on in the factory on Saturday night.' He stretched back in the seat and laughed. 'That old biddy. Her and her binoculars, I bet you she saw everything.'

68

Barlow arrived back in the house with Tom Rankin, safe in the knowledge that Vera couldn't nag him because Ernie was there as well.

Vera's mouth opened but she didn't say anything.

Barlow was quick with the good/bad news. 'There's two more for tea.'

'Four! I'm out of magic wands.'

Ernie held up a bag of meat and an even bigger bag of potatoes. 'We come bearing gifts.'

Barlow escaped past her into the kitchen, leaving Ernie to explain. Toby, for once, conceded him his chair.

He was asleep long before Ernie had finished.

Friday
December 23rd

69

Vera insisted on giving Barlow breakfast in bed even though he claimed that he was well enough to get up. He ate his scrambled eggs and toast and listened to her rattle around the house, preparing to go to work, and Toby's nails on the tiles and linoleum as he dogged her heels.

As soon as her footsteps faded down the drive, Barlow got up and tidied the house. When Toby returned from seeing Vera safe to work, he took him for a walk, and it was still only eleven-thirty. By twelve Barlow was back in uniform and heading for the station. He needed an update, he needed to know who was doing what, and where and why. After that he needed peace and a table and pad, and a pot of fresh-made tea to stimulate his thinking.

But first he walked on past the station as far as the railway bridge and turned left down Waveney Road. At the red-bricked fire station he asked to see the Leading Fireman from the night of the fire. The man was on duty and relieved to push a pile of papers to the side.

'The Lorrimer fire?' asked Barlow without any preliminaries.

The Fireman said, 'As for saving your interfering life, don't mention it.'

'Okay, I won't then. But thanks anyway.'

The fireman poured them both a cup of tea from a handy pot. 'We're still waiting for Forensics to confirm, but an accelerant was used to start the fire. Probably petrol poured through the letterbox.' He dug into a drawer and pulled out a packet of Fig Rolls. 'Help yourself.'

Barlow took one and backed it up with a second. After a couple of days of forcing himself to eat he was now surprisingly hungry. A fire like that in a hallway? It could have been the Belfast gangsters expressing their displeasure at the Lorrimers for some reason.

'An apparently outside job,' continued the Fireman. 'At least that's what the Lorrimers would like us to think.' His tongue worked to get the gummy figs out from between his teeth. 'You see, petrol cans, even with a spout, are unwieldy things. There's always a dribble that goes the wrong way. So you would expect the outside of the door to burn as well. That didn't happen in this case, and as for inside.' He made a flat motion with his hand. 'You pour petrol through a letterbox there is some splash effect but basically it spreads out in a large puddle.'

'Was there a lot of splash?'

'Too much splash spread too far.'

70

Peace was the last thing Barlow was going to get at the station. The Hart brothers were in the cells and singing their little hearts out. Very loudly and very, very off key.

Gillespie was in the Enquiry Office, leaning on the counter, his hands over his ears.

'Send them home,' shouted Barlow.

'Mr Harvey intends to charge them with disturbing the peace.'

Harvey came storming up the corridor. 'Gillespie, those awful men. The ACC wanted to know if our Christmas party had started early. Get rid of them.'

'If you think that's best, sir,' Gillespie said and headed down to the cells to effect the Harts' immediate release.

Harvey gave Barlow a quick up and down look. 'So, you're fit for duty again?'

'Er…'

'Christmas day, it's either you or Pierson for the double shift, and he needs the break.'

'He needs something, sir.'

Harvey marched back down the corridor. Barlow followed at a safe distance and slipped into Foxwood's room. Foxwood shifted awkwardly in his chair when he saw Barlow so the news couldn't be good.

'The Evon Flinton case, sir. Have you had R Shaw in for questioning?'

'There's no proof he was involved, Sergeant.'

'But there's motive. Framing Tom for the murder meant that he could get his revenge for being called a useless leech, and hold onto a cheap, willing worker in Rose.'

Foxwood shifted again. 'As a motive for murder, that's a bit farfetched.'

'And the fire at the house. The fire authority reckon it was an inside job, one of the family.' He sensed he was pushing uphill against immovable authority. 'You start talking to them about that and you don't know what else will spill.'

Foxwood touched one of his piles of papers. 'We obtained

preliminary statements from Rose and R Shaw. The father is still in Intensive Care: smoke inhalation coupled with blood pressure and emphysema. The prognosis is not good. Anyway…'

Barlow finished it for him. 'The Lorrimers are now part of the Special Branch enquiry into organised gangs.'

He made himself relax back in the chair and selected a Jelly Baby. Safer to grind that between his teeth rather than chew out the hapless Foxwood. 'You remember that bit of cardboard I found in the fireplace. Any luck there?'

'I'm afraid not. It was the top of a Woodbine pack, as you thought, but it was too badly burnt to make a positive connection between it and the pack found on Reg Corkey's body.'

I'll get a break in this case yet, if it kills me.

'And the writing on it?'

'Numbers. A four and what could be a three or an eight and maybe a seven.'

Barlow kept the casual tone going. 'We're having no luck here.' He emphasised it with a shrug. 'Special Branch getting involved has really stymied our investigations.'

'I don't like it either, Barlow, and I've said so in the strongest terms. I agree with your thinking. If we get the Lorrimers on the fire, they might be willing to turn Queen's Evidence in exchange for a lesser sentence.'

'So it's hands off and bugger Evon. After all she was only a prostitute.'

It was the one thing that kept him in the police when there were easier, better paid jobs out there. A desire, a drive almost, to make the law equal for all, and now a woman whose kindness had given him a future was being denied that justice.

He again forced down his anger against Foxwood. The man was being outgunned by a phalanx of senior police officers. There was little Foxwood could do other than, 'You are keeping in touch with Special Branch, sir?'

'Oh, yes, yes.' Foxwood was more relaxed now that he'd passed on the bad news and they were in agreement. 'Your friend, Michael Sinclair, has invited me to attend an update meeting tomorrow morning.'

Barlow nodded as if pleased. 'That's very good of Michael to keep us in the loop like that, and you can assure him that I will keep my word.'

Barlow slipped out of the room as quietly as he'd entered it. He would keep his word to Michael. If getting justice for Evon meant bringing down the Lorrimers, then Special Branch could sit on his word and swivel.

Meantime he had one final thing to check and he could hear Wilson's voice coming from the WPCs' office. He knocked the door and waited for the invitation to enter. Wilson sat in a chair, mug in hand while he chatted to Milton about dogs. Dogs: owned, loved and lost. He had the chair turned so that he sat sideways-on to WPC Hughes. She looked like the world had ended.

Barlow motioned him outside. 'A quick word.'

Two, really, but he wasn't telling Wilson that.

Wilson followed him out. 'Yes, Sarge?'

'Have you organised your days off over Christmas?'

'Kind of, Sarge. I finish my shift on Christmas Eve at eight in the morning and I can be in Belfast by nine to give Mum a hand.'

Wilson's mother was the housekeeper for a family in Malone Park. She was expected to produce the food for a large party on Christmas Eve and then a Christmas lunch for the extended family. The family gave her Boxing Day and the following day off in lieu. Wilson planned to help his mother over Christmas and then whisk her off to the Carrick Na Cule hotel in Portstewart for a couple of days.

'Good lad,' Barlow said and made the important question sound casual. 'Will you make the Staff Party tonight?'

'Yes, Gillespie came up with this idea of getting all the unattached officers to share the night shift and I got lucky in the draw. I'm on duty from eight to nine, then some of the others do an hour each until one when I take over for the rest of the night.'

'Good.' For Gillespie, Barlow meant. Gillespie couldn't run a draw straight if he tried,

'Why do you want to know, Sarge?'

'You're getting awful suspicious of my motives.'

'Sarge, you're the one who taught me to be suspicious of senior officers' and their motives.'

'That's good advice, son. Don't ever forget it.'

At that point, Barlow took another piece of advice from his old District Inspector: not to answer questions from someone who's acting suspicious. He had a full evening coming up of having to be nice to

Thompson, so he went home to take a couple of aspirins and rest up before the party, and to double check that the house was spotless.

With him safely out of the way for the evening, Vera was entertaining Ernie to dinner and there was even talk, by way of the merest hint, that a bottle of wine was involved. Which gave them: a meal, alcohol, a fire in the sitting room and a full-length settee.

Barlow hated thc dangcrs those images created in his mind. He intended to instruct Toby to attack Ernie: bite, savage and tear the young solicitor apart, if more than his jacket came off.

71

Johnny Scullion and his taxi were waiting for Barlow at the station door.

'First, 1 Riverside and then home to change for the party,' he told Johnny.

On the way they stopped at a flower shop. Vera had ordered him to buy a corsage. 'It's the done thing, Dad.'

His reply, 'But it's only Thompson,' cut no stick. Corsage it was.

He hopped back into the car, feeling a bit foolish carrying flowers and him in uniform.

'You're not taking Major Adair to the dance?' asked Johnny.

'At my age I don't need a chaperone. And don't you start.'

They found Edward sitting in the dark outside his hut, shivering with cold.

'My dear chap, how kind of you to visit at this festive period.'

Barlow said, 'I know they say death rather than dishonour, but death instead of staying dry doesn't have the same ring to it.' He heaved Edward to his feet. 'Get your toothbrush, I've a job for you.'

Even in the draining lights of the car Barlow saw Edward brighten and knew that he'd made the right decision. The man needed something to keep his mind off the free drinks he was missing in the Bridge Bar.

'Anything to oblige, my dear fellow, but where? What?'

'Bring a change of clothes for a couple of days. I'll brief you in the car.'

"Brief?" he thought. That took him back to a lot of bitterly cold Nissen huts during the war.

Mrs Collins was expecting them and opened the back door as the car swept into the yard.

She was anxious. 'Mr Barlow, do you really think I might be in danger?'

He said, 'I don't know, and that's why I'm keeping people with you until things settle.'

He made the formal introductions. 'Mrs Violet Collins, Major the Honourable Edward Adair.'

Edward's sweeping gesture needed a hat in his hand to make it perfect. 'Madam, it is my honour to be of service to such a beautiful and charming lady.'

The air in the back hallway warmed. The Captain was there and approved of the new arrival.

'Ah, one senses the presence of the unfortunate Cattle Collins,' Edward said.

Sometimes Barlow could kill Edward out of frustration. Right then was one of those times because the air became so bitterly cold that he had to rub his hands together for heat.

'Major, he doesn't like to be called that,' Mrs Collins said.

Edward looked in the direction of the door into the great hall. 'My dear chap, no offence intended. You will be forever remembered as the man who had greatness stolen from him by his unfortunate demise. Whereas I, having tasted from the cup, will be recollected, if at all, as the town drunk.'

The air warmed up to something approaching zero. Edward walked on into the kitchen.

Barlow asked Mrs Collins, 'How does he get away with it?'

She said, 'When he was a child calling with his parents, he'd tease the Captain so much that icicles hung off the chandelier.'

Barlow said, 'Wear your winter woollies, you're going to have a fun couple of days.

He said his good nights and went back into the yard where Johnny Scullion waited with the taxi. Johnny had turned the headlights off and what should have been darkness beyond the car had a faint glow of light. Someone was in the factory.

He made a motion for Johnny that he'd be only a minute, and went down the path and through the gate into the factory yard. This was one time he wouldn't have minded carrying his gun and truncheon, and having a few stout men to back him up.

The light came from the front of the factory. The General Office, he thought and became sure when he saw the outline of a Jaguar car at the front door. Mr Lorrimer owned a Jaguar, but he was in intensive care.

Barlow stepped quietly across the rough-stoned surface to the nearest window and looked in. Tom and Rose sat at a desk, their heads close together. Barlow was ready to storm in and order Rose to wherever was now home, and bollock Tom for not having more sense. Rose was barely out of hospital.

Then he realised. The next day, Saturday, was Christmas Eve. Both payday and the day the men got their Christmas bonus. Somebody had to work out the figures and R Shaw certainly wasn't going to do it.

He tiptoed away.

72

Vera saw Barlow out the door, making sure he didn't forget the corsage and gave his dress jacket a final brush down.

He settled himself in the car and held the plastic box so as not to crush the flower.

Johnny had driven the taxi straight up to the house. He reversed back onto the main road, strictly illegal, not that Barlow noticed. What he did see was a car parked in Meadow Lane across the way and a figure in the car ducking as the car lights swept over it.

Ernie waiting for the coast to be clear, he reckoned. With that sort of subterfuge, starters were likely to begin under the mistletoe, with Toby closed in the kitchen and the curtains in the sitting room already drawn. Maybe he should tell Johnny that he'd forgotten something and go back.

There'd be a row. She'd accuse him of not trusting her.

Of course, he did, hadn't he reared her proper. All the same?

He let Johnny drive on and arrived at the station to find the desk in the Enquiry Office propping up Pierson. Pierson rang through to Thompson in the Section House to say that Barlow was in and waiting for her.

'You're wasting your money there,' Pierson said. 'She only puts out for Superintendents and above.'

That remark and the accompanying smirk annoyed Barlow. He put his own boot in. 'You always volunteer for duty on the night of the Christmas party. I suppose that saves you from having to buy a round of drinks.'

He heard Thompson in the corridor and went to meet her. She wore a long tweed overcoat, buttoned high at the neck, and black high-heels. He suspected that her dress was black but couldn't see enough to be sure.

'You look radiant,' he said and presented her with the corsage.

'And you kind sir, are the gallant gentleman.'

She presented him with a carnation. Not the done thing and designed to cause some teasing among his friends.

She had a pin handy to attach it to his jacket. And a second for her corsage. She had to open her coat to pin it on. As he thought, a small black number that stopped just below her knees.

Her eyes challenged him to make a comment on her dress length. The current fashion for formal evenings was an ankle-length dress in a bright colour. He said nothing, convinced that it was going to be a fun evening. For other people.

Johnny Scullion drove smoothly and dropped them off at the Central Bar. They by-passed the main bar and went up the stairs to the function room on the first floor. They were among the last to arrive and the dancing had started. Wilson, he noted, had Keane on the floor for a quickstep.

On the landing the owner's daughter, Kathleen, waited to take their overcoats.

'That's one young lady who likes you,' Thompson said as they walked on.

'We both live on the Ballymoney Road. The father's in hospital, so she walks me home at night when she's working late.'

'I get it,' Thompson said.

The room had tables down both sides with the centre area kept free for dancing. Streamers and balloons and sprigs of holly made the room bright and festive.

Gillespie had kept two seats for them at his table. He spotted the carnation on Barlow's lapel and jumped up, hand outstretched. 'Congratulations, Barlow, I hope the two of you will be happy together.'

There were ladies present so Barlow restricted himself to, 'Shut your gub.'

The rest of the table, McGinn and a couple of the older constables and their wives, were as bad: shaking hands and kissing their congratulations.

'You're back,' Barlow said to McGinn.

Mrs McGinn butted in. 'Barely home in time to throw on his suit and come on.' She made a face that was part amusement, part annoyance. 'On the way here, he wanted to stop off to see Rex. The suit would have been covered in dog hairs.'

'I haven't seen my dog in almost two weeks,' McGinn said.

'All I got was footsteps on the stairs and a "Hi, Darling, sling the kettle, I'm gasping,' Mrs McGinn said.

Thompson had a pleased look on her face.

73

The three-piece band – a pianist, guitarist and a female singer – started a new set. Barlow took Thompson onto the floor, knowing that everyone was watching them. She had a light step but danced rigidly.

'I'm surprised you let me lead,' he said.

'Convention,' she said, and made it sound like a dirty word.

He danced Mrs Gillespie next. She loved the swirl of a quickstep and floated in his arms. Naturally she'd heard about Vera going to her mother's and of him doing a double shift on Christmas day.

'I'll plate-up a turkey dinner for you and send it around with one of the boys,' she said.

'You're an angel and you'd be next in line after Connie for my heart – if it wasn't for those lumps you raised.'

She laughed and they swirled on.

All the time, he was watching who was dancing with whom and what they were saying. In particular he looked for eyes that ached for a loved one to come their way. Hughes' eyes never left Wilson but, after dancing with Keane, Wilson retired to the bar with the rest of the wallflower officers. Harvey took Thompson for a dance. Her eyes remained fixed on the far wall, his between her breasts.

Sometime later, Wilson approached the table where the three WPCs sat. Hughes was all puppy-eyes but he asked Milton to dance. The wallflowers were waiting for a few more couples to start dancing before they approached the two remaining WPCs. Barlow stepped in and took Keane onto the floor. This time the music was indeterminate: waltz, jive, quickstep, whatever the couple fancied. Harvey danced with Mrs Foxwood, it had to be for the second time. She danced awkwardly, with her hips well back from Harvey's protruding groin.

Barlow kept their speed down. He had a long night of dancing ahead of him.

'Another Christmas,' Keane said, by the way world-weary.

'And your last in Ballymena.'

'What!'

'I had a word with Miss Macmillan.'

'Inspector Macmillan?'

'Yup. Traffic Branch.'

'Sarge!' She threw her arms around him and gave him a big hug. By the time she'd finished every eye was on them and there had to be lipstick on his face.

As they came off the floor he said, 'Keep it quiet. Mr Harvey doesn't know yet.'

'Not a word, Sarge.'

Barlow let couples settle then he went over to Harvey's table. Harvey shared it with the Chairman of the Local Police Committee, Captain Denton and his wife, Clarissa, Solicitor Moncrief and the town mayor and their wives.

Barlow planned to dance with Clarissa later in the evening, but for now... He snapped to attention before Harvey. 'With your permission, sir.'

Harvey had red splotches on his cheekbones and three empty brandy glasses in front of him. He gave a curt nod and Barlow held out his hand to Mrs Harvey. 'Mrs Harvey, I would be honoured.'

She smiled and rose and went with him. They were the first couple on the floor as the band broke into a semblance of the Missouri Waltz.

'Helen, you're looking strained,' he said.

'Everyone else tells me that I'm looking radiant.'

'They would.'

There were tears in her eyes. 'Things have been particularly difficult recently. Did you see the way he danced with Mrs Foxwood?'

'I did, but that's Foxwood's problem.' They did a full turn around the floor before he added. 'Don't forget my shoulder. It's always there for you.'

'John, without that shoulder, sometimes I think I'd go mad.'

'Kill him first, and I'll swear to justifiable homicide.'

She laughed. 'I didn't think anyone could make me do that tonight, laugh I mean.'

At the end of the set, she stood on her toes. 'May I add to the tally?' and added a lipstick-kiss to Keane's effort.

He saw Helen back to her seat and then picked up Thompson for a second set. They were hardly on the floor when he asked, 'Tell me, what duty arrangements have you made for the WPCs over Christmas?'

'I love it when men talk dirty,' she said and made sure she tramped on his toes.

He sucked breath and said, 'I take it you're having dancing lessons. What about the rest of them?'

'They've all families to go to, so I'm doing the double shift on Christmas day.'

'Just the two of us,' he said in a breathless, boyish whisper.

'And you can forget that.'

'Darlin' it never occurred to me.' After a pause to find space on the floor where they couldn't be overheard, he said. 'I've news for you. 'Keane is going to Traffic and Milton will be working with McGinn in a new dog unit.'

Her lips compressed in annoyance. 'Mr Harvey never told me that.'

'Mr Harvey doesn't know yet.'

Now she was really annoyed. 'You arranged all that for my WPCs without telling me first?'

'My WPCs. The next lot are yours to train in your own form and likeness.'

'How thoughtful of you.' They danced past WPC Hughes and a young constable. He was trying to smooch with her. Her eyes were across the dance floor watching Wilson dance with another officer's wife. 'I take it I'll still have Miss Broken Heart?'

'Nope. Wilson's getting his stripes and is being posted to Headquarters. He'll want her to go with him.'

'You're wrong there, Barlow. He's not interested, though there's no telling her.'

Barlow looked from Wilson to Hughes and back to Thompson. 'You think that?'

'Hughes begged me for the late night shifts between now and the New Year. That way she can be on duty the same time as Wilson, for all the good it will do her. He can't stand her.'

'I'll bet you a pound to a penny you're wrong.'

'Done,' Thompson said. 'And I collect on my bets.'

Time was flying and Barlow had a lot to do. He saw Thompson back to the table and made small talk until the ladies went to the bathroom in convoy. Thompson sat on.

74

Barlow went to ask Milton for a dance. A young constable got to her first, but Barlow held three fingers against his sleeve and told the constable to back off.

'Sarge, if only you'd said,' said Milton.

'Don't you start.'

He waited until the first dance of the set was over before he said, 'McGinn's back.'

'I know. He's collecting Rex first thing tomorrow morning.'

She had tears in her eyes. Then she surprised him by pulling a hand free and holding it out. 'I'm depressed and supper is coming. I need a gob-full of your sweets to keep me from comfort eating.'

He put a hand in his pocket, pulled out a pretend handful of sweets and tumbled them into her waiting hand. She put the hand against her mouth and her cheeks bulged.

'Thanks, Sarge.'

'It's rude to talk with your mouth full.' He waited for her to have a good chew before adding. 'That temporary rank of sergeant they gave McGinn for his trip to Hendon. They're making it permanent. He's setting up a branch to train dogs in search and rescue.'

'Ohh.'

She could have been looking at the most gorgeous dessert in the world, smothered in chocolate and topped with cream.

'And he needs a mixture of secretary, liaison officer and general helper. Someone who is good with dogs.'

'Sarge how could you? You let me eat all those sweets that I don't need.'

He staggered back when she threw herself into his arms. More lipstick landed on his cheeks.

He was at the bar ordering a round of drinks for his table when Hughes approached him flashing a book of raffle tickets. Any presents left into the station over Christmas were raffled, the proceeds going to a police charity.

He bought two strips off her even though her eyes were focused down the row where Wilson stood, pointedly turned away from her.

She gave him two more. 'They're little thankyous from Keane and Milton.'

'None from you?'

'So what am I getting then?'

'Wilson.'

'Sarge, he hasn't even given me a dance.'

'Stella.' Her eyes widened at his use of her Christian name. 'Man is a hunter, that means he chases. When the quarry circles around to track him, he gets uneasy, senses danger.'

She stood frowning at him for a few seconds. 'Oh,' she said eventually and tore off another line of tickets which she gave to Barlow, together with a wicked smile. 'Two can play hard to get.'

She sold tickets down the line of officers away from Wilson and disappeared among the tables. Wilson watched her go, a puzzled frown on his face.

By-the-way casually Wilson worked his way up the bar to Barlow. 'Hughes never came our way?'

'Hughes is selling tickets to half the room. You were in the other half, son.' Barlow changed the subject by asking. 'Milton, have you found out yet?'

'She talked around the problem, enough for me to guess. But I'd rather not tell you, Sarge, it was sort of confidential.'

'You've got her talking about it, good man.'

Wilson puzzled something in his brain for a moment. 'You know already, don't you?'

'All part of the training, son.'

Barlow patted him on the shoulder. The drinks order was ready. He picked up the tray and walked off.

75

Supper was carried into the function room: sandwiches, cocktail sausages and sausage rolls, and tea for anyone who wanted it.

Barlow crashed down beside Thompson with a sigh of relief. 'Make sure everyone at this table orders a cup of tea. I'll sup up whatever they don't want.'

'You look done in,' she said.

'And that music is not helping my head.' He swallowed an aspirin with his first cup of tea and watched the byplay as Wilson took a plate of sandwiches over to the WPCs as an excuse to join them. Hughes helped herself to a sandwich and then turned away and began a long conversation with Milton. After talking to Keane for a few minutes Wilson began a conversation diagonally across the table with Milton. Hughes immediately had something important to tell Keane.

'Keep that penny handy,' Barlow told Thompson as the band struck up again for the second half. Before Wilson could attract her attention, Hughes was on her feet and away. She relieved the owner's son, Frank, of a tray of empty cups and saucers and dragged him onto the dance floor. As far as Barlow could remember, Frank was somewhere between A Levels and First Year at University. Just the right age to think he'd died and gone to heaven when a leggy blonde favoured him. Wilson sat on and glowered.

Barlow danced with Thompson and asked Mrs Foxwood for the next set. Wilson had managed to grab Hughes. They jived to Barlow's sedate waltz.

'You're not a bad dancer,' he heard Hughes tell Wilson.

'What do you mean "not bad"?'

'You're all right, you know.' Accompanied by a shrug.

Thompson, he noticed, had picked up her purse and was doing a solo run to the "Ladies".

Wilson jacked up the standard of his jive. He and Hughes blurred in out and around each other. People were stopping to watch.

Harvey followed Thompson into the toilets. A minute later Helen Harvey followed, head high, her face set grim.

Barlow stopped dancing and aimed Mrs Foxwood towards her table. 'Get the Inspector. Now.'

'What?'

'Please do it.'

He left her standing and headed for the toilets. He whipped through the door almost on Helen Harvey's heels. The outer door led into a narrow corridor with two doors off.

Harvey had Thompson trapped against the back wall, pushing tight into her, his hands searching to reach beneath her dress. 'I know you're more than willing, Thompson. The boys told me.'

'Laurence!' said Helen.

'Go away,' he said without turning.

She clawed the side of the face. He swung an elbow at head height. Helen staggered back. Barlow used his body as *block* to stop her from falling.

'Bastard!' hissed Thompson. Her fist pistoned into Harvey's face. Harvey slammed against the door marked 'Ladies'. The door opened and he folded onto the floor. Blood from Helen's clawing trickled across the tiles.

Thompson's fist hadn't withdrawn after the blow. Her other arm joined it, her hands reaching out to clasp Helen. Helen's anger and pain disappeared. A soft pink merged with the red of the angry blow. Her hands came out as well.

Barlow stepped between them. 'No Helen.'

He held firm as she pushed against him. 'No. Helen.'

Thompson stood frozen. He pointed from her to the door. 'Get Foxwood and Gillespie, and don't come back.'

Thompson had to squeeze past them in the narrow corridor. Barlow turned with Helen when she tried to follow Thompson. He used his body to trap her against the wall.

When Thompson had gone, he released Helen and checked Harvey. Harvey lay motionless but his face had colour so he wasn't choking on his tongue. Barlow fought down the temptation to give the man a good kick between the legs. Ground him in more ways than one for a few weeks.

He cuddled Helen and soothed her tears.

She cried. 'I wanted babies, but this is too hard. Too hard.'

76

The music from the dancefloor crescendoed as Foxwood burst through the outer door. He stood open mouthed at the sight of Harvey laid out on the floor. 'Barlow, he'll have your stripes for this. Maybe even jail.'

'He slipped and fell,' Barlow said, heeling the door shut against curious eyes and the noise.

Harvey groaned into some sort of consciousness. He rolled onto his side and vomited up a foul stream of stale brandy. Foxwood hunkered down over him to make sure he didn't choke and finally registered the claw marks, the angry red blotch on Helen's face and the puffiness around her left eye.

Gillespie arrived and quickly took the scene in. He gave Barlow a concerned frown. 'Ye gods, what did you hit him with?'

'Mr Harvey had a fall in the toilets,' Barlow said with studied patience. 'When he comes to his senses he will be only too happy to confirm that fact.' He aimed Gillespie out the door again. 'Bring the car to the front door.' Turning to Foxwood. 'And you, sir. We'll put Mr Harvey between us and try and walk him out.'

Gillespie nodded and was gone.

Before Barlow helped get Harvey to his feet, he took Helen's hand and stared into a face ravaged by tears and loss. 'What do you want to do?'

'I chose my bed,' she said.

'Good for you,' he said, relieved that she had come to her senses and would not seek consolation in Thompson's arms. If she did, Harvey would divorce her and take the children.

Between him and Foxwood they hiked Harvey to his feet. He stood on rubber legs and they had to support him as Helen led the way out of the toilets. The set of dances was over and people were drifting to their tables.

Hughes and Wilson stood close. Barlow heard her say. 'Oh, all right. I'll admit that you're a very good dancer, but you're an awful show off.'

Wilson spluttered with indignation. 'Wait a minute, you were the one who…'

The first notes of the band starting up again drowned out the rest of his reply.

The exit from the function room seemed miles away as they helped Harvey across the room. 'He slipped on the tiles,' Barlow told more than one nosy parker. Mrs Foxwood displayed polite unconcern though the edges of her lips twitched. When Barlow thought about it, Foxwood was equally unconcerned.

At the top of the narrow stairs, Barlow said, 'I'll go first, Sir. We wouldn't want Mr Harvey to have another fall.'

'Not too far anyway,' muttered Foxwood, low enough for Helen not to hear.

With their help, Harvey wobbled his way down the stairs and out into the street. There Gillespie waited with Harvey's personal police car. The bitter night air helped revive Harvey who managed to stumble into the back seat on his own. Helen got in the front.

Foxwood told Gillespie: 'I'll follow in my car and help you get him into bed.'

Barlow's eyes were on a dark shadow loitering in a doorway two buildings up, and on the glow of light as the shadow sucked on a cigarette. He closed the car doors and saw everyone away before checking his watch. Nearly midnight and not worth re-joining the party. Anyway, people would ask questions that he didn't want to answer. He went back into the bar to collect Thompsons' overcoat.

Hughes was already on her way down the stairs with it. 'I saw Sergeant Thompson leave as well.'

'Great.'

He tried to take the coat off her but she held on. 'Frank… I mean Wilson has offered to run me home.'

He struggled to detach himself from one worry onto something more pleasant. 'And you said?'

'Nothing. I had to rush and get the coat, didn't I?'

Young love made him feel old.

He said, 'Milton lives the next street up from you.'

'So?' She was silent for a moment before the penny dropped. 'That way he gets to kiss the dog goodnight.'

'Something like that.'

'Lucky dog,' she said.

77

Thompson still stood in the doorway, dragging hard on the cigarette. The street lighting was poor but Barlow could see where tears had streaked her mascara.

'I didn't know you smoked,' he said.

'I don't.'

He draped her coat over her shoulders and felt the tremble in her body as he tucked it around her. 'Come on. I'll see you back to the station.'

'I couldn't… What a mess.'

'I'll stay with you for a while.'

He'd made the offer without thinking and realised that it was for the best. If someone didn't take her in hand, she'd spend the night tortured by old memories.

At the bottom of Wellington Street he guided her to the right along Mill Street and then across Linenhall Street onto the Galgorm Road.

The station was only three hundred yards away and he needed to get her talking. 'Helen wanted babies?' he said and phrased it as a question.

A yes sighed out of her. 'I never felt the same need.'

She stumbled a step as realisation struck her. 'You know?'

'I know Helen. That first day, when she walked into the WPCs' room and saw you, her face went from absolute joy to rock-bottom horror.'

She said, 'We met at university, York. I was a lecturer and doing my PhD.' She searched in her pocket for a handkerchief. He gave her his from his breast pocket. 'We had three years together.

'Three years,' she repeated with a sob. 'I thought it would never end and then Helen got her degree and her parents brought her home. They said she'd had her fun, and now it was time to think about getting married and settling down. They wouldn't have understood, thought it unnatural'

'And illegal.'

'Helen's hormones were kicking in. Every ovulation, she cried because she wasn't pregnant. Her parents kept introducing her to eligible young men, some of them very nice, but she couldn't do that to them. Marry and hate them every time they touched her, so she picked Harvey who needed a wife as cover for his disgusting lifestyle.'

They reached the corner at McCann's pub, not that she had any idea where they were. Barlow took her by the elbow and guided her across the road. She didn't pull away from his grasp so he held on. 'You came to Northern Ireland and joined the police, hoping to remain in contact with Helen that way?'

'Yes.'

He remembered his own empty marriage and the desire for someone to love and be loved in return and couldn't blame her.

She said, 'Not that I did, keep in contact I mean. Helen refused to even meet me. People in Northern Ireland live in tight little communities and are quick to jump to conclusions, so she didn't dare.'

He said, gently. 'They even began to wonder about you so you…' He stopped to let her finish.

'I pretended I'd do anything to anyone to get promotion.' She shuddered. 'Other Harveys who pumped their disgusting selves into me.'

'So when you hit Harvey tonight?'

Suddenly her voice had grit and determination. 'I was getting a lot of my own back.'

'Quite a punch?'

'My brothers were keen boxers. It was either learn to fight back or go under.'

'That's not in your file.'

'Very unladylike,' she said, and a forced laugh turned into another sob.

He stopped her in the outer hall of the station and checked her face. Mascara tracked her cheeks. He used spit and his handkerchief to wipe it off and found himself smiling.

'It's not that funny,' Thompson said.

'Not you. I'm remembering doing the same for Vera. With her it was either jam, or chocolate, or any amount of dirt from a tomboy childhood.'

'That's all right then.'

All the same she pushed his hand away and opened the door into the Enquiry Office.

Pierson was there on the phone. He held the receiver out. 'Barlow it's for you. I told them to try the Central Bar, now they're back on again.' He held onto the receiver when Barlow tried to take it. 'Tell your friends, this is a police station and I am a busy man. Ring here again and I'll do them for wasting police time.'

With a bit of luck it would be Michael Sinclair ringing with an important update. Barlow smiled, thinking of Pierson's horror when he addressed Michael as Chief Inspector.

He took the receiver.

A voice asked. 'Is that Barlow?'

The man had a Belfast accent but it wasn't Michael. Gritty. Ignorant enough to be a detective constable and there were background sounds as if other people were listening in.

'Yes,' he said.

'We've got your daughter. We want the jewellery. Either that or I use a knife to play X and Os on her face.'

He heard a voice, it had to be Ernie's, shouting, 'No.' The sound of a struggle and a distant sound of Toby's mad barking.

'An hour. Be at home,' said the gritty Belfast voice.

The struggle continued. Toby's barking turned into a savage growl. Men shouted. Vera screamed, 'No!'

Shots rang out.

The line went dead.

Saturday December 24th

78

Barlow stood with the dead telephone receiver in his hand and felt guilty because he should have held it closer to his ear instead of jerking it away when the shots rang out. Should have shared Vera's last seconds instead of worrying about his eardrums.

He dropped the receiver. Pierson fished it up by pulling on the cable and put it back on its stand. Thompson had taken his arm and was speaking, he could see her lips move but hear no sound.

Vera dead! VERA!

'Vera shot... Jewellery... What jewellery?' he tried to explain to Thompson as he shoved Pierson out of the way and grabbed the keys for the stand-by squad car.

He ran down the corridor towards the back door. The Duty Constable came out of the kitchen holding two mugs of tea. Barlow used his shoulder to blatter him and the tea back into the kitchen and ran on.

The back door was locked. He had to pull back the bolt and turn the Yale before he could burst into the yard and was clambering into the car when he realised that the back gates were closed over.

What jewellery?

A hard haul had the gates open. He lost seconds stopping their swing-back and had the car in fourth by the time it reached the road. Bell on, lights flashing and devil did he care who he woke up.

Up to the Pentagon. Scraped past a car that didn't give way quickly enough. A horn blared after him as he turned onto the Ballymoney Road. Cars were coming at him, their lights glaring.

Which one? Which one?

He tried to see who was in each car as they passed, how many people. Then he was at his own house and he'd missed them. He stood on the brakes and flung the car in a vicious sideslip to block his gateway. The front wing crunched against the pillar. No car stood in the driveway. None sat parked nearby. Through the open front door, he could see a body, bodies lying in the hallway.

'Vera!'

He screamed it out loud.

Barlow couldn't bear to see his daughter disfigured, dead. At the same time his feet were running up the driveway and in the door.

A lake of blood stretched across the tiles. One of the bodies groaned. Tall, lanky, wearing a suit.

Ernie.

Toby, the dog, lay still. His skull gaped open.

Barlow ran from room to room. Looked behind doors, searched under chairs. Even under the sideboard. Found himself stumbling over stuff that shouldn't be on the floor. Kicked his feet clear and ran on.

No Vera.

He grabbed a torch and scoured the garden, even checked the coal hole and the seldom used garage

No Vera.

Where where?

The wardrobes, the kitchen cupboards.

The torch still swinging, looking, he went back into the house.

Would they have taken her if she was dead?

He thought they might.

What jewellery?

He could list it: a string of pearls belonging to Vera. Little else, and all lying handy if that's what they wanted.

What jewellery?

He thought he knew. The stuff from the robbery in Belfast.

What made them think he'd got it?

The death of that schoolgirl had guaranteed them the rope. Killing Vera as well wouldn't even tighten it around their neck.

79

Now a third figure crouched in the hallway. For a moment he hoped – Vera? Then he recognised Thompson. She crouched over Ernie: overcoat off, hem of skirt barely clear of the blood. Someone, probably her, had put him in the recovery position.

'Head injury,' she said. 'No blood, so probably coshed or hit with the butt of a gun.'

'Have to ring,' he said.

She stood up and blocked him from tramping through the blood to reach the house phone. 'I rang Gillespie at the Central Bar. Help is on its way.'

'Pierson's useless,' he said.

Somehow it was important to tell her that.

'I know,' she said.

She kept guiding him until she had him in the kitchen and sitting on the two-seater settee. That close together, he could see the sweat stand on her forehead. She had run the whole way to get to him. That seemed important as well.

'You're in shock,' she said.

'What jewellery?' he asked.

'What are you talking about?' she asked.

'They said… I don't know… Exchange Vera for jewellery.'

He realised that the settee was uncomfortable, that he was sitting on bare wooden stringers. The cushions lay on the floor, their contents spewing out. The rest of the room was the same. Things thrown down. They hadn't much by way of ornaments but at least one had gone through the kitchen window.

He forced himself to focus. Someone, somewhere had mentioned an hour.

Then what?

Thompson brought him water. He could hold the glass and sip. He spoke out loud, more to get things straight in his head than actually tell her. Other people were there, listening in. 'They want to swap Vera for jewellery, that stuff from the robbery in Belfast.'

He made himself focus, stared hard around the kitchen and took in the mess. Everything that could be moved had been dumped on the floor, cushions gutted, mats thrown into corners.

'Is the rest of the house like this?'

'Worse,' said someone and crunched into the seat beside him.

Another second someone said, 'John, do one of your lists.'

That second someone was Gillespie. The last time Gillespie had called him John was wartime, when he'd managed to trap his leg under an unexploded 500lb bomb that ticked and stopped, and ticked and stopped. 'Don't move, John, we'll have you out in a minute,' Gillespie had said. "A minute" was three hours later and he could swear the bugger went off twice for a cup of tea.

The Belfast voice had said an hour, and the clock was ticking.

There was no time, no peace with people crowding around him. Pencil and paper lay buried in the mess on the floor, so he said it out loud.

'Dead: Reg Corkey
Evon Flinton
Shorty Corkey
Toby

'The dog?' questioned the man sitting beside him.

Barlow thought he should know the voice. He looked to see who it was. It was Solicitor Moncrief.

'Yes.' He didn't know how Moncrief knew the dog was called Toby or if Vera should be on that list or not. Couldn't bear to think that way.

''How's Ernie?' he asked to be polite, because Moncrief was being polite to him.

'Coming around, he's okay.'

'Good,' and now he could concentrate on the list.

'Accomplices: Mr Lorrimer
R Shaw Lorrimer'

Barlow supposed it had been Stan Holloway who'd spoken to him on the phone. The rough Belfast voice, the threats against Vera. The man who wanted *his* jewellery back.

Involved: Stan Holloway
Vera
Mrs Collins
Rose Lorrimer

Tom Rankin
Crimes: Kidnapping my daughter
Interfering with Mrs Collins' gas supply.
Murders
Jewellery theft
Burglary
Protection racket'

Listed that way it sounded like a complete crime wave.
It is!

Solicitor Moncrief said, 'You forgot Lorrimers' home.'

'Arson as well then,' Barlow said.

Thompson, he noticed, stood crouched at the kitchen table because the seats of all the chairs had been ripped apart.

She said, 'I recorded everything as you called them out.' She held up a piece of paper as if he could read it from across the room. 'They're not in the order they actually happened.' She looked at Gillespie as if he should know the answer. 'Should we read something into that?'

'Don't you go all psychological on the man,' he said.

The house had been wrecked by the Belfast crooks looking for the jewellery.

What made them think he had it?'

If only he had the peace and time to think he could work it out.

Foxwood had appeared from nowhere to stand over him, his hand out. 'Barlow, that stolen jewellery. I need you to give it to me now.'

80

This was normality, him being accused of something he hadn't done. Barlow's brain finally started to come out of his panic for Vera.

'I don't know where the jewellery is. I don't know why they think I might have it,' he replied.

And that was nearly a lie because an idea tickled the back of his brain. Very distant and almost lost in the morass of things that he didn't know. That was the trouble with this case. He had few facts to go on but a ton of guesswork.

It was the only way he could deal with Vera being in danger, turn the whole thing into an impersonal case to be solved.

Foxwood said, 'I thought that, Barlow, but I had to ask.'

Barlow puzzled for a moment. What was Foxwood on about? Oh, the jewellery.

He looked around the room. This time focus came easily. Captain Denton was there, a fleshy hand on his shoulder for comfort. Gillespie and Wilson stood beside him.

Solicitor Moncrief now hunkered down over Ernie who lay on a stretcher, groaning facts to McGinn. 'I arrived… They'd broken into the house… Kept asking Vera for it… Really nasty… Tried to drag her… Toby got out…'

Barlow realised that the car parked up in the side street had been the crooks and not Ernie.

If only he hadn't trusted Vera and gone back.

Something he had to know finally came out of the morass of unknowns. 'Solicitor Moncrief, did R Shaw and Rose Lorrimer call with you the other day?'

Moncrief's head whipped around. 'Barlow, that's confidential: solicitor to client.'

'Maybe, but it's sticking in my craw.'

It was and totally irrelevant to saving Vera, but knowing that might pull something else loose.

Captain Denton said, 'Moncrief, that's the way Barlow's brain works, coming at things sideways.'

Barlow waited. Either Moncrief would tell him or he wouldn't.

That cold-hearted man has never obliged him yet. All the same he was obviously concerned for Ernie.

Moncrief said, his eyes hard on Barlow. 'I'll tell you for Vera's sake, and only hers. On my advice, the Lorrimer family home was in the name of Mrs Lorrimer. When she died, she left it jointly between R Shaw and Rose. The business urgently needs additional working capital to meet their January bills. To obtain an increase in the overdraft, R Shaw and Rose have to assign the deeds in the family home to the bank by way of additional surety.'

'And?' asked Barlow.

'R Shaw came and signed, but not Rose.'

'Ooops,' said someone.

That piece of knowledge didn't help Vera. Not directly, however he sensed the tangle of confusion loosen as another part of the case became clear.

The Belfast men were strangers to the town. The only one place they'd know to hole-up in was Lorrimers' factory.

Foxwood would go by the book. Surround the factory and demand that the Belfast men surrendered. Meantime they'd throw bits and pieces of Vera out the window – he tried not to think what bits – as encouragement for the police to agree to giving them a car and a clear run to the border with the Irish Republic.

Barlow caught Gillespie's eye and jerked his head upwards. 'I need my uniform out of the bedroom, and my pistol is in the security box.'

Foxwood got between them. 'The pistol stays with me, and no uniform, Barlow. You're stood down, this is too personal for you to be involved.'

He'd thought that would be the case but it was worth trying. The hour the Belfast men had given him was nearly up and, pistol or no pistol, he was heading for the factory.

81

Barlow eased himself off the settee. For some reason every joint in his body ached. He knelt on one knee beside Ernie, by the way concerned for the boy. Really he was heading for the kitchen and the back yard.

Ernie lay with an arm over his eyes to hide the tears. Barlow pushed the arm clear. Ernie's face was covered in blood and the side of his face swollen. His cheekbone had to be broken.

'You'll be all right, Son.'

Fresh tears flowed. 'I'm sorry Mr Barlow, I couldn't stop them.'

'You did well.' He patted Ernie's shoulder. 'What's Vera going to think when we get her back and she finds you like this?'

'You will get her back?'

'Depend on it.'

He stood up, aware of suspicious eyes on him as he headed on into the working kitchen. He rattled a glass out of a cupboard and ran a tap while he unlatched the back door. A shadow moved against the wall. He looked back and saw Charlie Denton standing in the doorway, blocking everyone else's view into the kitchen.

'I recognised that face from wartime and the bombs you didn't want anyone else to tackle,' Denton said very quietly, then louder. 'Don't you worry, Barlow, we'll get her back.'

'Aye, sir, I know I can depend on my men.'

Denton spoke even lower. 'I've a gun at home that nobody knows about. Give me half an hour.'

'I reckon we're out of time.'

Denton spoke much louder this time. 'We've checkpoints set up on every road out of town.' Barlow slipped out the back door. Charles Denton kept on talking as if he was still there. 'And men coming in from every other Division to lend a hand.'

Barlow shivered from the cold in the yard that bit into his body and from his fear for Vera. He slipped around the side of the house and down to the front gate. There had to be a police car there that he could borrow. There was, but Keane sat in the driver's seat, the engine ticking over to give her warmth.

Barlow opened the door and swung in beside her. 'Geordie's,' he said.

With Keane at the controls, the car took off like a scalded cat. 'Whistle and bells, Sarge?'

'Everything.'

In spite of doing a U-turn on a busy road, she looked his way. 'Vera, if there's anything I can do…'

He patted her knee, realised her skirt had risen up and quickly took his hand away. 'You're already doing it, Love.'

It seemed to be no time before they were rattling over the bridge and out the Antrim Road. Then they were at Geordie's house.

Barlow was out of the car before it completely stopped. Geordie's front door was closed but not locked. He shoved the door open and ran into the kitchen. Geordie sat there, sharing a bedtime cup of tea with Connie.

'Geordie, I need you and your tools.'

'What tools?' aske Connie. 'We have no tools.'

'Connie, they've got Vera. I've only minutes left before they start hurting her.'

Geordie got to his feet. 'Do it, Connie.'

In most of a lifetime, Barlow had never before heard Geordie give Connie an order. She nodded and trotted down the corridor and out the front door. Geordie pulled on his jacket and the two men went out to the car. Connie was already back with a valise whose contents clinked when she handed it to Geordie.

'Take good care of my man, Mr Barlow,' she said, tears glinting in the uncertain light of the street lamps.

Barlow nodded. He knew that two of them would be coming back. The trick was to make sure that Vera was one of those two.

82

'Control to Kilo #2, return to base immediately,' said a voice on the radio.

Barlow asked Keane, 'Have you answered that?'

'Answered what, Sarge?'

He switched off the radio and pointed forward. 'The Larne Road, Mrs Collins' house, and quiet this time.'

When they were out of the estate and speeding up the Larne Road when he looked back at Geordie. 'You wouldn't have a gun in that bag, by any chance?'

'What do you think I am?'

That was the answer he'd expected but felt he had to ask.

Nearing the edge of town they came on a checkpoint. Keane put on the blue light but not the bell and they were waved through. About the same time Barlow became aware of the surrounding darkness and the brightness of their own car lights.

'Kill the headlights.'

'I'll have to slowdown,' Keane said.

'That's okay, we're nearly there.'

She turned off the lights and the darkness became a cocoon, the engine a quiet background purr. The car's dashboard-lights picked up every nervous twitch of the wheel as Keen used the sidelights to guide them from bush to bush along the road.

Geordie broke the silence, 'All we need is some old fart with no backlight on his bike.'

'Shut up.'

Nearing the Collins' house Barlow said, 'Turn off the sidelights.'

'Sarge?'

'And when you get there, go in the gate real slow and pull up at the front door without touching your footbrake.'

He could see the lights of two cars coming towards them. 'Now.'

'Can I wait until…?'

'No.'

She turned off the sidelights. The lights of the oncoming cars got brighter then became parallel as the second car pulled out to past the first.

'Oh,' Keane said and ran the patrol car as hard against the ditch as it would go.

'Barlow, you always were a mad bugger,' Geordie said.

His shape disappeared from the rear-view mirror as he ducked down between the seats.

'We'll be all right,' Barlow said. He'd feel remorseful about risking their lives later. If there was a later.

The oncoming cars were nearly on top of them. Keane flicked her headlights and the oncoming lights veered sideways. The patrol car lurched in the blast of their passing.

Geordie's shape reappeared in the rear-view mirror. His finger poked Barlow on the shoulder 'If we're dead, this must be hell because you're here as well.'

The Collins' front gates loomed out of the darkness. Keane swung the wheel hard and used the handbrake to slow the car as it crunched up the short driveway. It stopped just beyond the front door and they all piled out.

Barlow couldn't stop himself from pulling on the old bell handle though he knew it hadn't worked in a generation. He put his mouth to the letterbox and shouted. 'Mrs Collins. Edward… Mrs Collins.'

No one came. He shouted a second time, only now he added, 'Captain, would you tell them to open the door.'

Seconds later a glow of light showed in the great hall.

'Who's there?' asked a voice, Mrs Collins'. She sounded frightened.

'John Barlow, let us in please.'

Through the glass panels he saw her and Edward struggle with the bolts and bar securing the door. 'A deuce inconvenient,' said a voice. Edward's.

Finally the door swung open and they could step inside.

'John, son, if you don't mind, the next time come in by the back door,' Mrs Collins said.

'Sorry about that.'

'A young lady and Mr Dunlop. I'm honoured,' Mrs Collins said.

A scream of rage rattled every window in the house. A naval cutlass ripped itself off the wall and came at Geordie, point first.

83

Everyone stood frozen as the cutlass flew across the room towards Geordie. Somehow Barlow managed to step between Geordie and the cutlass. It stopped with its point tickling the hairs on his throat.

He tried to knock the cutlass away and down. It was like pushing against a brick wall and just as ineffective. 'Captain, I've enough on my plate without you worrying about old family disputes.'

Keane fled out into the night.

'What did I do?' Geordie squeaked, his eyes like two harvest moons.

'Nothing,' Barlow said to him. Then to the cutlass, 'It happened generations ago. Drop it.'

He refused to ease back even a fraction of an inch, though the sword point pricked his skin with every word. 'Okay, you were on your way to take command of HMS Cormorant. You didn't make it because you were killed by a herd of cattle driven by the Dunlops.' He risked a glance back at Geordie. 'Stolen cattle.'

He looked back at the cutlass, which quivered with the Captain's desire to ram it through him and into Geordie. 'As I say, you were killed and your old classmate, Thomas Saumarez, took command of the Cormorant, broke the chain blocking the river approach to Pekin and demolished the guns of the Taku forts, thereby earning undying glory: a knighthood, promotions and all the rest.'

Edward put his hand on the handle of the cutlass. 'My dear chap, who remembers Thomas Saumarez now? And if they do, his glory is tainted because it was earned during a totally reprehensible Opium War with China.'

Geordie came level with Barlow, the valise held up to his throat by way of protection. He said, 'The way I heard it from my grandfather, instead of having the manners to wait, you tried to ram your way through the herd. Your horse knocked down a calf, the mother had a go at your horse. You fell off and the herd stampeded.'

'Why don't you shut your mouth,' Barlow said.

Geordie ducked back behind Barlow.

'Drugs, they really are nasty things,' Mrs Collins said.

'Worse than drink,' Edward said. 'Though one has to admit, that one experimented in one's early days.'

The cutlass still held firm against Barlow's throat, and there was nothing he hated more than old rancour causing new rows.

He said, 'Look. My daughter's been kidnapped. She's in the hands of ruthless men who have already tortured and murdered people. You want to pick a row with the Dunlops do it with the next generation. I need Geordie alive and unharmed.'

Somehow, he now knew one of the reasons why Reg Corkey had been killed, and the likely killer.

He stepped around the cutlass and ran up the stairs into the almost complete darkness of the landing.

'Hey!' a frightened Geordie called after him.

'Stop that stuff in the valise from rattling,' Barlow called back and felt his way into the back bedroom. The one Mrs Collins shared with the Captain.

Her bedroom window was a grey rectangle in the darkness. Beyond it lay the garden, the boundary wall and the factory.

No lights showed in the factory, not a glimmer from any window.

Barlow had bet Vera's life on her being held there.

84

No lights showed in the factory. No Vera.

Barlow fought down his despair and tried to throw his thoughts out to her. Talk to me, Love. Tell me where you are.

He felt his way across the bedroom to the window and stared out. A cone of light hung over Ballymena and, way in the distance, a smaller cone over Antrim town. But nearby, where it mattered, nothing.

He stayed on watching because there was nowhere else to go, pleading, talk to me, Love. Talk to me.

And there it was. A pinprick of light on the roof that flared and died just as quickly. Not much of a light, probably a guard striking a match to light a cigarette, but the skylight had caught and reflected the glow.

Keep talking, Love.

Barlow ran out of the bedroom and down the corridor and crashed down the stairs in an out-of-control run. Everyone still stood in a group where he'd left them, only now Edward held the cutlass.

'Edward, find WPC Keane and tell her to contact the station. The Belfast men are in the factory.' He pulled at Geordie as he ran past them and out the door. 'You come with me.'

He sprinted around the front of the house, staying on grass to keep down the sound of running feet. Geordie came wheezing after him. At least the contents of the valise had stopped rattling.

Nearing the gate into the factory area he slowed and let Geordie catch up with him. 'You might have given Mr Edward your word to be good, but you'd still notice things.'

'It's as tight as a duck's arse,' Geordie said. 'Bars on the windows, rear doors lined with metal and secured with bolts and bars. A security alarm on the front door that can only be deactivated by a number.'

'Find a way for the police to sneak in.'

'It's got me beat,' Geordie said.

'Well un-beat yourself.'

Barlow led the way through the gate in the wall into the factory yard. He motioned for Geordie to go to the left while he turned right and, without trying to walk silently, went across the stoned ground to the front of the factory.

R Shaw's sports car sat tight against the wall where it couldn't be seen from Mrs Collins' bedroom. Seeing that, frightened him. Vera was in the power of R Shaw who had killed Evon, partly to keep her from telling what she knew about Reg Corkey and his involvement with the Lorrimers, and partly to destroy a better man than himself, Tom Rankin. Somehow that callousness was more frightening than a straightforward, ruthless crook like Stan Holloway.

At the front door, Barlow stopped and raised his hand to give a polite knock, then paused. That was not the way to do it.

He made a fist, intending to blatter the door, then had another thought and tried the handle.

The door opened.

Barlow stepped in. No alarm beeped. He felt along the wall until he found the bank of switches he knew were there and palmed on every light in the building.

He squinted into the sudden glare of light and roared, 'You lot upstairs.'

85

Barlow was on the third stair before a man appeared. He was tall, thickset and swung a crowbar in his hand. Not a gun, Barlow noted with relief.

'Where do you think you're going?' the man asked.

Barlow kept climbing. 'Are you the big hero who hit the wee girl over the head during the jewel robbery?'

'What jewel robbery?'

'Good answer, Son. It might save you from the rope.'

The man didn't like that reminder. He backed off a step.

Barlow built on that uncertainty, now was not the time to show weakness. 'I'm Station Sergeant Barlow. Tell your boss I'm here.'

Without taking his eyes off Barlow, the man backed across the wide landing until he came up against the door of the old butler's room. He opened it a crack. 'Stan, that copper's here.'

'Dad!'

Vera's voice sounded strong, so she was unhurt. He gave thanks for that as he reached the top of the stairs and crossed the landing. Standing nose to nose with the guard, Barlow got the stink of cigarettes on the man's breath.

'Are you going to open that door or not?'

The man swung the door open and Barlow found an excited Vera buried in his arms. 'I knew you'd come. Oh Dad!'

If the guard had followed them into the room, Barlow planned to send Vera flying down the stairs with instructions to run and keep running, while he blocked her pursuers long enough for her to get away.

But he hadn't and all Barlow could do was hold a protective hand over the back of her head. A heavy board, probably dating back to the wartime blackout, covered the window, which was why no light had showed. Barlow turned his attention to a battered looking R Shaw and the man the guard has addressed as "Stan".

"Stan", Stanley Holloway, was ageing and gut fat, with eyes that looked and assessed but showed no emotion.

'The jewels, Barlow.'

'What makes you think I have them?'

Stan nodded at R Shaw. 'We've talked to your man there a couple of times, and he knows nothing about it. Reg? Well Reg isn't around to discuss it and Shorty wasn't exactly the silent type but he had nothing to say either.'

Barlow made Vera stand against the wall at the door-opening side. For a quick escape if the opportunity should arise. He leaned against the door itself to keep the guard trapped outside.

'Is Ernie all right?' she asked.

'He's got a black eye and a fierce headache,' he said. It didn't hurt to underplay Ernie's injuries to the men responsible.

'He will be okay?'

'He's more worried about you.'

Vera, he noticed with pride, stood with a foot planted firmly against the wall, ready to go on the attack. More than ready, going by the glare she gave Stan.

Stan countered the threat by pulling a pistol from his pocket and holding it casually by his side. 'Talk, Barlow, and make it fast. I lose interest very quickly.'

Barlow said, 'You had a big robbery planned and you knew the police were likely to come asking questions. So you reckoned it best to get the proceeds out of town fast.'

Stan's eyebrow twitched, which indicated some interest in what he was saying so Barlow continued.

'So you arranged with the Lorrimers to send a fall-guy in the form of Geordie Dunlop, to bring the jewellery to Ballymena for shipping on to London, Amsterdam, wherever. And to be sure that Geordie or the Lorrimers didn't get smart you had Reg Corkey follow Geordie back here and stand guard over the jewellery until it was shipped out.'

Stan pretended to yawn. 'Tell me something I don't know.'

Barlow kept his voice steady, though he guessed he was running out of time. The aim of the pistol was starting to travel in his direction. 'Reg was muscle, not brains, and anyway you're a belt and braces sort of fellow. You made him write down a number to use when locking the jewellery in the safe overnight. A number you would know if anything should happen to him. When he ended up dead, you rushed to Ballymena and opened the safe and…' Barlow gestured with his hands. 'Poof, no jewellery.'

Now the pistol was steady on his midriff. 'You're still boring me.'

'I bet you don't know that we found the cigarette packet lying on top of Reg's body – the flap with the number on it, torn off.'

Stan didn't. For the first time his eyes flickered with uncertainty.

'Number four, either a three or an eight, then maybe a seven,' Barlow said, and pointed to the fireplace. 'I found it there a couple of days later.'

Now Stan had the gun cocked and pointed. Straight at R Shaw's head. 'You lying wee git.'

R Shaw ducked and screamed and used his arms to protect his head.

Barlow wouldn't have minded seeing R Shaw killed. He reckoned it was the best chance he had of making him pay for killing Evon.

But if Stan killed R Shaw, he wouldn't want any witnesses left alive to testify against him.

86

'It wasn't R Shaw who killed Reg,' Barlow said, and thought he might be right.

Stan steadied his aim on R Shaw's head. 'But he knows who.'

'The father,' Barlow said in a "who else" tone. 'He's protecting his father.'

Stan lowered his aim. 'I'll settle for his balls then.'

Vera squeaked and covered her face but didn't turn away.

Her courage gave Barlow a boost.

Stan's aim went back to R Shaw's head. 'How can you be sure about that? They could have been in it together.'

'I'll give you two reasons.' Barlow was trying to think faster than his head could come up with a believable story. 'Reg had quite a day on Wednesday: Took part in a big jewellery robbery, bludgeoned a schoolgirl to death for no reason.'

He paused deliberately to let Stan say something.

'He did,' Stan said. 'Hit her for no reason whatsoever. I could have killed him myself for doing it.'

Someone else was trying to avoid the rope.

'You have daughters and granddaughters yourself?' he asked Stan.

'I have. Get on with it.'

'So he lands here all hyped and ready for anything.' Barlow wished he could block Vera's ears for the next bit. 'So he puts his hand up Rose Lorrimer's skirt and nearly deflowers her with his fingers.'

'He did. He did,' R Shaw confirmed shakily.

He looked up, saw the pistol still aimed at him and ducked back under his arms.

'So what?' asked Stan.

'So, Rose goes home all upset,' Barlow said. That made sure Rose wasn't implicated in the loss of the jewels. 'Meantime, R Shaw rushes off to pick up a local prostitute who is into rough stuff.'

'Honestly, I did,' R Shaw said from under his arms.

'Then comes Thursday and the furniture still isn't ready.' Barlow looked at R Shaw. 'It's a funny thing about suppliers. If you're slow to pay them, they're even slower to make the next delivery.' He turned his attention back to Stan. 'To keep Reg amused, Mr Lorrimer suggested that they get rid of old Mrs Collins next door by gassing her.'

For the second time that evening Stan's eyes flickered. This time with puzzlement.

'Oh you didn't know about Reg and Mr Lorrimer's little plan, then?' asked Barlow.

'What plan?'

'To take over the old manor house and turn it into a classy bordello.' Now Barlow felt he could raise serious doubt in Stan's mind. 'Now where would they have got that sort of money? Mr Lorrimer didn't have it for sure.'

'You're lying, Reg would never…'

'Cash the woman was offered. Hard cash.'

Stan stuck the pistol in R Shaw's face. 'So you know nothing about it?' Then in Barlow's, 'And you know everything except where the jewels are now.' His face went frighteningly blank. 'The only man I need to talk to is Lorrimer. The rest of you are… trouble.'

The blacked out window concealed the lights but the sound of a car engine outside was unmistakable. Tyres screeched as the car slid to a halt at the front door.

Barlow didn't dare close his eyes but he shook his head in disgust. He'd sent for help, expecting the police to arrive like Indians sneaking in, not the flaming cavalry at full gallop, bells, bugles and all.

87

Car doors slammed, the front door of the factory banged open and footsteps sounded on the stairs. The guard's challenge was answered by the impatient snap of a woman's voice.

Barlow jumped clear of the door as it swung open. Rose Lorrimer stormed into the room, hair flying, her face set in a snarl. She seemed to acknowledge the presence of other people but not what they were doing. She headed straight for R Shaw. He jumped to his feet.

'You pig. You selfish, greedy, self-centred pig,' she screamed at him and slapped him. The blow raised a fresh streak of blood on his face. 'You cleaned out the bank, every penny. There's nothing left to pay the men.'

Barlow looked back. Tom Rankin stood in the doorway, more keenly aware than Rose of the atmosphere in the room. The guard now stood facing in, the iron bar held ready to strike. There wasn't a chance for Vera to cut and run.

The guard shoved Tom on into the room and slammed the door shut.

R Shaw retreated backwards as Rose prodded him. 'How could you? You know we need that money to get us through the New Year.' The prod became a rat-tat-tat thump on his chest. 'I want it back, you couldn't have spent it all. Where is it?'

Keeping well clear of Stan and his gun, Tom limped across the room and trapped Rose in his arms. She struggled but finally gave in to his quiet. 'Enough.'

He made her turn until she could see Stan and his pistol. 'Oh!'

'Money?' Stan said. His pistol and his attention back on R Shaw.

Barlow reckoned he could have Vera out the door before Stan could turn and fire. It would cost him his life but could she cope with the guard and his iron bar, on her own? He thought not.

'Just be ready,' he whispered.

He also cared what would happen to Rose and Tom, and the cavalry were taking a long time to arrive.

'Just how much money?' asked Stan.

R Shaw glared his hatred at his sister. 'We're tight up against our overdraft limit, so a few quid.'

Stan turned his attention and the pistol on Rose. 'You tell me darlin', and if I think you're lying, your boyfriend won't have a bad leg to limp on.'

'Nearly four thousand pounds,' she said, her voice tight with nervousness. Even so she added, 'I need it to pay the men, so you hands-off as well.'

Four thousand pounds seemed a fortune to Barlow, though he supposed if you paid upwards on fifty men out of that and a few bills there wouldn't be that much left. However, it might be enough money for Stan to forget about the jewels and take off for somewhere safe. As R Shaw obviously planned to do.

He'd heard that Spain was a good place to hide because the dictator, Franco, didn't like the British. The people he knew who had gone there on holidays could only talk about: sun, sea and sangria – and how unfriendly the police were.

One thing he was sure of. Those Spanish cops would be Stan's best friends compared to what he planned to do to Stan given half a chance.

88

Stan swung his pistol around in a great arc to remind people who he was and what he had in his hand. He smiled for the first time, at R Shaw. 'Now, where is that money?'

'It's…'

The pistol boomed. The bullet tore into the floor at R Shaw's feet. He cringed into a corner. Vera threw herself into Barlow's arms. Tom hugged Rose.

Stan said, 'The next bullet will go through your foot so no lies, I want the truth.'

Barlow reckoned Stan had five bullets left in the pistol to use against five captives. That was assuming he had reloaded the gun after shooting Toby.

R Shaw wheezed breath as if at the end of a ten-mile run. 'It's in the car, under things. I was leaving tonight. I mean…'

'Oh, I know what you mean,' Stan said and frowned at each of them in turn, daring them to move.

Barlow made himself stand apparently compliant but eased a foot back to give himself a boost when he went for Stan and the gun. He sensed his chance coming because that money was Stan's means of escape from an almost certain hanging.

Stan used the pistol to waggle R Shaw out of the corner, then shepherded him and Rose and Tom towards Barlow and the door.

He was taking them all downstairs: five captives, two guards and a narrow stairwell. Barlow knew he couldn't count on R Shaw but Tom would back his play.

To have any chance he needed Tom to go first, himself last and Vera and Rose in between. All the same, there was something professional about the way Stan did the shepherding. The man had done it before.

'Door,' Stan said, and R Shaw rushed to open it.

Things started to fall into place. Barlow selected a Wine Gum to moisten his dry mouth as R Shaw went ahead of the rest. When he gave the word, Tom would ram R Shaw into the guard to unbalance the man, and they'd take it from there.

There was a general movement towards the now open door as people sensed freedom.

'Stop,' Stan said in a voice that had to be obeyed, and to the guard. 'Anyone who tries to get down the stairs, clock them good.'

The would-be escapees ground to a halt, the doorway solid with their bodies.

Stan grasped Rose by the neck and threatened Tom when he refused to let go of her. 'She stays with me.' He waggled the gun at Vera. 'You too darlin'.'

Barlow held onto Vera's shoulders, his mouth dry as if sucking salt. He ached to ram her through the crowd, past the guard and send her running down the stairs and away. But other people would get hurt.

He said, 'You don't need Vera and Rose. We're not going to try anything when you're holding a gun.'

Vera shook herself free of his grasp. 'It's all right, Dad.'

She went back and stood beside Rose.

Stan indicated with the pistol. 'Everyone, move out slowly. Men to the right, women to the left.'

Even without a fire in the grate the butler's room had been pleasant. The open hallway and dormitory seemed to collect every bitter draft. Barlow moved the reluctant Tom ahead of himself and to the right. He stopped tight to the wall. If Stan tried to pass him, he'd grab the pistol and force it down. With any luck, Stan would shoot himself in the foot.

He heard the pistol being cocked as Stan said, 'Barlow, I've got the gun right against your daughter's head, so don't get smart.'

In the far distance of the dormitory, a shadow moved. The cavalry were coming.

Barlow could only grit his teeth and pray that Vera stayed safe.

89

Rose appeared in the doorway. Barlow held Tom back from going to her. Then Vera with the muzzle of the pistol resting on her neck. Finally, Stan's gut, followed by Stan himself.

'Sorry, Dad,' Vera mouthed.

Whatever she'd had in mind to disarm Stan, Barlow could only be grateful that she hadn't tried.

He made himself sound positive. 'It'll soon be over.'

'Once I get that package,' Stan interrupted loudly. He was silent for a few seconds, wondering how to cope with guarding the prisoners while searching for the package. Finally, he said to the guard, 'See him,' pointing at R Shaw. 'He's got a package hidden somewhere in his car. Go with him to get it, and if he tries anything, start with the knees and work up.'

The guard looked pleased. 'The jewels?'

'A package,' Stan repeated and gave the guard a glare that made him quail. That sort of casual remark could get a man hanged as an accessory.

That glare and the guard's quail took their attention away from the prisoners, giving Barlow a momentary chance to grab the gun and shoot: first Stan and then the guard. He hesitated because of the risk of Vera being hurt, and the opportunity had gone.

He had a sense of that dark shadow coming closer, but high up along the ceiling, moving from rafter to rafter. If only he could risk a glance to see who it was and what they were doing. Help in some way to co-ordinate the counterattack.

Stan's full attention was back on the prisoners, the muzzle pressed against Vera's neck. 'On you go,' he told the guard and R Shaw.

The guard went first, walking backwards down the stairs, a hand on the bannisters for balance, the iron bar ready if R Shaw tried anything. The outer door creaked open, banged shut and they were gone.

Barlow stretched out a hand and took Vera's in his. Tom limped across and held Rose in his arms. Stan didn't stop him. Even saying no would have created noise and all their ears were tuned to what was going on outside.

A car door opened and closed, then a sucking-clicking sound that had to be the boot lid coming up.

A yell… metal falling onto metal… a car engine roaring into life.

'He's dead,' roared Stan.

Which one of the men he was talking about wasn't clear. Both, Barlow reckoned, if the package didn't appear soon. Not that he was worried about the package. His eyes were on the pistol. The muzzle had come away from the back of Vera's neck but was still too close to her head to risk anything.

The car engine screamed as someone took off in it. Then the engine became sweeter as the driver moved through the gears. A screech of brakes and the agonised grind of metal crushing metal.

Barlow heard the dying trill of an electric bell that could only have come from a police car.

Stan's whole attention was on the noise outside, and the pistol…

Barlow grabbed Stan's arm and jerked it upwards and away from Vera, shouldering her clear at the same time. She spun away as Barlow and Stan came together, gut against gut. Stan had the door-jam behind him and more weight. Barlow found himself being pushed backwards and down.

The outer door banged open and footsteps hammered up the stairs accompanied by voices. Female voices.

The pistol roared as Stan finally found the space to flex his finger.

A dark body fell from the rafters. A flailing leg caught Barlow behind the knee, knocking him off balance. That and Stan's weight sent him crashing to the floor. They lay entangled over the fallen body. Barlow struggled to keep the pistol above their heads and Stan's gut from crushing the life out of him.

Still locked in each other's grip they struggled to their knees and then onto their feet. The pistol was between them and pointing upwards, liable to kill either man if Stan pulled the trigger a second time. Sweat dripped off Barlow but at least this time it was him against the wall and he couldn't be pushed back any further.

Barlow smashed his head into Stan's face. Stan's nose blossomed blood and he yelled. Barlow could have yelled as well because he'd caught Stan right on the bruise from the fireman's oxygen cylinder. Every vestige of headache erupted again.

Something hot and hairy hurled itself between the men and buried its teeth in a wrist.

Rex.

It took Stan screaming in pain for Barlow to work out that the dog had grabbed the right wrist. At the same time he saw WPC Hughes. She reversed the Lee Enfield rifle she held and slammed the butt into their tangle of legs, and again he felt no pain. Stan kept screaming. He lost hold of the pistol as he fell, taking Barlow and the dog with him. The pistol sailed through the air. Thompson appeared out of nowhere and kicked. The pistol sailed away into the dormitory area.

Hitting the floor with Barlow on top, knocked the last of the fight out of Stan. Barlow rolled clear and found himself lying beside Wilson.

Wilson lay on, not moving.

90

Barlow would grieve for Wilson. But first Vera.

Tom stood with his arms around both Vera and Rose. Vera's eyes were awash with tears, worrying about her father. Barlow winked. She saw him do it and her face blossomed a smile.

Thompson leaned against a wall, wriggling her right foot. Milton had Rex back on his lead but kept the snarling dog and its teeth close to Stan's throat. Hughes knelt over Wilson, wailing. 'Frank. Frank.'

Frank's body suddenly spasmed and he gulped air. 'I thought I'd never breathe again.'

Hughes said, 'You're not hurt?'

'I fell on my back.'

'I thought you were dead.' She started to cry.

Barlow looked over at Wilson and saw no dampness on his body, no trail of blood on the floor. 'You're not shot, son?'

'I slipped, Sarge. Sorry.'

'Slipped!' Hughes all but screamed. 'We're fighting for our lives down here and you fall over your big flat feet.'

Tom checked Wilson for broken bones. 'You seem to be intact, but if something comes through the skin you'll know I'm wrong.'

Barlow told him, 'You should be a doctor. You've already got the bedside manner.'

Thompson limped over. Barlow let her and Vera haul him to his feet and brush him down.

'Your dinner jacket's ruined,' Vera said, as if it was his fault.

Tom and Hughes helped Wilson up. Hughes clung to him crying. Wilson hugged her back. 'It's okay, Stella. It's okay.'

Tom snuggled Rose into him. He said to Barlow, 'You'd better call for a few ambulances.' And to Thompson. 'Sergeant, whatever your name is, loosen the lace of that shoe but don't take it off or you'll never get it on again.'

Barlow had Vera in his arms, safe and sound. All was well in his little world, but WPC Keane was outside and he didn't know about her.

Right then the door downstairs slammed open and Geordie's voice roared. 'Do you need a hand up there?'

Barlow roared back. 'Sending Wilson in by a skylight….. was that the best you could do?'

'He saved your bacon, didn't he?'

'Oh aye.'

Geordie appeared up the stairs holding the semi-conscious guard by the collar. WPC Keane came next, her face bloodied. Finally, Edward holding a cloth moneybag.

'The wages money,' Rose said. She grabbed it off him and wrapped it in her arms.

In the distance, they could hear the discordant clatter of police bells as Her Majesty's finest raced to their rescue.

Milton said, 'Would somebody mind cuffing this man? I'm getting tired holding Rex back.'

91

Sometimes it was nice to sit while everyone else busied themselves. A Station Sergeant doing his job, keeping others on their toes.

Barlow sat in the kitchen area of the staff sleeping quarters, eyes closed, a mug of tea in one hand, the other arm around Vera's shoulders. They'd spent a lifetime sitting like that and he hoped it would continue.

'Dad, I have to go and see Ernie.'

He opened his eyes to the reality before him. Stan had a suspected broken hip from Hughes' blow, high up near the ball-and-socket joint. He might never walk properly again. Ambulance men busied themselves securing Stan's injured leg for the transfer to hospital. Hughes and Wilson were sitting close together, not speaking but both looking content. McGinn had recovered a delighted Rex and Milton didn't know whether to cry at the loss of the dog or relish McGinn's talk about her new posting. Keane, bloody face and all, had insisted on taking part in the search for the fugitive R Shaw. Inspector Foxwood was giving Thompson a bollocking for risking the lives of women police officers. Not that that would appear in his official report: Displayed initiative in the Highest Tradition. All for the laudatory press releases. She'd probably get a medal.

Gillespie stood nearby. He looked sour.

Barlow said, 'You wouldn't be worrying about the cars if someone had been hurt.'

'Well they aren't so I'm huffing.'

Finally, Barlow winked at Vera as if he'd had a sly idea. 'Assault and kidnapping. We need an official report from Ernie in the hospital anyway.'

'I'll take her with me,' Gillespie said and scowled at Barlow. 'If I've a car left that works.'

'Ah go on with you.'

The Police Doctor stepped in front of Barlow. Barlow had been ignoring him, hoping the man would go away.

'Another bump on the head?' asked the doctor taking a good look at the bruise on Barlow's forehead.

'A head-butt,' Thompson said.

Barlow said, 'You'd be better employed digging out that penny you owe me.'

'And a headache,' the Doctor said. It wasn't a question. 'You've got concussion and I can't risk it.'

'Risk what?'

'You getting involved with Christmas drunks and New Year revellers. I'm standing you down from duty for at least ten days.'

Barlow's first thought was to object. He even had his mouth open but closed it again. The New Year. Plenty of sporting events, a bit of shooting and it meant that Pierson…

'Gillespie.'

'What?'

'The Hart Brothers. Send someone looking, I want them arrested.'

'You wouldn't do that to Pierson? Two full shifts of them singing flat as pancakes?'

'Oh, I would.'

He followed Vera and Gillespie down the stairs and into the yard. He didn't know why Gillespie was moaning about there being no transport. With men pouring in from outlying districts to help in the search for the fugitive R Shaw there were plenty of police cars sitting around.

Barlow watched Vera and Gillespie wind their way through a batch of new arrivals in unmarked cars. Special Branch from Belfast come to grab some of the glory, he reckoned. Rather than be caught up in meetings he went back into the building. The General Office this time, rather than upstairs.

Rose and Tom sat at a desk, heads close, working on a list of names. Geordie and Edward sat at another desk dealing out pound notes. The notes fluttered in the breeze coming in the door.

Geordie clamped his arms over the money, 'Shut that door, there's a breeze.'

Barlow booted the door shut behind him. 'And you're a quare man to be trusted with someone else's loot.'

'That R Shaw's a smart man,' Geordie said. 'Didn't he ask for lots of single notes to bluff the bank into thinking it was for the wages.'

'It is now,' Rose said. Her head cringed into her shoulders when she looked at Barlow. 'Could we finish here first?'

'Take your time, Love.'

Geordie said, 'All that money for a mere signature. It makes a man wonder.'

'Don't even think it.'

Barlow went over to where Rose and Tom worked. They were using a spreadsheet with all the employees' names listed down. Across the way was column after column of figures that made no sense to Barlow. 'What are you doing?'

Tom said, 'Lorrimers is finished. Rose wants to divide the money among the men, depending on their wages and how long they've worked for the firm.'

Barlow tapped the page. 'There's a name missing, your own.' He held up fingers in turn as he made his points. 'Junior management, unfair dismissal, loss of earnings.'

'Would that be okay?' asked Rose.

'And your own as well.'

He put his hand on her shoulder as gently as he could. 'Your father's private office, could I have a word.'

She rose and kissed Tom and said, 'I'm sorry,' and led the way into a glassed off cubicle.

Barlow carefully closed the door behind her so that no one could overhear.

She held her hands out as if expecting to be handcuffed. 'I don't know what came over me. I wasn't thinking straight. I'm so sorry. You could have been killed, you and that fireman who rescued Father.'

92

Barlow pushed Rose's hands apart and made her sit down because her whole body shook. Tom was looking their way, half out of his seat. He could see her distress and wanted to be with her.

Barlow moved to block his view. 'The way I see it, Rose. Your father and R Shaw conspired to ruin the reputation of the man you loved. Then R Shaw deliberately crippled Tom. If he didn't have a future in the English league then you two couldn't marry. Your father needed you around to run the business. As for R Shaw, I reckon R Shaw had other more selfish reasons.'

'He wanted the money from the house.'

'Not just his own share. If you had died in the fire he'd have got yours as well.'

'But I started the fire,' she said, and waited for him to jump back in horror and disgust.

'You did,' he said and kept anger out of his tone because that anger wasn't directed against her. 'You started the fire and you went up to your bedroom and blocked the door with your dressing gown to keep the smoke out. Then you got into bed and waited for R Shaw to raise the alarm. You planned to rush in and get your father up. You'd both escape and the money from the fire…?'

He paused wanting her to say it.

'If father would settle for a smaller house, with the insurance money and the sale of the site there'd be enough left over for me and Tom to make a fresh start.' She was so anxious to convince Barlow that she grabbed his hands. 'Tom doesn't know a thing about it, honest to God. It was all my own idea.'

'I know that.'

'When R Shaw didn't raise the alarm, I knew God intended for me to die as punishment for my sins.'

He gripped her hands back, trying to convince her of his own fundamental belief. 'God is never vindictive. That comes from the evil in men's hearts. In this case, R Shaw wanting the lot.'

He began to wonder if he'd come up with another solution and another threat. He had to leave, and fast, but first.

'Rose, the only proof we have of you committing that arson is if you make an admission under an Official Caution. Keep your mouth shut and no one will ever be able to prove a thing against you.'

'But I have sinned.'

He admired people with Fundamentalist beliefs, but sometimes that belief made them stupid to the reality of life.

'Yes, you have sinned, but look at it this way. Reg Corkey got injured in the Collins' house, which gave your father a chance to punish him for molesting you. Unfortunately, he hit Reg too hard and killed him.'

'Oh!'

'As for R Shaw, he'll be charged with things like Withholding Information and Accessory to the Fact, but not for the death of Evon Flinton. He was afraid she'd tell us of Reg's connection with your family.' He smiled down at her. 'So why should you be punished for a moment's madness?'

'But I have sinned and must accept God's punishment for that sin.'

In her innocence she didn't really get it. She wouldn't merely be charged with arson, which could be argued into a suspended sentence. She'd also be charged with causing her father Actual Bodily Harm which carried an almost certain jail sentence. Even worse, if her father died within a year and a day it would be manslaughter.

He said, 'I intend to give you a seven-year punishment that you must keep to yourself.'

'What? Anything? The Missions? Can I see Tom occasionally? If he wants to see me. He's so honourable he'll hate me forever.'

Barlow pushed her hands clear of his and stood as straight as aching muscles would allow. 'Rose Lorrimer, I sentence you to seven years of make do and mend, of struggle and doing without.' He smiled at her terrified face. 'During which time you will make Tom go back to school to get his A Levels. You will also convince Tom to forget about being a masseur and train to become a real doctor.'

She jumped up. 'Oh, that's not suffering.'

'Believe me, Rose, family life is not easy.'

Then he had to go, because someone's life could still be in danger.

93

Lorrimers' yard was full of people and cars, that turned Barlow's route to the gate in the wall into an obstacle course. Edward stood among a group of strangers, being very much: Major, the Honourable Edward Adair. G.C.; M.C., being effusively grateful, as only he could, for their prompt attendance at this little matter. A tall, grey-haired man waved at Barlow. Michael Sinclair wanting to introduce him to his team, but he ran on, breathless with fear for Mrs Collins.

He clicked the gate open and ran down the little path. The back door was locked, then he remembered that they'd used the front door.

He kept running though his legs seemed heavy. Down the side of the house, past the morning room to the front door.

He burst in, shouting, 'Mrs Collins.'

'In here, son.'

He crossed the great hall and went into the morning room. The lighting made the room bright and a fire roared up the chimney.

She looked embarrassed. 'I don't normally. I mean sit here like a great lady, but the Captain insisted.'

'And why not?' he said and looked at the Captain's portrait. 'Thank you for keeping her safe.'

Her hand fluttered over her chest. 'Safe? Who would want to harm me?'

Reflected flames from the fire leapt around the walls making the Captain's portrait grimace.

On the way out the door Barlow mouthed at the portrait, 'Keep her in here.'

A faint glow of lights from the cars around Lorrimers' factory guided him across the great hall. Before he was halfway there, the door to the servants' quarters swung open. R Shaw stood in the doorway. He held something heavy in one hand. It showed faint against the darkness of the back hall. A package was tucked under the other arm.

Barlow asked, 'Is that the wrench you used to kill Reg Corkey with?'

'My father did that.'

'You'd say that anyway.'

R Shaw stood hesitating in the doorway. He obviously didn't want to go out the back way and risk being spotted by the police. Now Barlow blocked the front door and his means of escape.

'Drop it, son. So far we've only got you as an Accessory After the Fact. There's no rope for that.'

R Shaw took a step into the great hall, the wrench still held raised. 'I'd be away and clear if it wasn't for you.'

'Maybe,' Barlow said, slipping off his jacket and holding it loose in his right hand. At the same time it didn't hurt to keep R Shaw talking. It might bring him to his senses. 'We figured Reg planned to gas Mrs Collins but couldn't resist a little larceny as well. It took a while to realise that the marks on the gas pipe came later, after Reg's death.'

He didn't like the way R Shaw came up on his toes. 'All that sneaking around as a child. You knew about the gap behind the metre, didn't you? Who'd ever think of looking there?'

R Shaw came charging at him, the wrench swinging at his head. Barlow sidestepped and swung the jacket. The dinner jacket was light, it didn't have the weight behind it of a uniform jacket, but the flick across R Shaw's eyes helped make the wrench miss.

Barlow heard a woman scream. It sounded in the distance but had to be Mrs Collins with her head stuck out a window. The only way that could have happened was if the Captain had forced the window open for her.

R Shaw ran on to the front door and tried to haul it open. It stayed shut.

Barlow said, 'I put on the deadbolts on my way in. They're a devil to find in the dark.'

R Shaw turned as he approached. Barlow held out his hand for the wrench. 'Give up, and we'll not mention this bit of attempted murder.'

R Shaw breathed heavily, his teeth showed behind rolled up lips. He charged at Barlow. This time Barlow tried to wrap the jacket around the flailing wrench. It caught but didn't hold and the wrench brushed his arm on the way down.

For the third attack, R Shaw didn't run but came at Barlow like a boxer, ready to duck and weave with Barlow's attempts to avoid the blow. Something appeared in the air between them that made both men jerk back a step: a sword, with the handle towards Barlow.

He took it. 'Thanks, Captain.'

The cutlass was surprisingly light in his hand and made a satisfactory *swoosh* when he did a few practice swings in R Shaw's face. All the same he'd have happily traded it for a loaded musket.

The wrench jerked out of R Shaw's hand and was replaced with a cutlass.

'Oh bloody hell.'

At the same time, the bolts on the front door snapped back and the door swung open. The Captain wanted a fair figh, but he didn't want blood staining his wooden wooden floor.

Mrs Collins was still screaming, 'Help! Help!'

Barlow trusted the Captain to keep her safe and edged slowly out of the house, wanting to be nearer his rescuers. R Shaw stood on transfixed by the appearance of a cutlass in his hand.

Barlow stopped when he stepped onto the gravel drive. Torchlight wobbled up and down the side lawn as people rushed to Mrs Collins' aid. A car turned in the front gate and lit up the front of the house.

R Shaw came charging after Barlow, cutlass swinging. Barlow blocked the blow and metal crashed on metal as R Shaw stumbled past, only to turn and stab at him. Barlow jerked clear of the blow and slashed and stabbed at R Shaw with no real chance of touching him. All the same R Shaw didn't like it, he kept backing off.

'Windy, are we, son?'

They circled each other, looking for an opening. Sparks flew when the swords clashed.

Someone shouted, 'Shoot,' only to have the order countermanded, 'Hold your fire.'

Edward advised, 'Parry and riposte, my dear chap. Parry and riposte.'

Gillespie was back. He said, 'Cut and thrust.'

Geordie roared, 'Stick the bugger.'

Barlow didn't want R Shaw dead that easily. He wanted him to suffer for Evon.

'You fight like you play football.' Barlow said and made a quick stab at R Shaw's throat. 'All fine when it's going your way.'

R Shaw slashed back. Barlow jumped forward and blocked the blow and held sword pommel against sword pommel as he pressed his weight against R Shaw's push.

He stayed close in on R Shaw and kept pushing and pushing. There was the remains of an ornamental pond in the middle of the lawn. He aimed that way, then hooked a foot against R Shaw's ankle and shoved. R Shaw disappeared into a glutinous mix of leaves and dirt and decaying creepy-crawlies.

94

Barlow thought that the moment would never come when his home finally emptied of helpful people. Vera had already left with Solicitor Moncrief to see Ernie safely home and then catch a train to Donaghadee.

He didn't know whether to be hurt or proud to see her go. She wasn't a teenager going to her mother's for Christmas. She was a young woman, in pearls and a twin-set, going off with her lover. By next Christmas they'd be married, he was sure of that in his waters, and be gone out of his day-to-day life forever.

Only Thompson remained. A penny, the settlement of their bet, lay on the kitchen table between them.

Mid-morning, a squad of men from Denton's brewery had come to the house to haul away all the broken furniture, followed by a squad of women, led by Clarissa Denton, to sweep up and tidy up. As the day wore on to dark, the lorry came back with bits and pieces of furniture to tide him over.

Barlow's only job, the one he insisted on doing himself, was to refill the cushion of his favourite chair and place it on the bottom of the grave for Toby to lie on. The chair itself was intact but he had it carted away with the rest. He'd buried Toby in the front lawn where he would be forever on guard. He hadn't cried but his throat burned as the soil covered the little dog.

Thompson asked, 'Did you get any sleep?'

'Aye, a couple of hours in one of the cells.'

'So that was you snoring? I was trying to catch forty winks in the next one.'

He knew she was trying to lift his mood. This house, once a nice size, was now too big for a man facing life on his own.

'You'll stay for tea?' he asked, rather than have that loneliness start straight away.

'Tea? It's more like supper.'

'Aye, it is.' He surprised himself with being hungry.

People had left in food but it was too late to start cooking or boiling. A meat pie still had some heat in it so he added bread and butter and sauces to the mix and they ate.

She wanted to help him with the washing up but he made her sit down again.

'That foot's giving you bother, though it was a quare kick.'

'I played football with my brothers.' She gave him a cheeky grin. 'That's not in my file either.'

He looked at her tired face and the time on the clock and the darkness outside. 'Christmas weekend and all, you'll not get a taxi and it's a long walk to the station with a bad foot.' He pointed through the wall in the direction of the bedrooms. 'Vera's bed is fresh made, if you want.'

'Thank you.'

They went along to the bedrooms. He left the hall light on in case she wanted to go to the bathroom in the middle of the night. He showed her Vera's room and went into his bedroom. Didn't bother turning on the light.

He was aware of Thompson using the bathroom and her footstep on the landing. She came into his room. He was already in bed.

'Your room's across the hall.'

'The thing is,' she said. 'I rang Inspector MacMillan this afternoon and resigned from the RUC.'

'What did you do that for?'

In the near darkness, with only the hall light creeping in under the door, he could see her unbutton her blouse. In other circumstances he would have scratched his head. Was he supposed to watch, or what?

She said, 'I've a friend in London A man, but a real friend. I stay with him and his wife sometimes. He's been at me for years to transfer to the Met. He says I'd have an easier time over there, people are much more acceptable of my sort.'

'Aggressive, bloody minded, willing to take a risk.'

'That too.'

The blouse was off now. The skirt followed. She was a richly shaped woman. Not that he'd doubted it. 'If you don't mind me asking?'

'What am I doing?'

She undid her suspenders and sat on the bed while she slipped off her nylons. Deliberately not looking at him, he realised, because her voice wasn't right. 'All these years, I've thrown myself at disgusting men. I'd like to finish with someone who respects me for myself.'

Barlow said, 'The truth is, Thompson, last night you went into the cells instead of into the Section House, and you didn't sleep then either, did you? In fact you haven't slept properly since you got here.' He had made room for her in the bed.

She slid in beside him. 'So?'

'Old hurts have surfaced like a nightmare. You'd do anything not to be on your own in the dark.'

Heat radiated off her body, her hand brushed across his chest. He wished she wouldn't do that.

'So?' she asked again.

'Tell me about the university,' he said.

Sunday
Christmas Day

95

Pre-dawn came peacefully for Barlow, though he still felt weary. Thompson lay curled in against him. She had talked forever through the darkness: about her love affair with Helen, about the men who thought they could buy her body with promises of promotion. The loneliness, her sterile life. Finally, her voice drifted off to silence and they'd slept.

Thompson came awake with the full dawn. Instead of pulling back from him, her hand curled over his chest. 'Barlow, I'm not being fair to you. The WPCs told me that you haven't a woman in your life, haven't had one for some time. So if you want to, I don't mind.'

He was tempted, ached to take up her offer. Instead, he gently pushed her hand away. 'In my life, even a "I don't mind" is quite an offer and thank you for it.'

She put a finger to his lips to still his refusal. 'Talking to you about Helen, the first time I was able to talk to anyone about our affair, was cathartic. Maybe I can go on from here and make something of my life.'

He said, 'I remember you saying something about Helen, but as soon as my head hit the pillow I was asleep. It had been a long day.'

She smiled down at him. Her lips formed the word *liar* but didn't say it. 'There will be no more men in my life but I'd like finish with one I can remember with pleasure.'

They made love. She guided him as to what pleased her, and he kept his weight off her as much as he could. She lay with her head thrown back on the pillow. He could see a glow of contentment in her cheeks, her mouth set in a slight smile that showed the tips of her teeth. Her eyes stayed closed. Who she was seeing, who was it she imagined she was coupling with, didn't matter.

The glow faded. He eased himself off and lay flat, both of them breathing easily. Snowflakes angled past the window, heavy enough to lie. It was a White Christmas, as Evon had predicted.

Thompson getting out of bed stopped that chain of sadness.

He knew she'd prefer that he didn't look at her naked so he closed his eyes and listened, and appreciated the gesture of her not slipping into the bathroom to dress. He heard clothes being picked up and the hiss of material sliding over her body. The crunch on the bed as she sat to pull up her nylons, the rattle and twist of shoes slipped on. The slide of the chair as she sat at the dressing table combing her hair. The pop of air as a lipstick canister slid open.

'Barlow.'

He opened his eyes. She stood before him fully dressed, fingers checking that her jacket buttons stood straight up and down. 'When I was on the phone to Inspector MacMillan, I told her that Ballymena doesn't need a woman sergeant. You are equally ignorant to all officers, both men and women.'

'I am that.'

'In fact, all WPCs from here get terribly bolshie on later postings if they're not allowed to walk the streets.'

He wondered where this was going to, as she finished straightening her buttons and brushed at a piece of lint on her clothes.

He said, 'I can't answer for their sex lives.'

That earned him a glare, but there was something soft about it. 'I plan to take a long sabbatical before I start my new job in London. Spend time with my English friends.'

His idea of a holiday was a long weekend in a trout stream. 'Each to their own.'

She stopped at the door. 'Last night didn't happen, never happened, couldn't possibly happen.'

He should get up and put the kettle on for her but didn't think she'd appreciate seeing him naked. 'Were you here at all?'

She opened the door and turned to him a final time. She had a smirk on her face that he didn't trust.

'Barlow, it's a good thing I wasn't here last night because my periods can be very erratic – and neither of us took any precautions.

She was out of the house and gone before he could throw on some clothes.

Acknowledgements

Way back in the far distance of time, what started out as a ten-minute writing exercise on the what-he-got-up-to tales of the real life Constable Barlow became a five stories, which became part of my submission for an M.Phil. in Creative Writing from Trinity College, Dublin, which became a one-off novel, *The Station Sergeant*, which became a two book contract with Portnoy Publishing.

The ending of the second book, *Barlow by the Book*, book kicked off the third book, *Barlow Laid Bare,* which took me onto the Antrim plateau and *Barlow Goes Forth,* which made me realise that the duties carried out then by women police constables were badly understated and undervalued, and this produced the latest and final Barlow book, *Barlow at Christmas.*

Thank you to everyone who has stayed loyal to Barlow and his vicissitudes over the years and especially to the people who willingly and generously gave of their time and expertise to help make the books that much richer.

And finally to my family: my wife Patricia, my daughter Lucie, and my son Daniel. They made the 'writing time' worthwhile.

John McAllister
johnmcallisterauthor.com

Ps to Kevin Hart. Sling the kettle. Now that Covid-19 injections are on the go, I'll be up any day now with the apple pie.

Printed in Great Britain
by Amazon